F
H18   Hammer, Richard.
          Mr. Jacobson's war.

Temple Israel Library
Minneapolis, Minn.

Please sign your full name on the above
card.

Return books promptly to the Library or
Temple Office.

Fines will be charged for overdue books
or for damage or loss of same.

MR. JACOBSON'S WAR

MR. JACOBSON'S WAR

• A NOVEL BY •
Richard Hammer

HARCOURT BRACE JOVANOVICH
NEW YORK AND LONDON

Requests for permission to make copies of any part of
the work should be mailed to: Permissions, Harcourt Brace
Jovanovich, Inc., 757 Third Avenue, New York, N.Y. 10017

Library of Congress Cataloging in Publication Data

Hammer, Richard, fl. 1969–
    Mr. Jacobson's war.
    I. Title.
PS3558. A4485M5   1981   813'.54   80-8750
ISBN 0-15-162828-9

Printed in the United States of America

First edition

B C D E

For
Allison Rachel Hammer
1975–1978
"If that would be all right"

And I shall thereupon
Take rest, ere I be gone
Once more on my adventure brave and new:
Fearless and unperplexed,
When I wage battle next,
What weapons to select, what armour to indue.

Youth ended, I shall try
My gain or loss thereby;
Be the fire ashes, what survives is gold:
And I shall weigh the same,
Give life its praise or blame:
Young, all lay in dispute; I shall know, being old.

ROBERT BROWNING, *Rabbi Ben Ezra*

MR. JACOBSON'S WAR

1

ON A BRIGHT, WARM MAY morning in 1946, five months before our shared birthday—his ninetieth, my ninth—my grandfather, Chaim Jacobson, walked out of the old people's home where he had been living for ten years. There were no shouts, no arguments, no rage. He dressed in a gray suit, knotted a blue patterned tie carefully under the collar and around the neck of his white shirt, fixed a black beret to cover the small, round bald spot in his otherwise full head of still-black hair, picked up his cane, and strode through the lobby and out the front door without a word to anyone. In the confusion of the midmorning, no one noticed him go. But then he was dressed as he always was, meticulously. He was not missed until lunch. It was another hour before Bernard Rubin, the director, got around to calling my mother. Mr. Jacobson (no one, not even those in his family, ever called him anything but Mr. Jacobson) had apparently gone for a stroll, he said, and simply lost track of time. He would certainly turn up before long. After all, a ninety-year-old man couldn't go far on his own. Still, Mr. Rubin said, he thought it was his duty to let my mother know her father was temporarily missing and the people at the home were making a thorough search of the building and the whole neighborhood, had been doing that for the last hour. They hadn't found him yet, but they certainly would and there was nothing for her to worry about. He would let her know as soon as there was any news.

My mother worried. She called my father. My father said that was all he needed to make his day. He was having enough trouble as it was trying to adjust to civilian life and the nine-to-five world of an office and paperwork after three years away at war. He really needed to have to start worrying about her father.

My mother said they were talking about her father, not some stranger.

My father said he knew that, they had been talking about her father since they first met. They never stopped talking about her father.

My mother said this was no joking matter.

My father said he knew that and he'd call the home and find out just what it was all about. He called Mr. Rubin and talked to him the way he used to talk to his privates when he was a captain in the army. He called my mother back to tell her there was still no sign of her father. What kind of a place is it, he said, that would have a nincompoop like Rubin in charge who would let an old man run around loose? Maybe it was time to call the police.

My mother said she had always thought Mr. Rubin a nice enough man despite my grandfather's complaints about him. It was just that her father was sometimes a little difficult.

God knows, my father said. Did she want to call the police?

The idea was a frightening one. She said maybe they ought to wait a little.

They were still on the phone, trying to decide, when the front doorbell rang. My grandfather was standing on the porch. With relief, and alarm, my mother relayed the news to my father, hung up the phone, ran to the door, and opened it. "Pa," she said, "where have you been? We've been frightened half to death for the last hours."

He only nodded to her and walked into the house, motioning with his head toward the street. A small moving van was parked at the curb. Two burly men were beginning to unload a collection of dusty boxes, the dust swirling with each movement, making a cloud that obscured and enveloped them and the van.

By the time I got home late in the afternoon from school and my piano lesson (I had been taking those lessons since I was six, my mother determined to expose me to culture early and, I think, drawing secret pictures of me on the concert stage as another prodigy, a second Rubinstein; so, three times a week I went from school to Miss Marcus, struggled under her eyes and often exasperated words and strenuous demonstrations for an hour, and seven days a week for another hour practiced on the secondhand Steinway baby grand in our living room; Miss Marcus kept telling my mother I had great promise, if only I would apply myself, and my mother believed her; I was sure that whatever promise I had and what talents there were lay somewhere else than the piano, but my mother was not interested in my opinions), there was no sign that anything unusual had taken place around our house. The street in front was empty and quiet as on most days. The moving van had long since gone and my grandfather's possessions, the saved relics of a lifetime, had been put away in the attic. He was taking a nap in the spare room next to mine on the second floor. I slammed through the kitchen door as always, shouting, "Mom, I'm home."

She rushed toward me, a finger at her lips. "Jerome," she hushed—she only called me Jerome, not Jerry, when she was annoyed—"do you have to make so much noise every time you come through that door? Grandpa's upstairs taking a nap and we don't want to wake him."

"Grandpa? Here?" I stared at her, thinking she must be making a joke. I had never seen my grandfather outside the home. He had gone there to live before I was born and the idea that it was not his natural environment, not someplace he had always been, that he might actually leave it, had never occurred to me.

"Yes, he's here, upstairs. He's going to be living with us for a while, so will you please try not to make so much noise."

It was dusk when my father's car turned into the driveway. We were waiting for him in the kitchen. My mother had already set the table in the dining room and was busy around the stove and the counters getting dinner ready. I was sitting across from my grandfather at the table in the breakfast area, watching with fascination as he sipped tea from a glass through a lump of sugar clenched between his teeth. He was settled so completely, so firmly in his chair that it seemed not only that he belonged there but also that he might never move.

My father came through the door. For the first time since he had returned from the war, he did not immediately wrap me in his arms in a tight grasp, let loose a glad roar, and lift me toward the ceiling as though I were still five. He stopped in the middle of the kitchen, staring at my grandfather. "Well, Mr. Jacobson."

My grandfather nodded serenely, continuing to sip his tea. "David."

"What brings you here?"

"The home. What else?" He raised his fingers and removed the lump of sugar from between his teeth, set it carefully in the saucer beside his glass.

"The home?"

"You think I came across town for the exercise, for a little visit, maybe?" After nearly seventy years in the United States, most of those years either in this corner of New England or a hundred miles north, around Boston, he retained hardly a trace of an accent; sometimes, when he was agitated, he might invert or convolute a sentence, and sometimes he might slip and substitute a *w* for a *v* ("A glass of wodka would be wery nice") or a *v* for a *w* ("There is a draft from the vindow on my neck"), but that was all.

"No, Mr. Jacobson," my father said, "I certainly don't think that. But this little excursion of yours has stirred up quite a little excitement, you know."

"An old man cannot go for a walk?"

"You walked? From the home all the way across town?"

"So, I rode. There is a difference?"

"You walked out of that place without telling anyone you were going. You didn't go back. Nobody knew where you were and nobody knew whether something had happened to you. You had everybody in a swivet."

"You think I am a child that I should leave notes every time I go someplace?"

"I think you should tell people, yes, especially the people who are supposed to be looking out for you."

"They were worried?" He pretended to be astonished; the pretense wasn't very good.

"They were worried."

"Good. It is the first time they have ever worried about anybody. It will do them some good, maybe."

"And how about us? How about me and your daughter and your grandson?"

"Why would you worry? I came to your house."

"Sure, but not until there'd been a dozen phone calls, and not until we were just about ready to call the police."

My grandfather looked at him and shrugged. "There were things to be done."

"There always are." My father shook his head in frustration. "All right, Mr. Jacobson, what was it this time?"

"I have done it before?"

"You've talked about it often enough."

"Talk is not doing."

"All right, so it's the first time. What was it?"

"The home. What else would it be? I have left the home, for good."

"I gathered that. Why? Why now?"

"You do not know?"

"I don't know."

"You have been there?"

"Of course I've been there. You know it."

"You think it is the Garden of Eden, maybe?"

"I know exactly what it is."

My grandfather made a gesture as though that was explanation enough. My father waited. My grandfather said, "Better I should have stayed in Russia and let the Cossacks murder me."

"Nobody told you to go there, Mr. Jacobson. You picked that place yourself if you remember, without consulting anyone. We warned you when you said you were going there. But you wouldn't listen."

"So, I made a mistake. In my life I have made plenty of mistakes. This was not the first one."

"It took you ten years to find it out?"

"Ten minutes it took me."

"And you stayed ten years."

"Ten years ago, I was stronger, I could fight better. Now, look, what do you see? An old man sits before you. An old man who can hardly rise from his chair. The taste for a fight, it is gone."

"Sure, I'll bet," my father said. "Since when? There hasn't been a day in your life when you didn't wake up ready for a fight with somebody. There hasn't been a day when you didn't spend half your time planning a fight with somebody."

My grandfather laughed, then shook his head, his face taking on a sad look. "When you get to be ninety," he said, "the desire is ashes, the effort is too much. An old man wants only a little peace, a little quiet. In that place, for peace I have to fight, for quiet I have to shout. So, no more. It is too hard."

"Okay. What now?"

My mother had been watching them warily, frozen over the cutting board, knife poised but unmoving, the half-prepared dinner forgotten. (I had been trying to make myself invisible, disappear somehow into the wall behind my chair so that no one would notice me and send me from the room, listening but not really understanding much.) Now she moved, just a step toward them, saying quickly, "David. Papa's going to live with us."

"So I gather," my father said.

"He won't be any trouble." Though the way she said it, I think she was trying to persuade herself as much as my father. "He can have the spare room, next to Jerry."

"Oh, sure," my father said. "And what happens if . . . ?" He did not finish the thought and I wondered what he was talking about.

"Oh," she said, "we don't have to think about that now, not for a long time."

"Do not worry," my grandfather said. "This affliction will not last long."

"Just what's that supposed to mean?" my father said.

"Methuselah I am not." He gestured toward me, and I think it was the first time they became conscious that I was in the room. "You think I will read Torah at this grandson's bar mitzvah?" He laughed. "Before Jerome begins to study with the *shammes,* even, the Yahrzeit candle will be cold a long time." He studied my mother for a moment, looked at my father, said, "And at the bris, if it is a boy, I will not drink the wine."

My mother looked stricken. She shivered. "Oh, pa," she protested, "don't talk that way. Just look at you. You're still a young man. You've got years and years ahead."

He shook his head at her. "Ruthie," he said, "you're a good girl. But sometimes you talk like your mama. Sometimes you see the mist and you think it is silk for a new gown." He looked at my father. "David, you understand."

My father nodded slowly.

"You have just come home from the war," my grandfather said, his tone suddenly serious. "It is not the same as when you went away. That I can see. The times are not easy for you. Well, you listen. You think I want to make more trouble for you? Never. You will help me and I will help you." My father was staring at him, protest forming. My grandfather waved a hand at him. "I have the old-age check from the state every month. I have a little money in the bank. So, I will pay my way. It will be even easier for you, maybe."

"You think I'd take your money?" My father was not just incredulous, he was furious.

My grandfather checked him. "I need money for what? For a few cigarettes, for the *Forward,* for a book. For what else? You think it should sit in the bank, I should put it under the mattress, in a cookie jar, so later you should have it? You should have it now, when it will help."

"Mr. Jacobson, you're welcome to come and live here as long as you like. But if you think I want your money in return, you're crazy."

"Who said anything about want? I said you will have it and have it you will."

"Not on your life."

My grandfather laughed. "We should argue over this? We should say it is there and that is enough."

2

SO, THAT SPRING DAY MY grandfather came to live with us. He chose us not because we were necessarily his favorites, though I think we were, but simply because we were his only relatives who still lived in Hartford, who still lived within a hundred miles. Twelve of his fifteen children, seven sons and five daughters, by his three wives were still alive, and there were thirty-four grandchildren, most, except for me, adults with families of their own, and forty-one great-grandchildren, but they were scattered across America, from Boston to Miami, from New York to Los Angeles. We were, then, not just a natural choice because of love and closeness, but the only choice when he decided it was time for him to leave the old people's home.

I suppose when he said that first evening that he had lost his taste for combat, that all he wanted now was peace and quiet, he was sure he meant it. I know my mother and father did not believe him. My mother had grown up with him and she sometimes said that she had never known what people meant when they talked of peace and quiet and serenity in a home until she married my father and moved into her own home. My father, remembering his first encounters with my grandfather and all those times before the war when he was witness to the man's passions, once said that my grandfather was like Don Quixote, waking in the morning, putting on his armor, and riding forth in search of a daily battle; though unlike Don Quixote, my grandfather rarely lost a battle with a windmill, or with anyone or anything else. My father was sure that the only time Chaim Jacobson would give up either the anticipation of a fight or the fight itself would be when he died, and even then he'd probably find some way to revive long enough to war against the undertaker over some injustice.

My grandfather settled into the room next to mine and my mother and father tiptoed around the house waiting for the explosion they were sure had to come, sooner and not later. A day of calm, two days of peace, three days of quiet, and they grew edgier, exchanging glances filled with growing concern, and an electric, bristling tension sparked the air in the house. I knew they were waiting for something, that they thought something was wrong; they snapped at me for little or no reason; everything I did seemed wrong to them. But I did not know how to do what they considered right, could not even, despite my best efforts, remain inconspicuous, do exactly what I was supposed to do, stay out of the way and out of trouble. There was always something. My grandfather just ignored it all, wandering contentedly, placidly, through those first days as though this was just what he wanted and expected. He gave no offense and looked for none, said nothing harsh about anyone or anything, acted satisfied and comfortable. He got up with us in the morning, joined us at breakfast, helped my mother with the dishes, despite her attempts to make him sit down and stay out of the way, after my father had left for work and I had gone to school. Every morning he took a four-block walk to the drug-candy-miscellaneous store to buy his newspaper (and after the first day, the owner managed to have a *Daily Forward* ready for him when he arrived) and his ten Lucky Strike cigarettes (in those days, it was still possible in small stores like that one to buy cigarettes in quantities of less than a pack; some years before, my grandfather had decided to cut down from his two-pack-a-day habit and limit himself to ten a day; if there were cigarettes around, he could not do it, so he bought half a pack every morning and rationed himself through the day). He walked home, sat in the backyard in an old lawn chair when the weather was good, in his room when it rained

or was too cold, read the newspaper or a book, smoked his cigarettes down to the last minute end, until there was nothing left
to hold to his lips. Early in the afternoon, after lunch with my
mother and me and after I had gone back to school, he took a
nap for an hour, then went back outside. When I got home, he
would come back into the house and sit in the living room, silently listening to me practice the piano, making no comments,
just listening. He had dinner with us, sat in the living room later,
reading, listening to the radio, talking about the news with my
mother and father. About ten, he went to bed. Nothing seemed
to ruffle him.

On Sunday, my father went to the old people's home to collect
the clothes and books and other things my grandfather had left
behind. An hour later, he turned into the driveway and took from
the car two heavy suitcases and a small cardboard box, the kind
you get from a liquor store, tied with rope. He carried them into
the house, up the stairs, and into my grandfather's room. My
grandfather climbed the stairs directly behind him and, even before my father had left, he began opening the suitcases and the
box and putting his things away.

Fifteen minutes later, we could hear his feet thundering down
the stairs, the sound alone signaling rage. He towered in the
archway to the living room, face apoplectic, his whole body stiff
with fury. "And the rest?" he demanded of my father.

My father looked up from the Sunday paper. My mother stared
with alarm from the section she was reading. I looked up from
the floor where I was sprawled over the comics. My mother
looked at my father. My mother was pale, her face tense. My father grinned, relaxed, and even I could see that the glance he
gave my mother said, don't worry, everything's going to be all
right now. "That's all there was, Mr. Jacobson," he said mildly.

My grandfather stared at him with disbelief. "All? All?"

"Everything was packed and ready when I got there, waiting
for me at the desk. The two suitcases and the box. That was it."

"You did not go to my room?"

"Why? I told you, they had everything ready and waiting."

"You trusted them? You did not check?"

"I didn't think that was necessary. Is something missing?"

"Something?" My grandfather glared at him as though he were sure something must be missing from my father's brain. "Something? My books. You want a list by titles so you should know? My ties. You want the colors and the patterns, even the spots and the stains? The four white shirts I bought new at the department store downtown last year. They are where? You should believe they are not in the suitcases. Socks. Underwear. You want a list? You want me to write them down? A list I will give you. You could not count the things. Those thieves, those robbers. And you trust them?" He expelled a cloud of disgust, stood stiffly erect, towering, appearing even taller than his normal six feet, even more menacing than at his most furious moments. "And my chair? Do you see it? Did you bring it? Is it still in the car?"

"There wasn't any chair, Mr. Jacobson," my father said.

"Aha!" he crowed in triumph. "No chair. I have had that chair for sixty years. I have sat in that chair for sixty years. Four times in sixty years I have recovered that chair, myself. Everyplace I have gone that chair has gone with me. Now they say there is no chair? I tell you, they are thieves, they are murderers, they are Cossacks. They would steal even my chair."

"Calm down, Mr. Jacobson," my father said, trying to placate him. "If you're so upset because you think a few things are missing, let's just call the home and tell them. I'll bet somebody, whoever did the packing, just overlooked them."

"Overlooked them? You listen, they forget nothing, they overlook nothing. Who you should call is the police, that's who." He spun in the archway with unexpected agility and stormed from the room.

A panic was growing in my mother. I suppose, having witnessed scenes like this all her life, she should have been used to them. But my grandfather's fury when aroused was not something she could ever accept with equanimity, and now that he was so old, she feared for him. "Pa," she cried, starting from her chair, "where are you going?"

He was on his way toward the front door. He did not pause in his march. He shouted back, without turning, "You do not know?" And he was through the door, slamming it behind him.

My mother turned toward my father. "David, stop him. He's

going to do something foolish. You know he is. You have to stop him."

My father grinned. "You want me to stop him? It would be a lot easier to stop a herd of wild horses."

"You just stop that grinning," she said, though suddenly I noticed in an exchange of looks between them that she was having trouble covering a smile of her own that was twitching the corners of her lips. "Or at least," she said, "go after him. You know what he's like when he gets this way."

My father was already rising from his chair. "Don't worry," he said, "that's exactly what I was going to do." He looked over at me. "Jerry, how would you like to go for a ride and watch grandpa tilt at a windmill?"

"You're going to take Jerry?"

"Sure. Why not? He might even learn something."

She started to object.

I said, leaping from the floor to my father's side, "Aw, mom."

My father put his arm around my shoulders. We left the house together and got into the car. By the time he had backed the car out of the driveway and turned it into the street, my grandfather was a rapidly shrinking figure, poised at the corner at the end of the block, tapping his cane impatiently against the curb as he waited for a car to pass so he could cross. We pulled up alongside. My father reached across and threw open the door. "Get in, Mr. Jacobson."

My grandfather glared at him, making no move toward the car. "Help I do not need."

"Who said anything about help?" my father said. "I'm offering a ride, that's all."

"A ride I do not need. I will take the bus."

"You're going to have a long wait. This is Sunday, if you remember. The bus runs once an hour and it must have passed about ten minutes ago."

"An hour I can wait."

"Oh, for God's sake, Mr. Jacobson," my father said with a touch of annoyance, "just get in. It's not going to hurt you to accept a ride. I'll drive you to the home and once we're there, you're on your own, you can do whatever you want. I promise, I won't interfere."

My grandfather studied him carefully, then nodded with one sharp movement of his head. He climbed into the backseat, sat rigidly erect exactly in the center, staring straight ahead, his cane planted on the car floor between his legs, all the way across town. At the entrance to the home, he shifted, grasping and pulling the door handle, opening the door even before my father had brought the car to a complete stop, got out, and strode belligerently toward the front door. My father parked the car and we hurried after him, going through the door perhaps a dozen feet behind.

The woman at the front desk was staring at him with shock, with surprise. "Why, Mr. Jacobson." He gave her a curt nod and went by, down a corridor. The woman looked a question at my father. "What a surprise," she said. "I didn't think we'd see Mr. Jacobson again so soon."

"He forgot a few things," my father said. We went by and down the corridor. I looked back. She was frantically lifting the phone.

My grandfather reached a door halfway down the corridor, flung it open. The sign on the door read: Bernard Rubin, Director. My grandfather was just halting before a woman behind a desk as we went through the door behind him.

"Why, Mr. Jacobson," she said. She was just hanging up the phone, but still, there was surprise in her voice.

"Mrs. Silverstein." He nodded brusquely.

"I thought you'd left us," she said.

"You thought right," he said.

"Oh," she said.

"I have returned," he said.

"Oh," she said.

"Not to stay," he said. "To see Mr. Rubin."

She put on a mournful expression. "Oh, Mr. Jacobson," she said, "I'm so sorry. You've just missed him. He left about fifteen minutes ago."

"Then I will wait."

"Oh, but he won't be back until tomorrow."

He stared at her grimly, nodded to himself, not to her, stepped around her desk to another door, rapped his cane against it once sharply, shouted, "Rubin, it is Jacobson. Do you think you can hide behind a door? Are you a coward you cannot face me?" He seized the doorknob and threw open the door.

There was a desk in the middle of the office, facing the door. A middle-aged man, soft, pale, with thick glasses that hid his eyes, with a fringe of graying hair around a scalp that reflected little rays of light, looked up with a startled expression. (I assume now that he must have been in his early fifties, though in those days all adults between twenty-five and old age appeared roughly the same age to me, adults, bigger and more powerful, the gradations and distinctions not yet clear.)

My grandfather pointed with satisfaction, with triumph. "Aha," he shouted. "I knew it. You think you can hide from Jacobson? You are not the invisible man. I could find you in the dark."

Mr. Rubin's normally pale complexion turned a little ashen. "Mr. Jacobson," he said. "What a surprise. How nice to see you again." (It took me about ten seconds to grasp that this grown man behind the desk might actually be afraid of my grandfather at this moment. I stared from one to the other, trying to understand.)

"You think it is nice to see me?" my grandfather said. "You will not think it is nice for long."

Mr. Rubin seemed to shrink. "Is something wrong?"

My grandfather glared at him. "You do not know?"

My father stepped between them. "It seems," he said, "that Mr. Jacobson thinks that some of his things are missing."

My grandfather looked at my father. "Be quiet," he said. "You think I need help?"

"Of course not," my father said.

Mr. Rubin swallowed hard. "Really?" he said. "I can't understand it. I gave the orders personally for your belongings to be packed. I sent one of the aides to do it. I told him not to forget anything. He assured me that all your things had been put in your suitcases and in a box. I can't understand it."

My grandfather snorted, a noise that seemed to ricochet off the walls and reverberate through the room, knocking Mr. Rubin back in his chair. "My chair," my grandfather said. "He put my chair in the suitcases? In a box from the liquor store?"

"Your chair?" Mr. Rubin looked surprised.

"My chair. You remember my chair?"

"How could I forget it?"

"So, where is it?"

"It wasn't with your things?"

My grandfather laughed sarcastically.

"I don't understand it," Mr. Rubin said.

"And my books. My shirts. More. You want a list?"

"No, no, Mr. Jacobson," Mr. Rubin said quickly, waving an ineffectual hand toward my grandfather, "of course not. I'll take your word that the aide forgot to pack a few things. I'm sure it was just an oversight, just an accident. I'm sure it wasn't deliberate. I'm sure we can straighten it all out in a jiffy."

"You may be sure," my grandfather said, contempt coloring his voice. "I am not so sure."

"What do you mean, Mr. Jacobson?" Mr. Rubin protested.

"You do not know? I have to explain it on a billboard?"

"You don't really think anyone here would . . . would steal anything that belonged to you?"

"I do not think," my grandfather said.

"You're not suggesting . . ."

My grandfather laughed without humor.

Mr. Rubin glanced over at my father, a silent appeal.

My father said, "It seems to me that the quickest way to get this whole thing resolved would be for Mr. Jacobson to go to his old room and take a look."

"Of course," Mr. Rubin said with a little relief. "I was just going to suggest that myself." He looked at my grandfather. "Would that satisfy you, Mr. Jacobson?"

My grandfather stared at him but said nothing.

"You don't think anyone's hidden anything, do you?" Mr. Rubin was appalled at the idea.

My grandfather snorted again, stood staring at Mr. Rubin for a moment, then turned quickly and strode out of the office. We followed. He marched down the corridor. Several old people were gathered outside the dayroom. They saw my grandfather approaching. They stared at him with surprise, with a kind of shock, with a semblance of awe and respect. One old man nodded gravely, said with deference, "Mr. Jacobson."

"Mr. Cohen." My grandfather nodded as he passed by.

"You have come back?"

"I am here. You are not looking at a ghost."

Another man said, "You have come back for good?"

My grandfather looked at him over his shoulder and did not bother to answer. We reached the door to what had been his room. His name was still on the white card in the slot on the door. He took the knob and pulled the door open, stepped inside. A tiny, frail man, ancient as dusty scrolls (though, I learned, ten years younger than my grandfather), was sitting in a rocking chair by the window. He looked up, gasped, "Mr. Jacobson."

My grandfather stared at him, nodded severely. "Mr. Katz."

Mr. Katz seemed to grow older, to shrivel under the look. "Well you are looking," he murmured with effort.

"Better I will be," my grandfather said, his voice suddenly turning into a lash, "when you move your buttocks from my chair."

Mr. Katz aged another ten years, shriveled another six inches. He struggled to propel himself from the chair, could not find the strength, sank back, pushed again, finally managed to lift himself and hobble a few feet away to lean for support against the wall. "The chair," he stammered, trying to explain, fluttering his hands. "The director, Mr. Rubin, the chair he said I might have. He said the chair you had left behind and mine it could be."

My grandfather stared from him to the chair and back. "You know this chair?"

Mr. Katz nodded, pleading.

"You think I would leave it behind?"

"I did not think. The director said."

"Rubin said. And you believed?" My grandfather shook his head sadly. He went across to the chair, seized it with both hands, and tried to rock it, to drag it toward the door. I recognized the chair then, once Mr. Katz was out of it and my grandfather was in possession. It was an old mahogany-framed rocker, the wood dark and satiny with age, use, care, love, the seat and

back a rich maroon brocade, a little worn and faded and indent-
ed by the years. My grandfather had been in that chair every time
I had come into this room to visit him; it was part of my earliest
memories of him.

Mr. Katz pressed himself against the wall as though he would
find a secret door and vanish through it. "Other things, too," he
whispered. "The director said I might have. Whatever you had
left. You would not need them. He told me."

My grandfather turned toward my father. "Aha," he crowed.
"Did I tell you? You did not believe?" He turned back to Mr. Katz,
looming over him. "Where?" he demanded.

Mr. Katz struggled, could not get words out. He gestured toward the closet. My grandfather nodded, opened the closet door,
peered inside, his eyes moving from side to side, up and down.
He stood in the closet doorway, looking back at Mr. Katz. "My
shirts," he said. "You could wear them?" (I looked from my
grandfather to the quaking, tiny Mr. Katz. The idea of Mr. Katz in
my grandfather's clothes seemed a joke. I laughed. My grandfather glared at me, stopped my laughter.)

"No, Mr. Jacobson," Mr. Katz murmured. "Fit they would not."

"My socks. You could put them on? My underwear, too?"

"No, Mr. Jacobson."

"My books. You would read them?"

"No, Mr. Jacobson."

"Still, you keep them."

"The director said."

"The director said you should jump off the roof, you would
jump off the roof?"

"No, Mr. Jacobson."

"But the director says you can have my things, so you take my
things." He reached into the closet, pulled out a handful of ties.
He flung them across the room toward Mr. Katz. "Here," he said,
"Jacobson says you can have these. A gift from Jacobson."

The ties fell in a heap around Mr. Katz. He looked at my grandfather. There were tears in his eyes, pleading in his manner. "Mr.
Jacobson," he said, "too much it is."

"I give them to you." He reached into the closet again, came
away with an old sweater. "This I give to you. It should keep you

warm." He threw it toward Mr. Katz. It landed at his feet. He reached into the closet and pulled out a few other things, threw them toward Mr. Katz. "These, too, I give to you."

Mr. Katz looked as though he would burst into tears.

My grandfather looked at him, shook his head, softened. "Katz," he said with resignation and pity, "you are not a bad man. A weak man, yes, a bad man, no. For you, I feel only sorry." With that, he dismissed Mr. Katz. Mr. Katz waited a moment. My grandfather ignored him. Mr. Katz sidled along the wall to the door, disappeared through it. My grandfather turned to my father. "Boxes we need," he said.

My father grinned and nodded. "Boxes you'll have." He left the room. My grandfather ignored me for a moment, disappeared into the closet, emerged with an armful of books. He looked at me. "Jerome," he said, "you should stand there like a statue?"

"No, grandpa."

"Then come and help."

I went into the closet and together we removed more books and clothes and other things. My father came back with an aide carrying two large packing cartons. My grandfather stood over them, supervising while they packed, watching carefully, stopping them several times when they were about to put books into the cartons. "These," he said, "I give to the library," making sure they were put to one side. When all his possessions had been packed, he followed behind the aide, who carried the containers down the corridor and out to the car, stayed with the aide while he went back to the room, and then shouted warnings and instructions as the aide, sweating, heaving, muttering, lugged the rocking chair down the corridor and out to the car, wedged it into the trunk, and tied the trunk down over it with heavy rope.

Satisfied at last, my grandfather marched back into the home. We followed. He went back to Mr. Rubin's office, ignoring the secretary, flinging open the door, standing in the entrance staring at the director. "Now," he said, "it is done."

Mr. Rubin looked at him. "You've got everything, Mr. Jacobson?"

"Everything. The rest I give to the home." He paused, his eyes not leaving Mr. Rubin. "To you," he said at last, "I give a good-bye." He turned away then and strode back down the corridor and out to the car.

In the car, my father looked over the front seat at my grandfather. He grinned. My grandfather nodded serenely, leaned back. He was asleep before we were even out of the parking lot.

We drove most of the way home in silence, though about halfway, I looked up at my father and said, "Grandpa must really love that chair."

My father looked quickly down at me. He smiled. "I suppose he does. He's had it long enough."

"I mean, how can an old chair be so important?"

My father looked at me. He said, "With your grandfather, it wasn't just the chair, Jerry, or the books or the other things."

"I don't understand, daddy."

"I know. And I'm not sure I could explain it to you now so you would. Maybe, someday, when you're a lot older, you'll know."

"I felt sorry for that Mr. Katz."

"So did your grandfather."

"He didn't look it."

"But he was."

"Mr. Rubin, too. The way grandpa was with him, I felt sorry for him."

"Don't feel sorry for Mr. Rubin, Jerry. He and your grandfather were playing a game. They've been playing that game for years."

"What kind of a game, daddy?"

My father shook his head and grinned. "Their own special game."

3

A LONG TIME LATER, REMINISCING with me, my father said that he had always been sure that the reason my grandfather never became senile while people a dozen years and more younger lapsed into that half-world of vagueness and uncertainty was simply that he had always been too busy and so he just didn't have the time. There was always another windmill just ahead for him to charge.

For a while, I thought that Mr. Rubin and some of the others at the home, especially those in charge though not the other residents, must have been glad to see the last of him. During his ten years there, he had been what a lot of people would have called a troublemaker. He would have scorned that characterization if it had been put to him, and, I think, so would most of the others who were trapped in that institution for their last years. If he had ever thought about it, he would probably have said that what he did was nothing more than what any man should do if he is able, which is to try to right wrongs, to fight injustices, to help not only himself but those who are too frightened or too weak to help or defend themselves. But I don't think he ever put a name to it or thought much about it. He merely went his own way, doing the things he was sure he had to do if he was to live with himself and call himself a man.

When he first showed up at the home, I'm certain no one was completely prepared for him even though he had a reputation in the community. But he was eighty then and they must have thought that he was merely another lonely old man with nowhere else to go who would, out of loneliness and fear and advancing senility, be like all the others, compliant, even subservient, anxious to please, afraid to give offense, grateful for the small favors. They were wrong, of course, and it should have been evident in the very manner in which he arrived to take up residence.

My grandmother, whom I never knew, died about a year after my mother and father were married. For a couple of months, my grandfather continued to live in their house. But the silence, the peace after more than thirty years of never-ending battle and tumult, were too hard to bear. The house was empty, the children all grown and gone, my grandmother dead. He was not used to taking care of a home by himself, had no taste for domesticity. He could have gone to live with one or another of his children, but that was something he would not do. My mother and father were just married and he would not inflict himself on them at that stage. All his other children had moved far away and he had no desire to be a stranger in a strange land; he had been through that before. So, without consulting anyone, without even telling anyone, he had explored the four Jewish old people's homes in the city, had settled on the Zion Home, he said later, because he knew a number of the people who were already there and for a lot of other reasons he couldn't explain even to himself. On his own, he sold the house and most of the furnishings, put the things he treasured into storage, and then, with his clothes in suitcases, some prized books, and his old rocking chair, showed up at the home one morning with the revelation that he had come to stay. He sat in the lobby surrounded by his baggage until a room was found for him.

He was there when I was born, there when I first remember meeting him, there all the times I saw him until the spring he came to live with us. Through my first eight years, I would guess I saw him about once a week, though he was, for me then, only a distant, forbidding man who seemed to have little time or interest in a very young grandson.

We would drive across town to the home every Sunday afternoon, my mother, my father, and I until my father left for the war, and after that just my mother and I until my father came home. We would walk through the entrance, down the corridor to his room. My mother would push me ahead of her through the door, shouting, "Pa, hello, it's me, Ruth."

Invariably, he would be sitting in that rocking chair beside the window, reading his newspaper or a book or sometimes staring out the window, with its view then of grass and trees and a wood in the distance (today, all that is a subdivision of low-income apartments and a hundred small, identical houses), and sometimes bent over a lined pad writing intently and rapidly. He would look up at the sound of the door opening and my mother's cry, would glare, would snap, "I know it is you. Who else would it be? You do not have to shout. I am not deaf yet."

She would push me toward him, still shouting. "I've brought your grandson, Jerome, to see you. Say hello to grandpa, Jerome."

"You think I do not know my own grandson so you have to tell me his name?" He would glare at her, then stare at me, his eyes magnified by the lenses of his glasses always seeming huge, menacing, so at first I would shy away. He would put on a smile. "You are getting to be a big boy already, Jerome."

So, at my mother's urging, her finger driving a hole into the middle of my back, I would murmur, "Hello, grandpa." The finger, the hand pressing against my back would thrust and I would be propelled forward toward him and my lips would touch his bristly cheek. For the next hour, I would sit on the bed, wander around the room, look out the window, be bored and anxious to escape, while my mother reported the latest news of the family to him, read letters from my father, from my uncles, from my aunts. He would listen with mounting impatience and even a show of his own boredom, asking few questions, offering only terse and unilluminating answers to her questions. An hour would go by and my mother would finally rise, say, "Well, pa, we have to be going now. We'll be back to see you next week." She would thrust me against him for a farewell kiss on the cheek, which he seemed to suffer. He would nod his good-bye, though with an expression that said he wished we were gone already so he could get back to his reading, his writing, his thinking. Yet, I think he did look forward to those weekly visits. My mother, his youngest child, the child of his old age, loved him and he loved her, and we were the one regular personal contact he had with the blood of his past. My uncles and aunts and cousins appeared now and then, but their visits were infrequent and, during the war, when travel was all but impossible, rare indeed. Their letters and occasional phone calls may have helped, but we were his touch with the reality of his family.

But I hated those visits even while knowing there was no way I could avoid them. They were as much a part of the ritual of my life then as waking in the morning, eating, going to school, playing with my friends, taking my piano lessons, and practicing. It was not that I hated my grandfather or even hated being with him. It was simply that I hated going to that place, hated the sight of the gloomy bulk of that shabby old brick building that could as easily have been some ancient, nearly abandoned prison as an old people's home. I hated going to the neighborhood; it was falling apart, the houses needing paint, tilting as though they were about to slide back into the earth through lack of repair and care; the lots and fields and the nearby woods that looked so fresh and green from the distance were, up close, weed-choked and littered with old bottles and cans and newspapers, debris of every kind. I hated the smell that assaulted me every time I went through the doors and down the corridors to his room, a smell I realized later was antiseptic, dirt, decay, old age, and impending death all blended, but which I thought then was only the smell that came from being old.

And so, even if it had been possible, even if there had been a reaching out, I would have resisted in those years and that place any real knowing of my grandfather. He occupied his space which was not my space and the distance between us was more than years, was unbridgeable.

Once he came to live with us, everything changed. There was no longer that awful drive across town and that dreaded, endless hour every Sunday afternoon. He was always with us now, every day, the whole day, no longer just an austere, forbidding figure in an old rocking chair but a man who rose in the morning, ate meals with us, talked, listened to the same radio programs we did, went to bed. The distance between us began to close, the wall between us began to crumble. We were thrown together more and more, began, without thinking about it, even to seek each other out, to relax with each other, to know each other.

I was only vaguely aware of it at the time, but this was a difficult season for my father and mother, and not just because of my grandfather. My father had come home from the war at the end of the last summer, expecting to pick up his life where he had left it when he joined the army after Pearl Harbor. But he was no more the same man he had been in 1941 and 1942 than the world of 1945 and 1946 was the same world. In the army, he had been an officer, a captain, had given orders, commanded men, made decisions about life and death, been in danger, seen and experienced things he would never talk about but which had left him with premature threads of gray in his hair and a melancholy deep behind his eyes. Now he was back behind the same desk in an insurance company, discovering that those who had once worked alongside him or even under him and had stayed home had prospered, had advanced large steps beyond him, were now supervising him, giving him orders. He felt himself trapped behind that desk with no hope of advancement or change, buried in a world of actuarial tables that had lost all meaning. His life was frozen in a mindless routine, his days an endless scraping of fingernails across a blackboard until his nerves screamed and his temper raged—at the world, at his job, even at his family at home. He could no longer tolerate his job and yet, because of my mother and me and now my grandfather, too, he was sure he could not leave it.

But the steam inside that pressure cooker built up with no escape valve until the lid had to blow off. A few weeks after my grandfather came to live with us, I got home from school to discover the car in the driveway. My father and mother were in the kitchen, talking in low, anxious tones, their bodies leaning toward each other in agitation. It was a few minutes before they noticed me in the doorway. They stopped talking, shooed me out of the house. Go outside and play, they both told me. We're busy. I stared from one to the other. For once, nobody mentioned the piano, which both pleased and mystified me. I turned and left the house. But I knew something was wrong and so I got my ball and stationed myself beneath the kitchen window, throwing the ball against the cellar hatchway though I was more interested in and intent on trying to hear what was being said. Words and phrases drifted to me through the open window and I began to piece together a little, to begin to understand.

He said, "I blew my stack. It was about time."

He said, "That little son of a bitch had the nerve to tell me . . ."

He said, "Then I told him to go to hell."

He said, "God knows, it wasn't anything sudden. It's been building since the day I got home. This was just the last straw."

He said, "I told him he knew what he could do with the job, with the whole damn company for that matter."

He said, "I told him the hell with the end of the week, I'd be out of there in an hour."

He said, "You think I'm sorry? Like hell. I feel like I've been carrying ten tons on my back and now I've kicked it off."

He said, "I tell you, it's the best thing that could have happened. I should have done it long ago. Hell, I never should have gone back there in the first place."

My mother said, "But what are we going to do now?"

He said, "Tighten our belts. What else can we do?"

She said, "But how are we going to live?"

He said, "We've got some savings. We'll have to use them until we get straightened out. Everything will work out eventually."

She said, "But what are you going to do?"

He said, "What I should have done last fall, when I got home. Open my own office. I'm a damn good accountant and there's going to be plenty of people who need good accountants now, you'll see."

She said, "I know. I believe in you and I know you can do it, you can do anything you set your mind to. But what are we going to do while you're getting started?"

He said, "We'll just have to play it close to the vest, cut down everywhere we can and try to get by. Don't worry. We'll make out all right."

She said, "Don't worry? Of course I'm worried. We've got the mortgage. We've got people to feed—you, me, Jerry, my father. We've made plans. What are we supposed to do?"

He said, "Well, the first thing we do is cancel the plans for the summer, and that means no vacation, no cottage in New London, no camp for Jerry. We'll just have to stick around here this year."

She said, "But what will Jerry do? All his friends will be going away."

He said, "He's a resourceful kid. He'll find plenty of things to do."

She said, "And the baby?"

He said, "There's plenty of time to get on our feet before that. Everything will be okay by then."

She said, "God, I hope so."

He said, "It will be. Believe me."

She said, "Maybe we ought to ask pa to help. He offered and as long as he's here with us . . ."

He said, "No. There's no way in the world I would ask your father. Let him keep what he has; it can't be much and he can use it for himself. Do you really think I'd do that?"

She said, "But if we have to, if it becomes necessary?"

He said, "If it's necessary, we'll talk about it then. But it won't ever be necessary."

She said, "I suppose, if it becomes really necessary, we could always ask your father."

He said, "Are you kidding? Do you think I'd ever go begging to that stiff-necked . . . ? Do you think even if I got down on my hands and knees and crawled, he'd do anything but say he'd told me so and he always knew the day would come? I'd rather starve than ask him for a red cent. And, believe me, we won't starve."

A lot of what they talked about passed right over me. The baby, for instance. There was no baby in our house then and nobody had said anything to me about one coming. I heard that, thought about it for a second, and then dismissed it.

What my father said about my other grandfather, his father, I simply accepted as fact, as truth, as something nobody would ever question. There was always a kind of awful tension, a barely veiled hostility toward us, whenever we were around my father's parents, Joseph and Frieda Greif, though we were not around them often. They never came to our house and the only times we went to theirs were for the first seder on Passover and the feasts on the eves of Rosh Hashanah and Yom Kippur. Those visits were invariably preceded by some kind of argument between my mother and father.

My father would say, "Maybe we ought to skip it this time, just call and say somebody's sick and wish them a happy holiday and leave it at that."

My mother would say, "Oh, David, they're expecting us."

My father would say, "Sure, they want us like they want the plague. If we don't go, they'll say a couple of extra prayers, of thanksgiving."

My mother would say, "Oh, David, that's not so."

My father would say, "Oh, isn't it?"

My mother would say, "We hardly ever see them. Just two or three times a year."

My father would say, "And whose fault is that?"

My mother would say, "They're your mother and father."

My father would say, "Don't I know it."

My mother would say, "We have to go."

My father would say, "I don't see why."

My mother would say, "You know why."

And so, eventually, we would go. If I was reluctant to visit my grandfather, Chaim Jacobson, those Sundays when he was in the home, I was physically afraid, nearly sick to my stomach, whenever we went to visit the Greifs. He was a jeweler, and a successful one, with a large store in downtown Hartford; his family had been jewelers in Leipzig and he had learned his trade there before coming to the United States as a young man with a new bride at the turn of the century. His house was filled with precious and valuable items, a terrifying museum to a small boy. From the moment we walked through the front door, about the only things either he or my grandmother ever said to me were, "Jerome, don't touch that, you'll break it. Jerome, keep your hands to yourself. Jerome, stop talking this instant, children should be seen and not heard," though I was sure they felt the less I was seen the better. In his study, my grandfather kept his books in glassed-in cases. Once, I took a book, carefully opening the glass door and removing it from the shelf. I've never forgotten the title: Kipling's *The Light That Failed,* in a maroon leather binding. While I was looking at it, my grandfather came up on me, his face turning crimson with rage, pulled the book out of my hands, smacked it hard across the side of my head, thrust it back into the bookcase, shouting, "How many times do you have to be told you are not to touch things in this house?"

I was not exactly his favorite. But, then, the only times I ever saw him smile, the smile so unfamiliar and tight it seemed to crack lines in his face, was at my younger cousin, Barbara, the daughter of my father's sister, his only sibling. Despite those attempts at smiles, Barbara was as frightened of him as I was. My mother he simply ignored, never spoke to her, rarely even looked at her. My father he scorned loudly and insistently, for refusing to go into the jewelry business with him when the offer was made after my father graduated from college (while his son-in-law jumped at the chance and soon became my grandfather's favorite, more a son than my father ever was), for not being rich, for daring to disagree about politics and almost everything else, and, especially, for daring to marry my mother, who was not rich and who was the daughter of one of those uncivilized Orientals, a Russian. His wife, my grandmother, seemed to share his every idea and attitude, would sit and beam at him, nodding agreement at whatever he said, attending to his every wish even before he expressed it.

My father's refusal to consider turning to his father for help in a time of need, then, was something I instinctively accepted. I would have been surprised if he had done anything else.

What did have real meaning for me in that conversation I overheard that afternoon was the fact that I wouldn't be going to camp that summer like some of my friends, or to the beach or the mountains like most of the rest. I understood only a little the real meaning of a tight budget, of cutting down everywhere, just that it meant that the things I had looked forward to for the summer were not to be. But there was a kind of excitement, too, in the idea of my father opening his own office, of his going into business for himself.

Though I didn't know it at that moment, what the summer at

home, with all my friends away, would really mean for me was that my grandfather would become my closest companion and my friend. With so few other choices, we would discover each other in ways that would not have been possible at other times and in other circumstances.

When I got home from school, and later when vacation started, he would call me to come and sprawl on the lawn in the backyard beside his old canvas chair, which he had set in the shade of a tall old elm and where he relaxed and read and talked when the weather was hot and clear. When it rained, there were days he seemed to wait for me just inside the door to his room and when I passed in the hall, he would beckon to me to sit beside him as he rocked in his old chair. For the next hour or more, until he tired or until something pulled me away, he would fill me with the stories of his wars and of his past, would summon up passions and images and suspense to hold me transfixed, unaware of the passing of time, thirsting for more.

There is, I think, a special affinity that grows between the very young and the very old, between those at the beginning of life and those nearing its end, when they are thrown together without barriers, without interruptions, for long periods. Perhaps it is that the very young are open and accepting, are eager to learn because they have experienced so little, while the very old, who have experienced so much and have so much to tell, have lost all other listeners. Perhaps it is, too, that the very young, if they are not subjected to lectures and sage advice, will listen and absorb and remember the tales of adventure; and the very old see in the very young a continuity of life, the possibility, and maybe the only possibility, that their memories, the magic they discovered in living long and doing much, even their own existence, may stretch out beyond their own time.

Perhaps it was all these things and perhaps there was something more and different, but during that late spring and through the summer, a special bond grew between my grandfather and me. It was a bond that went beyond the fact that we were members of the same family, beyond the fact that we were born on the same day though eighty-one years apart. It grew, I think, from the realization that he had stories to tell me about himself, about real people, some of whom I knew personally and many of whom I knew at least by name, and that he would not, like my parents and most other adults, pretend to an omnipotence and imply a knowledge and a wisdom that should guide my life, that he would not fill me with endless lists of what I should do and what I shouldn't do. He would talk and I would listen and discover and so I would come to know my grandfather better, I think, than anyone in my family.

There was a parade on Memorial Day, the first Memorial Day since the end of the war. The parade would wind the mile and a half along Main Street from the town hall to the old cemetery, where there would be speeches and wreaths laid on the graves not just of the Civil War dead, as in the past, but this year on the graves of the dead of all the wars, the Spanish-American, World War I, and World War II. It was to be the biggest Memorial Day parade our town had ever seen, with veterans of all the wars putting on their uniforms and marching, and at the head, driven because they were too old now to march, our three living veterans of the Union Army.

My father promised to take us—my mother, my grandfather, and me. I was sure he would put on his own uniform and maybe even march in the parade so we could wave to him from the curb when he passed. I hoped he would, wanted desperately for him to do it. I had seen him in the uniform only a couple of times, when he was on leave before going overseas, which I barely remembered, and the day he had come home, when he had taken it off as soon as he was in the house and hung it out of sight somewhere at the back of his closet. But, when we were ready to leave, he came downstairs in an old pair of slacks and a sport shirt. My grandfather was dressed, of course, as always, in a suit, white shirt, and tie. I looked at my father and I guess my disappointment was written in large letters all over me.

He saw it, asked with concern, "What's the matter, Jerry?"

"Aren't you going to wear your uniform, daddy?"

He shook his head. "No. Why?"

"The fathers of all the other kids who were in the army are going to wear theirs, and some of them are even going to march in the parade. I thought you would, too."

"No," he said, "it didn't even occur to me. I'm not even sure where the uniform is anymore."

"It's in your closet. Way at the back."

"I see. You've been looking."

"I thought you'd need it today."

He looked at me and he was serious. "I hope I never need it again."

"But everybody else is going to be wearing theirs."

He studied me for a moment, then sat down on the bottom step and pulled me down beside him. "For some people," he said, "being in the army and fighting the war was the most important thing in their lives. They never get over it. I suppose they don't want to get over it. So every chance they get, they dress up like they were still soldiers and they march in a parade. Maybe it makes them feel young again or maybe it makes them feel important and maybe it makes them live that time again. I don't really know. But, Jerry, for me, you see, going to war was something I had to do so you and your mother would be safe. I didn't want to go but I had to. Now the war's over. I hung up that uniform when I came home and there isn't any reason for me to put it on again. I don't have to show anybody I was in the war. What's important are the things I'm trying to do now for you and your mother, not what I did then. That's over and done with. If other men want to play soldier, that's their business. But it's not for me. Do you understand?"

I tried to. I nodded slowly, uncertainly. "But," I said, "I told all the other kids you were going to put on your uniform, that you were a captain and everything, and that you were going to put on your uniform and march in the parade."

"Well, you shouldn't have told them that, because I'm not going to do it."

"Won't you do it for me, daddy?"

He sighed and shook his head. "No, Jerry. It's something I can't do. Maybe fifty years from now, if I'm still around, when I'm the last veteran, I'll dig it out and put it on. But until then, it's something I'm just not going to do, not for you and not for anyone. Someday I hope you'll understand."

My grandfather was standing in the hall listening, watching us. He nodded several times. I looked to him for help. He said, "You listen to your father, Jerome."

"But, grandpa," I said, "he was a soldier in the war. He has a right to wear his uniform. He ought to wear it today, like everybody else."

"I'm not everybody else," my father said.

"A man does what he must do," my grandfather said.

My mother came from the kitchen, calling impatiently, "What's holding you up? Come on, we don't want to be late."

"In a second," my father said. He studied my face. "I'll tell you what we'll do," he said. "I'll go up and get my garrison cap and you can wear it. How about that?"

I stared at him. My mouth fell open. "Can I, daddy? Can I really?"

"Sure. Why not?" He got up and went back up the stairs, came down in a few minutes holding his army hat. He put it on my head. It fell down over my ears, over my eyes so I couldn't see. He and my grandfather began to laugh. He took the hat off my head. "We'll have to fix that," he said. He carried the hat into the kitchen and we followed. He took some newspaper and stuffed it around the sides of the hat, then set it on my head again. This time it fit, though it was uncomfortable.

My father found places for us in the front row of the spectators along the parade route. We had to wait about a half hour for the line of march to reach us. The spaces around us filled. Several people noticed me wearing my father's hat, laughed, made comments, until finally I was embarrassed and took it off and just held it by my side.

The parade started. We could hear the drum rolls approaching, the bugles, the band striking up martial music. The car with the three Civil War veterans came into view. The three old men in their blue uniforms which no longer fit very well were perched on the backseat. They looked ancient and tiny; a strong gust of wind would have blown them right out of the car and turned them into dust. They were very serious. They did not look left or right, only straight ahead. There were loud cheers from the crowd as they passed.

I stared at them and waved my father's hat, but they did not look toward me. I looked at my grandfather. He was staring at them, too, with a sad expression. I reached out and took his hand. He looked down at me and smiled a little.

"Grandpa," I said.

"Yes, Jerome?"

I pointed to the passing old men. "I'll bet they're older than you."

He laughed then. "You would win that bet," he said. "I was just a little boy like you when they were fighting in their war."

It had never occurred to me until then that he had even been alive when the American Civil War was being fought. I asked, "Did you know about the Civil War when you were my age?"

He shook his head. "In my village in Russia, we did not know about the Civil War in America or about Abraham Lincoln or about the slaves until many years later."

I looked at him to see if he was serious because I found that hard to believe. "How couldn't you know? Didn't everybody know?"

"In Russia, we did not know. We knew only what the czar wanted us to know. And the czar would not have wanted the Russian people to know about a war to free the slaves."

"Why?"

"Because the people might have thought the czar should make all his slaves free."

"Were there really slaves in Russia when you were a boy? Like in the South?"

He thought for a moment, then slowly shook his head. "You will not understand, Jerome," he said. "It was not like in the American South. The slaves in Russia were not Negroes. The slaves in Russia were Russians. They were called serfs. When I was a small boy, a new czar said they should be free. But he did not really mean they should be free and the serfs were still slaves."

"I don't understand."

"I told you you would not understand. Even the serfs did not understand. They thought the czar had made them free but they found they were still slaves."

He had lost me and I told him so. Then I asked, "Were you a serf, grandpa?"

He laughed. "No. I was a Jew. A Jew was not a serf. For the Russians, a Jew was lower than a serf."

"How could anybody be lower than a slave?"

"A Jew in Russia understood."

4

"TELL ME ABOUT RUSSIA, GRANDPA," I asked a dozen times that summer.

"There is nothing to tell about Russia," he said.

"I mean, what was it like?"

"You think it was the moon? When you are a boy, one place is like another because it is the only place you know. Jerome, you tell me about America. If I asked you, what would you say?"

I thought about that and wasn't sure how to begin or what to say.

He answered for me. "You would say it is a place with trees, houses, fields, forests, rivers, people. What else? What else would make it different from another place? You could not tell me because you do not know any other place."

"Oh, I understand that, grandpa. But you know lots of places so you know the difference. What I mean is, what was it like to grow up in Russia when you were a boy and there were serfs and slaves and czars and everything?"

"It was like it is for you to grow up here where there are rich people and poor people and presidents."

"Oh, grandpa, that's not so and you know it."

"You think so? You go to school every day. I went to the *cheder* every day. You will go to the high school when you are old enough and then to the college. I went to the gymnasium, which is like the high school only more. When you are a small boy, Jerome, every place is the same because you live in one very small place with your mama and your papa and you do not know what is different. You cannot even think what could be different."

"But when you're grown-up, you know the difference because by then you've been to lots of different places, so you have to know. Isn't that right, grandpa?"

"When you are grown, you know, yes. But then you forget the other. You forget what it was like when you were a small boy. A boy's memories are a boy's and a man's memories are a man's. To tell you what it was like to grow up in Russia when I was a boy, I would have to remember what it was like to be a boy. I am too old to do that."

He would not be pushed. He had his own tempo, his own rhythm, his own patterns, and he would tell me what he would in his own time. About his life in Russia he did not want to talk then. Bits and pieces would come out in other stories, but he was concerned with other tales.

And so, "Slop like a peasant in the old country would not throw to his pigs, even," he said one afternoon. "That they put on the tables in the home, and they said it was a place that was kosher. They said, eat, eat, it will be good for you, you should eat and be healthy and live long." He made a wry face, as though the memory of that slop even then turned his stomach. "You think your grandpa is making a joke, maybe? You listen, Jerome. About food, that I know. Maybe other things not so much. But about food, there is nobody who knows better."

He was not talking about the taste of food, though that was part of it, of course. He was no gourmet with a finely developed palate who could savor the taste of a well-prepared meal for hours and then recite in exquisite detail years later exactly what had been served. The way he rushed through meals, often with a distracted expression, made me wonder at times if he was really tasting what he ate, if actually he didn't consider eating nothing more than what a man had to do if he was to survive. It was, rather, that he had spent more than thirty years in and around the wholesale food markets, for he had been a peddler of fresh fruits and vegetables, and so had developed an instinct, could recognize without thought, by sight, smell, feel, and the indefinable, the quality of the food he approached. It was not born in him, but learned because it had to be learned. And he had not begun learning it until he was in his forties, until he had been in America for twenty years. It was only one of a dozen twists and changes of direction in his life, beginning—and then I began to discover—when he was a boy in Russia.

His father, my great-grandfather, had been an innkeeper in a village called Nezhin, which was near Kiev in the Ukraine. He was a hard man, a difficult man, who ruled his home and his inn like the czar ruled Russia.

"In my father's house," my grandfather said, "we did not speak unless my father said we might speak, and then we spoke only the words he wanted us to speak. We did not go out and we did not come in unless my father said, go out, come in, and if we went out, we went only where he said we might go."

"What did he do if you didn't do what he wanted?"

"We did only what he wanted. He had sticks like the trunks of trees. He had a knout that stood by the door. He had a strong arm like steel and a hand like a hammer. We did not disobey him."

"What about your mother? Sometimes when daddy's mad at me, mom can say something to him and everything's all right."

He laughed. "You are talking about America. It was not so in my home in Nezhin. My father was the czar and my mother obeyed him just as we did. She would not think to interfere with his wishes."

His mother's place was in the kitchen. She cooked for the family and she cooked for the travelers who stopped at the inn. She cleaned. She took care of my great-grandfather. She had his children, seven of them, five boys and two girls. She raised them as her husband dictated. She kept her silence. My grandfather was the oldest child. At first, his father determined that his place would be in the inn. But my grandfather was smart in school, showed a thirst for knowledge, and in a Jewish boy such a penchant was to be cultivated, not thwarted. So my grandfather went to the *cheder* and then he went to the gymnasium, and it was expected that he would someday be a scholar, a teacher in the community. His life was to be books, his only diversion a flute his father bought him and forced him to learn to play, as my mother forced me to learn the piano, telling him that someday he would understand the value of that musical instrument. When he was growing up and learning the flute, my grandfather always puzzled at why his father was forcing it on him, and why he forced his other sons to learn other musical instruments. They did not play for the guests; there was no orchestra in the village; there seemed no use in learning the instruments except for learning them. Still, they knew enough not to question their father.

"I didn't know you played the flute, grandpa."

"I don't," he said.

"But you did. You learned."

"I have not played the flute in seventy years, maybe," he said.

"Was your father right? Did it help you?"

"Someday I will tell you. Not now."

My grandfather's career was not the only part of his life his father had marked for him. When he was still an infant, he was betrothed to a distant cousin named Ruchele. All the time he was growing up he knew exactly whom he would marry and when. At fifteen, they were marched to the *chuppa,* broke the glass, and moved into a room for themselves in the inn. Before he left Russia six years later, they had three children, Gershon (my Uncle George), Fagel (my Aunt Frances), and Yussel (my Uncle Joseph).

He was twenty-one when he left Russia suddenly, leaving Ruchele and the children behind.

"Why did you leave, grandpa? What happened?"

"Don't ask," he said. "Sometime I will tell you, maybe. Not now."

He got on a ship, sailed across the Atlantic for more than two weeks, wondering, he said, in the retching sickness of overcrowded steerage, whether the stories that the world was flat and eventually you would fall off the edge weren't, after all, true. Finally, when he had about given up hope of ever seeing land again, there was land ahead. "You wouldn't believe, Jerome. Everybody stood on the deck, trying to see. I thought some people would fall over into the water they pressed so hard, they leaned out so far. Everybody cheered. You could not hear yourself the shouting was so loud."

The ship docked, as all ships to New York carrying immigrants did in those days, at Castle Garden. My grandfather had only the vaguest idea of where he was, where he was going, what he would do. In his pocket, he had only a few coins; he had spent everything else for his passage and for an English grammar he had studied all through the voyage, when he could concentrate, so that he would have at least a few words of English when he reached America. He knew the name of only one man in the United States, a friend from Nezhin a little older who had reached the New World a few years before and written back of its wonders and opportunities. He knew the name of the city where the man had settled. It was in a place called New England, but he did not know where New England was.

"What did you do, grandpa?"

"I tell you, Jerome, when the boat stopped, I was afraid to get off. So many people you never saw. Not in Kiev, not in Saint Petersburg, not in Moscow, even. The men from the ship, they came and said, 'Get off, go ashore.' They pushed us off the boat so we had to go onto the land, into this big building. There, a man said, 'What is your name?' I told him. Other questions he asked and I answered. He said, 'Go into that room.' I went. Another man said, 'Take off the clothes.' Everybody took off their clothes. A man who said he was a doctor came and gave a look, asked a few questions, wrote on a piece of paper. He said, 'Put on your clothes.' We put on our clothes. He said, 'Go into that room.' We went. A man gave me a piece of paper that said I could come into America. Then he pointed and he said, 'Go.' So, I went, through the door. There was a long street marching away from the water and I started walking up that street. Several people I stopped and showed them this piece of paper where I had written the name of Lev Dubinsky and the name of the city, Lowell, where he was living. They looked at it and they looked at me and some of them laughed and kept going about their business, and some of them tried to tell me things but I did not understand what they were saying. The English I had studied on the ship was not the English they were speaking. Then I stopped a man and I showed him the paper and he spoke Yiddish. I tell you, Jerome, I could have fallen on my knees and kissed his feet I was so glad to meet a man who could speak a language I could understand."

The stranger read the paper and he looked at my grandfather and he laughed. "Greenhorn," he said. "You've come to the wrong place."

"The wrong place?" my grandfather said. "How can it be the wrong place? I am in America."

"You are in America, all right," the stranger said. "But not the part of America you want to be. America's a big country."

"So, Russia is a big country," my grandfather said.

"Yes," the stranger said, "but if you wanted to go to Moscow, you would not land in Odessa."

"A fool would know that," my grandfather said.

"So, you're a fool," the stranger said. "Where you want to be is Massachusetts. Where you want to be is near Boston. You should have taken the boat to Boston, not New York."

My grandfather said, "What do I know from Boston? You want to come to America you get on a boat and it takes you where it will take you."

"So, it took you to the wrong place," the stranger said.

"So, it took me to the wrong place. How far is the right place, this Boston?"

"Two hundred miles, maybe even a little more."

"And which way is this Boston?"

The stranger laughed at him. "Greenhorn," he said, "you want to go to Boston you walk up this street a couple of miles and you come to the train station. You get on the train and it will take you to Boston, only make sure you get on the right train or you'll get off in Philadelphia or Chicago, even."

"And if not the train?" my grandfather asked.

The stranger looked at him and shook his head. "Greenhorn," he said, "you know nothing. You could walk a little more and come to the stage station and get on the stage and ride to Boston that way. You could buy a horse and ride to Boston by yourself. You have strong legs? You could walk to Boston."

"And in which direction would I go to walk to Boston?"

"You would walk north."

"There is a road?"

"There is a road. It is called the Post Road."

"And I could find it?"

"You could find it without trouble. It begins over there," and he pointed.

"But you took the train, didn't you, grandpa?" I asked.

He shook his head. "For the train you need money and money was the thing I did not have. I went where the man pointed and I began to walk on the road he said I should walk on."

He walked for more than a month, steadily north, following the Boston Post Road. He slept in fields and forests. He foraged for whatever food he could find. He stopped strangers to ask directions, to make sure he was on the right road, going in the right path. The strangers stared at him oddly, did not understand what he was asking as he did not understand what they were telling him. He showed them the paper. They read it, nodded, pointed up the road, so he knew he was moving in the right direction. A few times he stopped and found work on farms, cleaning barns, helping plow fields for a meal and a bed.

A month after he had left New York, he saw Lowell in the distance. "I was on a little hill. I looked down and I saw this city spread out in front of me. I thought I had come to Sodom or Gomorrah, even. The sky was on fire and the smoke was thick and black so I thought it must be midnight over the city even though it was only noon on the hill. I looked at the city and I said, Chaim, turn, go back to Russia where they do not have places like this."

He did not go back, of course. He walked on slowly into the city of fire and smoke, a city of factories. He had not realized how big it would be, how many people there would be in it. He had thought he would merely have to enter it to find Lev Dubinsky. Now he wondered how he could possibly find Dubinsky, if he could ever find him in this midnight place. All that day he wandered the streets, searching, asking people if they knew his friend, getting only uncomprehending stares as an answer. He had no idea where Dubinsky worked or lived, and he began to wonder if Dubinsky was even there any longer.

"It turned into real night, in the city and everywhere," he said. "The streets were filled with the people of the city. Never have I seen so many people in one place all at once. You could not walk on the street without bumping into people. They were people who did not care. They were people who did not have a word, a nod, even a look for a stranger. They bumped into you and they walked by as though you did not exist. I tell you, Jerome, never have I been so alone in all my life, not even when I was alone when I left Russia. I was hungry and I was tired and I did not know what I would do. I had not eaten since the morning and I had been walking since the morning and now I had nowhere to go. I stopped in the middle of the street. A horse charged at me. I thought he would knock me down. I thought he would kill me. I would not have been sorry at that minute. I jumped out of the way of the horse. The man on the horse yelled at me and I did not understand what he yelled, not the words, but I knew what he yelled. Somebody else yelled. I heard the shout and I could not believe what I was hearing. You know what I heard? I heard, 'Chaim! Chaim Jacobson! Is it really you? Here?' Who was coming down the street toward me but Lev Dubinsky."

He slept that night on the floor of Dubinsky's room. It was not the palace Dubinsky had written to Nezhin about. It was one tiny room on the third floor of a rickety wooden building, up a flight of rocking outside stairs from which several rungs were missing so that he almost fell climbing them. There were gaps in the walls that let in the night breezes and that must have channeled the gales and the snows of winter when the weather turned, changing the room into an ice palace. There were gaps in the floorboards and my grandfather could look into the room below, could see a man and a woman copulating on a bed, could hear their sounds and words as though he were in the room with them.

Dubinsky talked to him late into the night, until the people in the room below yelled up for them to be quiet. Dubinsky told him it was not as bad as it looked. He was working in a shoe factory and there was plenty of work for anyone who wanted it. The pay was not bad, better than they could make in Russia, and nobody cared whether you were a Jew or an Irishman and an Italianer or what. Dubinsky said he was putting plenty of money away so that someday he would be rich, so that someday maybe he could start his own business.

My grandfather listened and in the morning he went with Dubinsky to the shoe factory. It was still dark when they groped their way down the stairs, but the job began at dawn and lasted until it was too dark to see any longer. My grandfather was hired and went to work that morning. He was put behind a machine whose functions he did not know, was given a perfunctory lesson in its operations, handed some leather, and told to begin. He discovered he was being paid a few cents for every pair of shoes that came off his machine. He had been raised to be an innkeeper, then a scholar and a teacher, had never done manual labor, and now he was a manual laborer, bent over his machine twelve, fourteen hours a day, just so long as there was enough light to see. Quickly, perhaps for the very reason of surviving, he found that his hands had a dexterity and a skill he had never realized they possessed and that his brain moved ahead of his hands no matter how exhausted he was. It was not long before he was turning out more shoes than anyone else in the factory.

He stayed with Dubinsky for a week and then found a bed in a small room at the rear of the local synagogue, paying for that bed and that room with his own labor, sweeping out the synagogue and the study hall every night when he returned from the factory, then reading, studying to learn English, to learn about America for an hour before falling into dreamless sleep. He spent nothing of what he earned except for meager meals and cheap clothes, putting all he could into a shoe box that he hid in a niche carved in the wall of his room and then covered over.

It took him three years and then he had enough to buy passage and send for Ruchele and his children, to rent and furnish a small flat for their arrival. He waited eagerly, reading the papers every day to make sure he would be at the pier the day the boat docked. On that day, he went to Boston, dressed in a new suit bought specially for the occasion, went down to the harbor, and stared as the boat reached land. He stood on the pier and watched the people disembark, searching for a familiar face. He did not recognize Gershon, Fagel, and Yussel, though he was sure it must be them when he saw three children, two boys and a girl. He approached, saw the papers pinned to their clothes, read their names printed in Yiddish and English on the paper. They looked terrified, but there was something beyond fear of a strange new place. He strained to pick Ruchele from the crowd but he could not find her. His concern growing, filled with trepidation, he went toward the children. They saw him approach and hugged closer around the long skirts of a young woman. She hovered over them protectively. When she saw him, she smiled with obvious relief.

"Are you Mr. Jacobson?" she asked when he reached them.

He nodded. "Yes, I am Chaim Jacobson. These are my children, my Gershon, my Fagel, my Yussel?" They both spoke in Yiddish.

"These are your children," she said.

He reached for them, to take them in his arms. They shied from him, clinging more tightly to the young woman's skirt. He was, after all, not their father but a stranger, someone they had not seen in years, a man they barely recognized if they recognized him at all.

"This is your father, children," she said to them, pressing them toward him. They buried their faces in her skirt, would not look at him.

He understood. He did not press. He looked at the woman and asked, "Who are you? Why are you with my children? Where is my Ruchele?"

"My name is Sarah Meyerson," she said, "from Vinnitsa. I am very sorry, Mr. Jacobson, but I have very sad news for you." Ruchele was dead.

My grandfather said he felt as though God had struck him across the face, leaving a mark that would last forever. He said he had tried to hide his feelings, had kept his face as stiff and stoic as he could while he asked Sarah Meyerson when and how Ruchele had died.

"Why, I do not know," Sarah said. "How, because she suddenly became very ill with something no one could put a name to. When, two days before the ship sailed from Bremen."

"You were with her?"

"I was with her." They had met in Bremen during the week both waited for the ship's sailing. They had been staying in the same rooming house near the port and had become friends. Ruchele had told Sarah that she was on her way to join the husband she had not seen in many years, and that he was working in a factory in a place called Lowell which was near Boston. Sarah had told Ruchele that she herself was on her way to join her three older brothers in Boston, where they had been living since leaving Vinnitsa seven years before, when she was still a girl in her teens, and where they now ran a very successful store that sold clothing and shoes and all sorts of dry goods. During that week of friendship, they had exchanged confidences and hopes, had become close friends, had promised they would see each other in America if that was possible, and Sarah had helped Ruchele care for the three uncertain and bewildered children. Then, without warning, Ruchele became ill, was burning up with a fever, was irrational. Sarah called the doctor. He examined Ruchele and shook his head. There was nothing he could do. Before morning, Ruchele was dead.

"So far from home," my grandfather said, "with no family, with no holy ground to lie in."

"No, Mr. Jacobson," Sarah said, "she rests in holy ground."

"How is that possible? There was no one."

"I was there, Mr. Jacobson. I was her friend. When she died, I went to the synagogue and I went to the burial society. The society came and washed the body and prepared her for burial. The rabbi came and conducted the service. We arranged with the mourners in the society to say the kaddish. And she was laid to rest in the Jewish cemetery."

My grandfather heard her and saw her no longer as a stranger. "Can I thank you?" he said. "Can Ruchele thank you? Can anyone thank you?"

"I do not need thanks," she said. "What I did was for a friend. What I did was what anyone would do."

"Not anyone," my grandfather said. "I can name you some who would not do as much for a brother." He looked toward the children again. "And my children. You cared for them after Ruchele died. You cared for them when they had no one. You cared for these orphans on the voyage across the ocean that was like the voyage of Jonah inside the belly of the whale. You cared for my children like they were your own. I can see now they look on you as a second mother."

"No, not as a mother, Mr. Jacobson," she protested. "Only as a friend."

"More than a friend, Miss Meyerson," my grandfather said, trying really for the first time to see her clearly through the veil of mist that blinded his eyes. "Much more than a friend." He looked away then, scanning the harborside. All around them, the newcomers were being met, were being embraced by relatives, were beginning to move away from the waterfront. He looked back. "No one is here to meet you, Miss Meyerson?"

She shook her head. "My brothers, they could not leave the store." She reached into the purse made of heavy brocaded carpet she carried on her arm and removed a piece of paper. She held it out to him. "But they wrote down the directions so I should not get lost."

He took the paper from her, examined it. "I will take you there," he said.

"That is not necessary, Mr. Jacobson," she said. "You have the children and you have a long journey. I have the directions and I will find my way."

"I will not hear of it. You should not travel by yourself in a strange place on your first day." He retrieved the luggage and, despite her continued protests, led her and the children away from the dock, herded them onto a streetcar, and rode with them to her brother's home. There, he handed her into the care of Abraham Meyerson. For another hour, at the insistence of Meyerson, he sat in the parlor and drank tea, met Sarah's two other brothers, Moses and Daniel, summoned within moments by Abe Meyerson's daughter, Deborah, received their thanks with the disclaimer that he needed no thanks, that what he had done was what anyone would have done, that it was small repayment for what Sarah had done for him and his children.

He put his children to bed late that night in the home in Lowell he had planned for them and their mother, knowing that now it would be a home without a mother, without any woman, knowing that somehow he would have to find the way to cope by himself. He tried to be gentle with his children, understanding that to them he was still a stranger. They were frightened of him and they cried themselves to sleep in their new beds in this new, alien world. He sat up late, constantly moving to stand over their small sleeping forms, staring down, wondering what he would do, how it would be possible for him to care for them.

In the morning, he was faced with the reality of the day, the summons of the factory, the necessity of work. He could not evade that call, yet he could not leave his children alone on this, their first day in the New World. He made them breakfast, tried to talk with them to put them at ease, to win just the trace of a smile, to persuade them he was their father and he would take care of them, would make sure that no more evil befell them. They ate and stared back at him with huge expressionless eyes, their faces frightened, resigned, an aura of defeat all about them.

"You must go to work, papa?" Gershon said at last, and these were almost the first words any of the children had spoken directly to him.

"Yes, I must. If I do not, we will have no place to live, we will have no food to eat, we will have no clothes to wear."

"What will we do when you are at work?"

"What will you do?" And my grandfather knew. "You will do what all the children in America do. You will go to school and learn all they teach so in America you can be what you will be."

He took them to the local school that morning and enrolled them, waited until they were in their classrooms, talking to them without stop, trying to chase the fear, to give them a sense of adventure, a sense that this day was a door opening into the future, a future without limits, available nowhere else in the world.

Then he went to work. He was late. He tried to become invisible as he edged through the factory gates, into the factory, down the aisle to his machine. Just as he began on the first pair of shoes, the foreman came up to him, stood over him.

"Well, Jacobson. I see you managed to get here finally."

"Yes, your honor."

"I suppose you've got a good alibi. You people always have."

"My children, your honor. They arrived in America yesterday, on the ship from the old country. I must put them in the school this morning. So, that is why I am late. It will not happen again."

"You people," the foreman said with scorn. "You're always comin' up with some wild story. Yesterday, we gave you the day so you could meet your kids. Today, you have to wipe their snouts for them. If you was to ask me, I'd make a bet you was out drinkin' a little too much schnapps last night. Am I right?"

"No, your honor," my grandfather said. "What I tell you is the truth. It is my children who have just come to America. I could not leave them until I had put them in the school."

"Yeah, sure," the foreman said. "You stick to your story and me, I'll believe what's the real dope."

"I speak only the truth."

"Since when do people like you know what's the truth? You listen to me, Jacobson. We ain't runnin' a charity institution here. We expect you people to be on time and put in a full day's work."

"I do not work?"

"Oh, you work, all right. That's the only reason I ain't throwin' you out on your can right now. But what I'm gonna do is this. I'm gonna dock your pay three dollars. Maybe then you'll learn we ain't runnin' a charity here."

"Three dollars?"

"You don't like it? The door's right over there. There's plenty more waitin' outside would give their eyeteeth for your job."

My grandfather remembered the children. He held himself back.

"Just remember," the foreman said, "this is the last time. You come in late again and it's out you go, before you can say Jack Robinson. You understand me, Jacobson?"

"Yes, your honor."

My grandfather would not be late for work again, as he had never been late before. He needed the job too much. Every morning, he rose when it was still dark, made breakfast for his children and shared it with them at the table, prepared a lunch for them to take to school. He found a neighbor willing to let them tag along after her children to school and home again in the afternoon, who agreed, for a small price, to watch after them, at least casually, in the afternoon until he got home from work. In the evening, he made dinner for them and, despite his fatigue, sat with them, eating and talking, asking about their day, talking about the future. He sat with them in the light of the oil lamp and the candles while they studied their lessons, and he studied with them, read their books with them, mastered English alongside them, mastered the elements of an American education and of America.

But he worried about them. He was trying to be both father and mother to them and that was not possible. He worried about his failure and could think of no way to right it. Though the children did well in school, seemed to hunger for knowledge, a hunger that could not be satisfied, still there was a melancholy about them that could not be missed. They ached for their mother and she was gone forever. Perhaps they even ached for the familiarity of the old country, for the friends they had left behind, for all that had once been their lives; but all that was gone, too, and was not to be recaptured. He had brought them to this strange land and was forced to leave them as strangers for much of the day, to find their own way while he labored at his last.

They had been in Lowell for nearly a month when he received a letter from Boston, from Sarah Meyerson. She wondered about the children, how they were getting along. She wrote that she missed them, that they had become so close to her and so much a part of her life during those weeks on the sea that something now was absent and there was an emptiness in her existence. She longed to see them again. Perhaps Mr. Jacobson might be willing to bring them to Boston if he had a free day, to share a meal with her and her family.

He wrote back that the children talked about her often, that they were doing well in the new country but obviously missed old friends and would be greatly pleased to see her again. He would bring them whenever it was convenient for the Meyersons. He was free every Sunday.

She wrote that she and her brother would expect them the following Sunday.

He sat once more in the Meyersons' parlor, sat stiffly and uncomfortably. The children had embraced Sarah and run off with her into the yard, animated, laughing, expansive as they had not been in their month in America. He watched them through the window, pulling his eyes away only to answer in monosyllables Abe Meyerson's questions about his work in the factory, about his plans for the future. He was sure Meyerson was cross-examining him for a purpose, but he put that purpose to the back of his mind.

"So, Mr. Jacobson," Meyerson said during the afternoon, "soon you will have been here long enough to be a citizen."

My grandfather was not completely sure what Meyerson was talking about. When he had gotten off the boat in New York, somebody had mentioned something about citizenship but he had not paid much attention. And the men at the factory in Lowell sometimes talked about it, but he listened with only part of his mind. He said, "I am here, so I am an American already."

"You have your papers?"

"My papers? What papers are those?"

Meyerson shook his head sadly. He looked at his brother, Moses. "A real *griner* we have with us, Moses," he said. "Such a greenhorn never before sat in my parlor." He explained to my grandfather that a man could not be a citizen just because he got off the boat and decided he would stay in America. There were things a man had to do before he could become a citizen.

"And what is it I should do?" my grandfather asked.

"First, you must go to the courthouse and tell them you would be an American. You must tell them you have been here for two years and they will give you what they call the first papers. Then you must study and learn the English and learn about America, and when you have been here five years you must go back to the courthouse and answer their questions and put your hand on the Bible and raise your other hand and swear what they say is an oath that you will be a good American. Then they will give you a paper that says you are an American, a citizen."

My grandfather listened and nodded slowly. "The English I am learning already," he said. "About America, I am learning with the children from their books from the school. About the courthouse, when should I go?"

"You should go now; not today, because the courthouse is not open on Sunday. So you should go tomorrow and if not tomorrow, then the next day."

"And my work? You think they will let me off from my work to do this thing?"

"You should tell them what you must do and they will let you off. Maybe a day's pay you will not get, but they will let you off. You ask and you will see, it will be."

The next morning, my grandfather approached the foreman and made his request. The foreman studied him, at first seemed about to refuse, then, with some reluctance, agreed to give him the day off to make the trip into Boston to get his first papers. "I'll let you go," the foreman said at last, "but you won't get no pay. You do it on your own time, Jacobson, and we'll expect you to make up for it when you get back. We'll expect you to turn out double the shoes."

"Pay I do not expect if I do not work. And double I will make. But to become an American, it is a necessary thing to do."

For a year, my grandfather and the children made the trip to Boston every Sunday to visit the Meyersons, dressing in their best clothes, walking to the station, riding the train and then the streetcar. It became a weekly ritual, the one thing to look forward to, the one break in the otherwise unvarying routine of the week over the last in the factory. It was a day of renewal so that the next week could be faced. The children laughed and played with Sarah, held back tears when it was time to leave. My grandfather sat in the parlor, talking with Abe and Moses and Daniel Meyerson and sometimes their wives, too, beginning to feel easier with them, listening as they told him how they had come to America, become citizens, become successful merchants, listening as they told him that in America every door was open, to him as it had been to them, that in America even a Jew could go and do what he would.

It was not Abe or Moses or Daniel with their stories and their advice, with their offered friendship, who really drew him back to that house in Boston every Sunday. It was not even the joy Gershon and Fagel and Yussel, becoming now George and

Frances and Joseph, revealed at the prospect of seeing Sarah and being with her, though for a long time my grandfather told himself that was why he made the trip. It was Sarah herself, seeing her and being with her, and finally he came to realize that. Toward Sarah, he felt an emotion he had never experienced before, an emotion to which he could put no name. His father and Ruchele's father had chosen Ruchele for him when they were still children, and they had grown up knowing they would marry, had never questioned that fact, had understood that their futures were linked. With Sarah, it was different. He was drawn to her by something over which he had no control. He wanted her as he had wanted nothing before in his life. He needed her as he had never needed anything before.

"Miss Meyerson," he said on a Sunday afternoon just before they would leave for Lowell, feeling suddenly shy and hesitant, feeling something unfamiliar churning in his stomach, realizing he was afraid of rejection, "Miss Meyerson, something I must say to you."

She fell silent, his eyes widening. She peered up at him and nodded with seriousness. She waited.

"Miss Meyerson, I should be honored if you would say yes."

"If I knew the question, I might say yes, Mr. Jacobson."

"The question? The question is, I would like to marry you if you would like to marry me."

"You love me, Mr. Jacobson?"

He stared at her. It was an unfamiliar word. "Love? From love I am not sure. About love I do not know. But to marry you, of that I am sure. To live with you, of that I am sure. To come home at night to you, of that I am sure. To wake up to you, of that I am sure. If you say that is love, then I love you."

"That is love, Mr. Jacobson. About you, I feel the same."

"Then we will marry."

"We will marry. But first, my brothers you must ask."

He went to Abe and Moses and Daniel, told them he would marry their sister.

"And how will you live, Mr. Jacobson?" Abe asked.

"We will live."

"You will support our sister, our Sarah?"

"I will support her."

"On the money you make as a shoemaker?"

"In the beginning, yes. She will not starve."

"You have plans?"

"I have plans."

"You will tell us your plans. We can help you, maybe."

"I will tell you my plans when I am ready. I am not ready yet."

"Still you would marry our sister now?"

"Now I would marry her. What will come will come when it is the time."

"So, when it is time, we will tell you our decision."

"And when will it be time?"

"When you come next Sunday, maybe that will be the time. Maybe it will not be the time. We will see."

The next Sunday was the time. They gave their permission and their blessing, and two weeks later, my grandfather and Sarah stood under the *chuppa* and my grandfather broke the glass with the first stamp of his heel.

He took Sarah back to Lowell, back to the small, cramped flat that was only a little bigger and little better than the one he had shared with Dubinsky that first night in the mill town. But now it was a home, a real home as it had not been before. Sarah was all he could have wished for himself and his children, and more. Now he knew the meaning of the word *love* between a man and a woman. In her presence he found pleasure, found fulfillment in the sight of her, could imagine no life without her. She listened to what he said as though the words were new and no other man had ever said them, listened to his dreams and hopes as though no other man had ever had them. She could argue with him, but always with such good humor and such sense that there was no offense and he could never become angry with her. And she loved the children and was as much a mother to them as though they had been born to her. She made that flat a home for all of them, made it seem a palace and all that she desired. With her to share his life, even the routine of the factory no longer seemed so arduous or mind-sapping.

Within a year, their first child, Samuel, was born. Over the next decade, they would have six more—Rachel, Benjamin, Reuben,

Joshua, Rebecca, and finally Miriam, though Benjamin was sickly at birth and did not last a month, and Rebecca was stricken by scarlet fever and died at two.

"It was right after Benjamin was born," my grandfather told me. "My brother-in-law Abe Meyerson was at the flat for a visit. He said to me, 'Mr. Jacobson, next week you will be ready?' "

"Ready?" my grandfather said. "I should be ready for what?"

"You do not remember?"

"What should I remember?"

"Next week, it is the time you will become a citizen. You did not remember such a day?"

And then my grandfather remembered. Once more, he asked for a day off and once more, reluctantly, it was granted, without pay. He and Sarah and the children dressed carefully that morning, rode the train to Boston, where they were met by Abe and Moses, who would stand up for my grandfather and swear to his good character. They rode to the courthouse in Abe's carriage, walked up the courthouse steps and into the clerk's office. Sarah took the first papers from her purse and handed them to my grandfather.

The papers in his hand, he marched up to the clerk. "A real Yankee, with a sour face like a prune he was, Jerome," my grandfather said, "in a coat and a shirt with a collar like you wear to a funeral. Over some papers he was bent. At me he did not look. So, I said, 'I am Chaim Jacobson and I have come to be a citizen of America.' Still at me the man would not look. In Russia, in America, in all the world even, you give a man a title, you call a man an official, he has no time for anyone. So, again I said, 'I am Chaim Jacobson and I have come to be a citizen of America.' "

The clerk looked up finally. He studied my grandfather. He waved a hand. He said, "I heard you the first time. Go and sit over there. I'll call you when I'm ready."

My grandfather went across the room and sat with the Meyersons, with Sarah and the children. He waited. He waited more than an hour. The clerk ignored him. Eventually, the clerk looked up, beckoned. "You. You can come up here now. I'm ready to deal with you." My grandfather approached. The clerk took out a register, opened it, looked at my grandfather. "Your name?"

"I told you already."

"Tell me again."

"Jacobson. Chaim Jacobson."

The clerk wrote. "You have your first papers?"

My grandfather handed them to him. He read them, studied them carefully. He wrote.

"They are all right?" my grandfather asked.

"They're in order." The clerk looked at him. "Where were you born?"

"It says on the papers. In Russia."

The clerk wrote. "Have you ever been convicted of a crime of any kind, here or in Russia?"

My grandfather glared at him. "You think I am a criminal you should ask such a question?"

The clerk looked at him. "I have to ask that question. Just answer yes or no."

"Then I answer no."

The clerk wrote. My grandfather glared at him. The clerk asked, "I suppose you have a job?"

"You think in the streets I beg?"

"That's not what I asked. I asked if you had a job. Just answer yes or no."

"Then the answer is yes."

The clerk wrote. He paused, studied my grandfather. "What kind of job?"

"In the shoe factory, in Lowell."

"Did you bring along witnesses to vouch for your character?"

My grandfather gestured toward Abe and Moses. "My brothers-in-law I brought."

The clerk called them. They approached. "Are you men American citizens?"

"We are, your honor," Abe said.

"And you are prepared to swear that this man is of good character and will not become a public charge?"

"We are, your honor," Moses said.

The clerk wrote. "You can go back to your seats," he told them. They went. He turned again to my grandfather. "If you are granted citizenship in the United States, are you prepared to renounce all allegiance to your native land, Russia, and to all foreign princes, especially the czar of Russia?"

"I would be here if I wasn't?"

The clerk looked at him. "I don't need any comments. Just answer yes or no."

"Then I answer yes. You think from Russia I should want anything? You think from me Russia wants anything?"

The clerk glared at him. He wrote. "Then you are willing to renounce all claims to Russian citizenship?"

My grandfather snorted. "I should renounce what I never had?"

The clerk was growing impatient. "You said you were born in Russia. Isn't that right?"

My grandfather nodded. "In Russia I was born."

"Then you are a Russian citizen."

"A Russian citizen I never was, so how can I give up what I never had?"

"If you were born in Russia, then you are a Russian citizen until you declare otherwise." The clerk drummed on the ledger, his voice testy.

"A Jew I am," my grandfather said, his tone not merely explaining but becoming patronizing. "Maybe not a good Jew, but still a Jew. A Russian citizen? Never. In Russia, no Jew is a citizen. The czar would not let such a thing be. So. Mr. Clerk, tell me, how can I give up what I never had?"

The clerk glared. He pushed the ledger to one side. "You're wasting my time," he said.

"How am I wasting your time? A question you ask, a question I answer. When I cannot answer, I tell you."

"You call these answers?"

"You would call them what?"

The clerk looked toward the Meyersons. "If you want this man to become a citizen," he said, "then I would suggest that you tell him just to answer my questions without all his explanations and shilly-shallying. If he keeps giving me these arguments, I'm going to send him packing. I'm not here to play these games with people like him. This is a serious business and he'd better realize it. Becoming an American citizen is no joking matter. If he thinks it is, then maybe he ought to go back where he came from. He'll find out just how the czar handles people like him."

Abe Meyerson rushed to my grandfather's side, pulled him away. "Mr. Jacobson," he whispered, imploring, "you should stop what you are doing. Just answer what the man asks."

"A question he asks I can answer, I will answer. What else have I been doing?"

"You want him to say you cannot be a citizen the way you are acting? You want he should send you back to Russia? You want he should send Sarah and the children back to Russia?"

"The way he is acting, in Russia I could be already."

Meyerson stared at him, aghast. "You can say such a thing?"

"I can say it. You give a man a title, it don't' matter where he is, he acts the same."

Meyerson shook his head. "Mr. Jacobson, think, use your head, use the brains God gave you. In Russia, an official, he would ask you a question you could answer? You, a Jew, he would even ask a question?"

My grandfather considered that. He nodded slowly. "You are right, Mr. Meyerson. In Russia, he would not ask."

"In Russia, they would let you, a Jew, become a citizen?"

"You are right. In Russia, a citizen they would not let me be."

"In Russia, you could vote for the czar? You could vote for who you wanted to be the czar?"

"You are right. In Russia, the czar is the czar and no one votes to say he should or he should not be."

"Especially not a Jew."

"Especially not a Jew."

"But in America, a citizen can vote for who he wants to be the president, who he wants to be anything."

"You are right, Mr. Meyerson."

"In Russia, a man can be what he wants to be?"

"In Russia, a man is what the czar says he should be."

"But, in America, a citizen can be whatever he wants to be," Meyerson shouted in triumph.

My grandfather nodded slowly. "So, Mr. Meyerson, I should do what?"

"You should answer the man's questions is what you should

do. You should not argue with the man is what you should do. Then, maybe, he will let you become a citizen."

"I will do what you say, Mr. Meyerson."

"So, Jerome," my grandfather said, "I went back to the clerk and I said I would do whatever he wanted and I said I was sorry if I had said anything I should not have said. A few more questions he asked me and this time I did not try to explain, I answered his questions yes and no. Then he took out a book and he opened to a page and he told me to read to see if I could read the English. What he showed me I had already read in the books that my children had from the school. But I did not tell him that. I read from the book for him. You know what I read? I still remember it: 'We, the people of the United States, in order to form a more perfect Union, establish justice, insure domestic tranquility, provide for the common defense, promote the general welfare, and secure the blessings of liberty to ourselves and our posterity, do ordain and establish this Constitution for the United States of America.' When I had read, he said that was enough. Then he told me to put my hand on the Bible and to raise my right hand and he read some words to me that I should repeat and say, 'I do,' and then he said a citizen I was. He took a big piece of fancy paper with fancy writing on it. He filled in blank places. He told me to sign my name and he signed his name. He gave me the paper and he said, 'Now, Mr. Jacobson, you are an American. Never lose this paper. It will show everyone everywhere that you are an American citizen.'"

"Do you still have the paper, grandpa?"

"I still have the paper, Jerome. I have always kept it."

"Can I see it sometime?"

"You can see it." And later that day, he came to my room with the certificate. It was very large. The paper was a heavy parchment of a kind I had never seen before and have rarely seen since. The writing was all in script, and you knew, looking at it, that the script would fade and vanish long before the paper finally disintegrated into dust. In fact, the script was already fading and the ink in the places where the clerk had written and where my grandfather had signed his name had turned brown with age and there were some letters that could no longer be made out, that had vanished with the years.

So, my grandfather had become a real American, and with him, Sarah and the children had become Americans. With that precious document in his hand, they went back to Lowell. The next day, he went back to work at the shoe factory, and nothing had changed and everything had changed.

As his family grew, the pressures on my grandfather increased and his responsibilities multiplied. He had always known he would not stay at his last forever, not if his dreams were to become reality, not if his children were to have a chance to go as far as they could go in this country where all of them were now citizens. The children were growing faster than he would have believed possible. They had to be fed, yet no matter how much they ate, it was never enough. They had to be clothed, yet the instant they were in new clothes, the clothes wore out, became too small. They needed schooling, thirsted for knowledge, and he was determined he would deny them nothing, would give them the best he could. The boys would all go to college, would become men of stature, perhaps doctors or lawyers or engineers, perhaps even businessmen if that was where their desires led them. He was sure they would all go far. The girls would learn what girls had to learn and maybe even a little more so they could marry well and help their husbands and give him grandchildren to make him proud. But such dreams could not be realized behind a machine, no matter how long and hard he worked, no matter how many pairs of shoes he made each day. He was sure that he had learned enough, as much as there was to learn, about the making of shoes; he had even thought of ways, which he kept to himself, to cut costs and still maintain and even improve the quality. It was time to make the change.

If it was time, still there was the question of how to take advantage of the moment. He had only a minuscule savings, nowhere near enough. He talked with Sarah, elaborated on his dream. She listened, told him he could do it, told him he should do whatever was necessary to make it happen, told him she was sure her brothers would help, told him she would go with him to Boston and talk with her brothers. They went to Boston, spent an entire Sunday with the three men, explaining in detail what my grandfather proposed. The brothers listened, nodding approval. It was about time, they said, that their brother-in-law showed ambition, that he did something to ensure the future for Sarah and the children. They would lend him what money he needed to get started; they would set up a special department in their store to sell the shoes he made; they would talk to men they knew in Springfield, in Hartford, in Providence, in Bangor, in Portland, all over New England, and persuade them to carry his line when he was ready.

"So, we went home to Lowell," my grandfather said, "and I knew it was the time. But I said to myself, Jacobson, a lot you know, but not enough. Sometimes it is better to have two heads than one. So, you should have a partner."

He went to his friend Dubinsky. It was a rainy Sunday in the early spring and he took Dubinsky for a walk in the rain into the country outside Lowell. Dubinsky complained about the weather, complained about the rain, complained that he was getting soaked and would end up in bed with pneumonia so he wouldn't be able to work and then how would he live, if he survived the sickness. My grandfather said it was better they talk in the fields in the rain where nobody would hear them. Besides, Dubinsky was a strong man and a little rain never hurt anyone. He needed a bath anyway.

"So, Jacobson, what is it you want to talk?"

"What I want to talk about is a factory."

"We work in a factory. What is there to talk about that?"

"We should talk about a factory we should own."

"Jacobson, in your head you have borscht instead of brains. You want to start a factory? You would make what?"

"Shoes. What else would I make?"

"Shoes? Jacobson, you should see a doctor. Crazy you are."

"Don't run away, Dubinsky. The Cossacks, they are not chasing you. Stay and listen." They walked on through the soaking fields, ankle-deep in water and mud, while my grandfather explained his plan to Dubinsky.

"Jacobson," Dubinsky said when my grandfather finished, "do I hear you? You think a Jew can fight the Yankees where the Yankees live and own everything?"

"This Jew can do it."

"Jacobson, I do not know. It would not be easy."

"About easy, who said anything? Hard it would be, but we could do it."

"Do I hear you or are my ears playing tricks? You are saying we?"

"Of course I am saying we. You think if I was not saying we I would be talking to you in the rain?"

"You want me to leave the factory? You want me to work for you? Crazy you are."

"Who is talking about working for somebody? I am talking about partners."

"Partners? You want me to be a partner?"

"Czar Alexander I am not asking. Queen Victoria I am not asking. President Cleveland I am not asking. You, Dubinsky, I am asking."

"What should I say?"

"You should say yes."

"I should go to the insane asylum I should say yes."

"You want you should work for the Yankees for the rest of your life for pennies and when you are too old they should throw you onto the street and not even say good-bye? That is what you want, Dubinsky?"

"It would not happen if I become your partner?"

"It would not happen."

"No, on the street I would be before I am old."

"You are afraid?"

"I am afraid."

"Dubinsky, be afraid of a gun when it is pointed at you. Be afraid of a lance in the hands of a Cossack. Be afraid of the ocean if you cannot swim. But do not be afraid to take a chance to be rich."

"You think we would be rich?"

"I think so. But you, why should you worry? You have a little money. Put it into the business. I have a little money. I will put it into the business. The rest, what we need, my *mishpocheh* will lend, and contacts they will give us, too. You, what do you have to lose? A little money? That is nothing. You have no wife, you have no children, so what should you worry? You should not have to think, even. Let us be partners, Dubinsky. We will stop being serfs to the Yankees. We will start a place of our own. We will be our own bosses. Think, Dubinsky, think. Who else should do it? Who else knows the shoe business better?"

"So, for you I will think. But I will not promise. Now, let us get out of this rain before we get pneumonia and it is too late to think."

Whether Dubinsky would ever have said yes on his own, my grandfather was never sure, though he thought in time he probably would have. But the decision was made for him. Someone must have seen them talking so intently together and done some arithmetic, or a store owner approached by the Meyersons must have told another store owner who told someone who told someone else, and so the rumors started and the word was out. Whatever the cause, about a week later, in the middle of the morning, my grandfather and Dubinsky were hauled away from their lasts, told the company had no place for malcontents, troublemakers, and traitors, and then thrown out the door and onto the street, not even paid what was owed to them for the week's work.

"We stood on the street outside the gate to the factory," my grandfather said. "We looked at each other. We nodded. We shook hands. I said, 'Dubinsky, my partner.' Dubinsky said, 'Jacobson, my partner.' "

They found an abandoned, run-down plant in Lowell, bargained with the bank that owned it, bought it for what my grandfather said was a little song. He and Dubinsky took off their coats and went to work and fixed it up. They filled it with secondhand machines and my grandfather spent the next month adapting them for some new manufacturing ideas he had. They went to suppliers and bought leather and other raw materials, paying cash that first time to establish their credit, for they had no credit then, of course. They hired a dozen workers, mostly Jewish immigrants who had arrived after them. And then they began making shoes.

The first year and a little more was not easy, was harder than my grandfather could have imagined when he began. He had been sure they would succeed with the first pair off their machines. There was a lot he had not reckoned on. He knew manufacturing, more even than he realized. Dubinsky had an innate sense of styling. But they knew almost nothing about pricing, shipping, merchandising, and so much more that goes into establishing and running a successful business. They had to learn as fast as they could as they went along, with the constant help and advice of the Meyerson brothers.

"A thousand times that year I said to myself, Chaim Jacobson, you are a fool. You are heading for the poorhouse on an express train and you will be there before you can turn around and you can blame only yourself. A thousand times Dubinsky came to me and he said, 'Chaim Jacobson, look what you have done. Better off we would be with the Yankees. With the Yankees, we had pennies at least. Now, we have nothing and pretty soon it will be more nothing until there is only nothing times nothing.' "

What kept them going while they mastered the tricks of business, the shortcuts, the techniques of success was that my grandfather had been right in at least one thing: he knew how to make a better pair of shoes than his competition and at cheaper prices. And his brothers-in-law and their friends who handled those shoes were soon selling them as fast as they could get them in stock.

So, the reputation of the Jadin shoes, the name my grandfather and Dubinsky adopted for their company, spread around Boston and across southern New England. Eighteen months after they opened their doors, they wrote the first entry in black ink in their ledgers. The ink grew blacker, the profits climbed. They bought more machines, hired more workers, paid off the loans to the Meyersons, discovered that wherever they went they had credit.

"So, now Dubinsky sees me and he says, 'Chaim Jacobson, we are two geniuses. We have an idea and we start our business and look what happens. The Yankees will have to learn from us if they want to stay in the shoe business. For us, the leather is turning to gold.' "

Still, my grandfather was nagged by a sense that all was not right. He could not forget his own days at the last, those long hours, twelve, fourteen of them six days a week, and the few pennies they earned him on payday. He wandered through his factory and studied the workers bent over the machines, sagging with fatigue at the end of the day, still numb with fatigue when they started again in the morning. There were accidents in the plant and he was sure, from his own experience, that they were the result of minds destroyed by weariness. He noticed, too, that by the end of the week, the output of the plant was measurably lower than at the beginning, and there were often flaws in the shoes, the quality not as good.

He went to Dubinsky. He said, "Dubinsky, we are going to do something you will not like until you think about it."

Dubinsky said, "What now, Jacobson? Things are not good enough?"

"Things are not good enough. So, I tell you, this is what we are going to do. We are going to cut our hours. The men in the plant, they will work only ten hours a day from now on. More. We are going to raise the pay. We will raise it a nickel a pair."

Dubinsky was appalled. "Jacobson," he said, shouting, raging, "your mind you have lost? You want to drive us from business? You would pay people more for working less? Jacobson, a doctor you need."

"Dubinksy, you listen to me for once."

"I listen to you too much. That is the trouble."

"Listen, Dubinsky! Be quiet for a minute and listen with your ears and your head. You remember in the factory in the old days what it was like? By the end of the week, you were so tired it was lucky if you made one pair of shoes in an hour. How many times did you cut off your hand almost, you were so tired? So, think. The men work less, they will work harder, they will make more shoes, they will make better shoes. The men work less, they will not be so tired, they will not have accidents. The men work less, they will make more shoes, they will earn more money, they will be happier and better workers and we will make more money."

"Jacobson, go see a doctor."

"Dubinsky, we will do as I say."

"Jacobson, you are crazy. You will put us in the poorhouse."

"Dubinsky, I will put you in the rich house."

Dubinsky stormed. My grandfather stormed back. They raged at each other all that day and the next, for a week. My grandfather prevailed. The hours were cut, the wages were raised, and, as my grandfather had predicted, output increased and so did quality, while accidents fell sharply.

It was not long before word of the new hours and wage rates at Jadin was all over Lowell. There were lines at the factory every day of men seeking work. My grandfather and Dubinsky had their pick of the best shoemakers in Lowell, and in all the nearby cities and towns.

A delegation of the other factory owners came to see my grandfather. They were enraged, of course. They told him he was destroying the whole manufacturing system in the United States. They called him a radical who wanted to overthrow the country. They told him he ought to go back to Russia. They told him he was a traitor to his class, by which, he assumed, they meant the capitalist class of which he had become a member. He listened to them. He said he wanted to throw them out of his office, but he did not. He sat behind his desk and heard what they had to say. He said he laughed at them finally and told them maybe they ought to do what he was doing because he had no intention of going back to the old way. He told them that if they followed his example, maybe they would have the same kind of success he was enjoying. They told him that someday he would regret it. He told them he didn't think that day would ever come no matter what happened. They told him that when it did, he shouldn't come to them looking for help. He said that when he was working at a last for them and needed help, they hadn't given him any, so why should he expect any help from them now or ever if he was to need it. He told them he had to get back to work and maybe they ought to get back to their own work. They told him he'd be sorry he ever crossed them. He said, so he'd be sorry, but maybe they'd be sorrier.

They went back to their own factories, but they did not forget or forgive and they did not give in. Jadin Shoes was branded an outlaw by its competitors, and as an outlaw, it was to be driven to the wall and then into the grave at all costs. Pressure was put on suppliers not to sell leather, lace, and other raw materials to my grandfather and Dubinsky, or, if they sold, to sell only for cash on delivery, to extend no credit. Bankers were told that if they lent money to Jadin, they would lose the business of the other manufacturers. Retailers were ordered to drop the Jadin line or lose the other shoe lines they were handling. Jadin's workers were threatened. The competitors cut the prices of their own shoes. And they spread rumors that Jadin was shaky, that it would soon collapse.

My grandfather fought back and a war was under way in the shoe business. "To the suppliers, I said, so we will pay cash like we did when we started. Only, you should remember, when we win this war, we will not forget and somebody else to supply us maybe we will find. To the bankers I said, so, you will not lend to us? At the beginning you did not lend and still we did all right. When this is over and you want our business again, maybe some other bankers someplace else we will go to. The retailers, they laughed at the Yankees. My brothers-in-law made sure of that. People wanted to buy our shoes, not the shoes the Yankees were making, so they would handle our shoes. And, you know something, Jerome, now we were getting bigger orders than before, especially when I said to Dubinsky, 'The Yankees want to cut their prices, we will cut our prices, which are lower than theirs already, and we will see who will fall off the mountain and break a leg first.' To the workers, I said, 'You don't want to work for us anymore because you are afraid, I give you permission to quit, but this is America and my permission you do not need. Outside, there are plenty of people would like to work for Jadin.' Let me tell you, Jerome, nobody quit. And for the rumors, at them I laughed."

The war lasted nearly a year. Two shoe companies—one in Lowell and one in a nearby city—went under, closed their doors, unable to sell at the low prices and still make a profit, yet unable to sell at their original prices now. Jadin suffered only a little. Its profits were not as large as they had been, but there was still a profit. And its cash reserves had to be tapped, but my grandfather had always insisted there be plenty of cash reserves for emergencies; he had built his company to last, to weather any storm. The peace came without discussions or treaty, without any word to my grandfather that peace had arrived. He realized it only when a delivery of leather arrived at the gates and the supplier said cash was not necessary, Jadin would be billed for the leather on the first of the month; when a banker dropped by to ask how things were going and whether, perhaps, Jadin might need a loan to finance expansion or new purchases. My grandfather said he only smiled a little and went back to work.

One day, my grandfather realized that he was rich, and it was time to do something for his family. He bought land on the outskirts of Lowell, built a house big enough for Sarah and the children, bought a milk cow that Sarah tended every morning, bought a rooster, hens, and chicks, bought a horse and a carriage to take him to work every morning and home every night. There was enough land, too, for Sarah to raise flowers and to grow vegetables. For a few weeks in the summer, he rented a house for Sarah and the children on a lake in the White Mountains of New Hampshire (no hotel would take Jews then), though he did not go with them. These things he did for his family, and more. For himself, there were only some clothes—he had by then taken to wearing a suit, white shirt, and tie at all times, a habit he was never to lose—and work. He still rose before dawn and was at the factory before anyone else. He stayed at the factory all day until after dark, was always the last to leave.

But not Lev Dubinsky. He luxuriated in his new riches. "You think you have seen a peacock?" my grandfather said. "Until you saw Dubinsky, you never saw a peacock. A different suit every day, a different shirt, a different tie, never the same twice, colors you wouldn't believe. And suits like you never saw. He had them tailor-made by hand by the best in Boston. They cost him hundreds, and in those days, hundreds were thousands."

And Dubinsky went courting, though my grandfather was not aware of it at first. He was aware only that Dubinsky was leaving work early two and three days a week, that he was coming in late several mornings, that he talked about seeing shows in Boston, about eating in restaurants in Boston, talked constantly about Boston.

One day, he arrived at work about noon. He strode into the office, wearing a huge, self-satisfied smirk. He went to my grandfather's desk, stopped, said, "Jacobson, say congratulations."

My grandfather looked up at him. "And why should I say congratulations? Because you came to work today? Because you came before it is time for lunch?"

Dubinsky laughed. "Jacobson, just say congratulations."

"So, congratulations already. And for what are the congratulations?"

Dubinsky said, "Lev Dubinsky is going to stand under the *chuppa* at last."

"Under the *chuppa*?" My grandfather stared at him. Dubinsky was not a young man anymore; he was older than my grandfather; he was already past forty. "You have found a woman?" he asked.

"Such a woman like you never saw."

"Women I've seen plenty."

"Not like Hannah. A girl she is, like no other girl."

"At your age, Dubinsky, a girl is one thing you do not need. A woman, maybe, but a girl, never."

"Jacobson, you should understand. If anyone, you should."

"I understand already."

"At my age, a man needs a family."

"At your age, a man needs a doctor."

"Jacobson, you are making jokes. This is no joke. You should meet her and you would see."

"So, introduce her already."

"This girl, you should be so lucky. From a good family, the best. In America twenty years already, maybe more. And money like you would never believe."

"I believe. So, when am I going to have the honor?"

"At the wedding, of course."

"And the wedding is when?"

"Next week."

My grandfather and Sarah went to the wedding at a synagogue

in Boston the next week. They met Hannah. "A girl she wasn't," he told me. "About her good family, I don't know. But I could see with the first look that a girl she hadn't been for twenty years. She was as old as Dubinsky, maybe older. And with a family already. There were four daughters and the youngest was older than you, Jerome. Dubinsky said she was rich. But at the wedding, before Dubinsky broke the glass even, and it took him four tries with his foot before he could break it, it was, 'Lev, I want this,' and, 'Lev, buy me that,' and, 'Lev, you would not want me not to have the other.' That was only the beginning. I tell you, Jerome, I looked at Sarah and I held her hand and I thought, Chaim Jacobson, you have never been so lucky."

Dubinsky took his bride and her four daughters for a honeymoon to Niagara Falls. When they returned, he built them a house far bigger and grander than my grandfather's. He bought a horse and carriage for himself and another for his bride. He sent them to Boston and New York to buy completely new wardrobes, to buy the most expensive furnishings for the house. He took them on trips, to the mountains, to the ocean, took a month off in the summer so they could all board a ship and sail to England and France first class. He was, my grandfather said, spending money like he owned the Philadelphia mint. And he was doing something else that my grandfather knew nothing about then. He was gambling, on the horses, on anything where a bet was possible.

But my grandfather did not have time to worry about Dubinsky's new high style of living. And he did not have the energy or the emotions to consider the implications. Sarah was pregnant again, only this, her seventh pregnancy, was proving a difficult one. Several times she hemorrhaged and almost lost the child. She was forced to spend most of every day in bed, rising only for meals. She was pale, had little energy. My grandfather called in doctors from Boston. They told him they were worried but there was nothing anyone could do but wait and pray.

He waited and he prayed and he spent as much time as he could when not at the factory at her bedside. She told him not to worry, everything would be all right. She had had six children before and, though two had died, nothing had ever happened to her. "Don't worry, Mr. Jacobson," she soothed him, "I will live to be a grandmother, even a great-grandmother."

Her labor came. It should have been easy after all the children she had already delivered. But this child was a breech, the delivery excruciating and lengthy. At last, the baby, a girl, my Aunt Miriam, was born. She was fine and healthy and alert, setting out loud cries at the moment of birth. Sarah saw her, held her for a moment. Then she started to hemorrhage again. The midwife could not stop the bleeding. My grandfather rode as fast as he could, whipping his horse to near death, to the doctor. By the time the doctor arrived at the house, Sarah was dead.

Tragedy is its own messenger; nobody has to be told bad news; it is carried on the winds, drifting where it will so that no one remains ignorant for long. The people seemed to know instinctively. Nobody gave orders but the factory doors were sealed the day of Sarah's funeral and the entire work force appeared at the synagogue; a delegation of workers came to my grandfather and cried its own grief at his loss. The Meyersons were at the house within hours of Sarah's death, stayed on, the women taking charge of the children, taking charge of the entire house. Dozens of merchants who had dealt with my grandfather showed up at the synagogue and the cemetery from all over New England, and so did suppliers, middlemen, and others. There was not room for them all in the synagogue and many had to stand outside the doors, which remained open so they could join in the prayers for the dead. My grandfather hardly noticed, but even some of his Yankee competitors, those who had railed the most ferociously at him a few years before, who had been the most threatening and unrelenting, put their bitterness to one side for that moment, appeared at the ceremonies, came to him and murmured soft words they hoped would comfort.

Only Lev Dubinsky, his wife, and her children were missing. They were in New York when Sarah died, did not learn of the tragedy until too late. Dubinsky raced to the house where my grandfather was sitting shivah the next day, tears streaming from his eyes. He came to my grandfather and embraced him, as though it were he who needed solace and not my grandfather.

"Jacobson," he sobbed, "what is there to say?"

My grandfather held him off, looked into his face. "Dubinsky," he said, "there is nothing to say."

"A tragedy like this the world has never seen," Dubinsky said. "Such a woman. Such a mother. Such a loss. How will you live, my friend?"

"I do not know, my old friend. I do not know."

"You should do nothing," Dubinsky said. "Do not worry about the business. That I will take care of. You should rest. You should comfort the children. You should comfort yourself. You should go away for a little, even. But about the business you should not worry. I, Dubinsky, will be as you and me, like both of us as one."

My grandfather was not alone; at least he had some help. His sisters-in-law stayed for days, and when they went back to their own homes and families in Boston, they left behind Deborah Meyerson, Abe's oldest and still unmarried daughter. She took charge as though she had been born to it, tending the children, sending them off to school, hiring a wet nurse for the baby, Miriam, hiring maids to come in and clean the house, doing the cooking herself. She took over so totally that it was not long before my grandfather could hardly imagine the house without her in it, without her running it, could not imagine the children without her to guide them and mother them.

He stayed home, sat shivah for the week, then went back to the factory. It no longer seemed very important. He sat at his desk but could not concentrate on the papers that piled up around him, could not deal with the problems that confronted him. They seemed of little consequence. Still, every morning he went to the plant, spent his day at the desk, though the hours went by and he did little before going home in the evening.

Dubinsky came to him. "Jacobson, go home," he said.

"I should go home? How? The business, it needs me."

"Jacobson, for the first time you should listen to me," Dubinsky said. "The business, it does not need you. Who needs you is your children, not the business. The business will need you when you need the business. You think it will blow away because you are not here? It runs itself, like a clock from Switzerland, even. And what needs a little winding now and then, I, Dubinsky, will wind. What else is a partner for? You should go home to your children and leave the business to Dubinsky."

For once, my grandfather did not argue. He was wise enough, even in his grief, to realize that he was no good to the company as he was, that in his state, decisions were beyond him. Before he could function efficiently again, he would have to come to some kind of terms with the loss of Sarah, would have to find his way back to life. After all his years with Dubinsky, he had faith in his partner's judgments despite those recent eccentricities. The business, he persuaded himself, would go on as always with Dubinsky in total command.

For the first time in his life, my grandfather put his business and the outside world to the side and devoted himself to his family. Though he still tried to spend a couple of hours a day in the office, he ate his meals with his children, spent most of every day with them, reading and telling stories to the younger ones, taking long walks through the fields with the older ones, listening to their hopes and their dreams, trying to get to know his children. One morning, he went to the barn and tried to milk the cow, and even enjoyed the mocking laughter of Deborah and the children. He went with Deborah in the morning to help collect the eggs and feed the chickens. He took them shopping to Boston. When the weather grew hot, he rented the house in the White Mountains once again, only this time he went with them for the two weeks and even tried to learn to swim, laughing along with his children at his ineffectual splashing in the shallow lake waters.

"Before," he said, "I worked like a dog in the shoe business. Every day I left the house, sometimes on the Sabbath even, in the dark. I got home in the dark. The children, they did not know me. I came in the door, they hollered, 'Mama, a stranger comes through the door.' You think I am joking, Jerome? It was the truth, believe me. Sarah had to tell them it was only their papa. I had no time to read the newspapers, so what was happening in the world I knew only when someone told me. Maybe five books I looked at in ten, fifteen years. There was only the factory. Everything was the factory. To myself in those days, I said, Chaim Jacobson, this is the way of the world; it is the life of a man so for his children things should not be so hard. Then my Sarah died and the factory, everything, was like a puff of smoke in my hands and I knew I held only the air."

By fall, he felt restored enough to consider returning to work full-time. It did not occur to him then that Deborah might have plans of her own, that she was not a permanent fixture in the house under the circumstances as they then were. When the children went back to school, he announced that it was time for him to take up the business once more.

"It is what a man should do, Mr. Jacobson," she said.

"So, I will begin tomorrow," he said.

"And I will go back to Boston at the end of the week," she said.

He was stunned. "You will go back to Boston?"

"I cannot stay here forever," she said. "I have my own life and it is time for me to see to it."

"What will you do in Boston?"

"I will live," she said. "I do not grow younger, Mr. Jacobson. It is time for me to think of the future."

He knew he could not let her go. When the children heard her plans, they pleaded with her to stay, told her they would be lost without her. Their father was going back to the factory, she was going back to Boston, the house would be empty. Who would take care of them? What would they do? She said a woman could be hired to come in and take care of the cooking and the cleaning and all the other things. She would find such a woman before she left. But she must go.

My grandfather did the only thing he could to keep her. He asked her to marry him.

"Mr. Jacobson," she said, "you do not love me."

"Love," he said. "What is love? You think I loved Ruchele when I married her?"

"But Sarah you loved."

"Sarah was different. Love is what you learn. It would be good for me; it would be good for you."

"To cook and clean for you and your children? To be a mother to your children? That is what you want?"

"What else is there?"

"For that you could hire a woman."

"It would not be the same."

"Mr. Jacobson, I must tell you. I want children of my own."

He nodded slowly. "If it is God's desire, then you will have children of your own."

So, my grandfather delayed his return to work another month, long enough to stand under the *chuppa* once more, now with Deborah, break the glass, and ride off for a honeymoon.

He came back to his desk to find a very worried Dubinsky. The country was sliding into recession and depression. Everywhere, people—merchants and consumers alike—were pulling back, afraid to buy, afraid to spend. The orders began to slow down, to dry up, and suppliers began to demand immediate payment, payment on delivery. A year before, credit had been easy; now everyone wanted cash.

Dubinsky was frantic. He waved a handful of outstanding bills at my grandfather even before my grandfather had time to sit down behind his desk. "Jacobson," he said, "look at these."

My grandfather took the bills, ran through them quickly. "So," he said, "pay them."

"Jacobson, you do not understand. Everybody wants money but nobody pays money."

"Dubinsky, what are you talking? Since when we haven't had money to pay? Always we have kept money to pay the bills even when people did not pay us so quick. So, what is different now?"

"The world, it is different," Dubinsky said. "For months, you have not been here. If you had been here, you would know."

"So, why you did not tell me before?"

"The way you were, it would have done no good. Besides, you could have done nothing. I have done everything and it is not enough."

"Dubinsky, somebody breathes, you think it is a hurricane. This business we did not build on quicksand. We built it on rock." My grandfather was sure the company could weather this economic storm, could weather any crisis. He had built it to last, had moved forward only when he was sure the footing was solid and he knew the foundation was safe, secure. They might have to contract, to lay off some workers, to shut down some machines, but they would come through. Their reputation for price and quality would see to that.

He said to Dubinsky, "All right, so we tighten the belt a little. Everybody will do that, so why should we be different? Everything will be okay, hunky-dory, believe me. These bills, we have the money, we will pay them. Then, who do we owe? Nobody, that's who. So, what can happen?"

Dubinsky only moaned. "Oy, Jacobson, you should only know."

He said, "Dubinsky, what is it that I should know that I don't know already?"

Dubinsky said, "The whole country is in big trouble."

He said, "So, the whole country is in trouble. You are telling me something I don't know already?"

Dubinsky said, "If the country is in trouble, we are in trouble, too. You don't know, Jacobson. You don't know."

"I know. You think because there is big trouble we should jump into the ocean and drown?"

"Oy, Jacobson," Dubinsky repeated with a frightened groan, "you should only know."

He said, "Dubinsky, what I know is we work hard and we don't be foolish. People got to wear shoes because they cannot go barefoot these days anymore. Lots of things they will give up, but not shoes. And who makes better shoes cheaper than Jacobson and Dubinsky? Tell me, who?"

"You know, Jerome," my grandfather said, "I could have been talking to the wall. You know why? Because I was talking to my partner, to Dubinsky. When he said I didn't know, he was right, I didn't know. When Sarah died, he said I shouldn't worry. Worry is what I should have been doing. When Sarah died, he said the factory would run like a clock and he would do the winding. He wound it all right, only he wound it and put it in his pocket. On a Monday morning, I went to the factory and there was no Dubinsky. I asked everybody, 'Where's Dubinsky?' Nobody knows. All morning I waited and no Dubinsky. So, in the afternoon, I get the horse and carriage and I ride to Dubinsky's house. Nobody is there. It is locked up so tight a mouse could not find a hole to get in. The carriages and the horses are gone from the barn.

The next day there is still no Dubinsky and the house is still locked like nobody is ever going to unlock it."

Dubinsky was gone, vanished into the darkness of the weekend with his family. But he had vanished with more than his family. He had disappeared with all the liquid assets of the company. Left for my grandfather were only chaos and debt beyond his comprehension. My grandfather went back to the factory, locked himself into the office, took all the books and records, and tried to go over them, to make sense of them. He spent days adding, subtracting, never arriving at anything he could understand. According to his calculations, there was no money in the bank, there was very little still outstanding from customers, only payments for what had been ordered and shipped over recent weeks; and there were months of unpaid bills, mortgages, other loans, and more. He could not believe what his eyes were telling him. Certain that somewhere he had made a mistake, he summoned his brothers-in-law from Boston; they, especially Abe (now his father-in-law, too) understood finance a lot better than he.

The Meyersons arrived, went through the ledgers, the books, the papers, everything, item by item, adding, subtracting, coming together in increasingly grim consultation. They marched out of the office and down to the bank, went from one bank to another, returned ashen and seething. They told my grandfather things were even worse than he had imagined. Dubinsky had cleaned out the company; he had emptied out all the bank accounts steadily through the last six months, using most of the money, they discovered, to pay off huge gambling debts as well as to buy jewels and more for his wife and her daughters. He had mortgaged the factory itself and all its machinery; he had borrowed against future orders. He had not paid any but the most pressing company bills, diverting the money for his own use, sliding it into his pocket.

My grandfather listened, only partly comprehending, trying not to believe. When the Meyersons had finished, he asked, "So, what's left?"

Abe Meyerson sighed. "Mr. Jacobson, you did not understand what we were saying? What's left? Nothing is left, that's what.

Nothing and more than nothing. Your partner, that Dubinsky, he took everything. What's left for you is bills and mortgages and loans, debts and more debts, that's what he left for you."

Dubinsky had done such a thorough job that the business was dead and there was no hope for a resurrection.

It did not take more than a few days for the news to spread. Creditors besieged the factory, threatening legal action unless they were paid. The workers, who could not be paid their wages that week, stormed out, threatening violence against the plant itself and against my grandfather; a mob of them marched on my grandfather's house, raged, threatened to burn it to the ground with everyone in it, were dispersed by the police. They marched on Dubinsky's house and, before the police could arrive, they did burn it and prevented the firemen from putting out the blaze until there were only ashes left.

The company, of course, was bankrupt, was only a memory. But there still remained the question of what my grandfather should do. The Meyersons, Deborah, the children, friends, everyone had only one demand: "You must go to the police. That Dubinsky must be found. He must be brought back in chains. He must go to prison where he belongs."

"That I could not do," my grandfather told me so many years later. "Who was to blame? Who had told Dubinsky to leave his machine and become a boss? Who had left Dubinsky alone to run the company while that woman and her daughters were saying without end, 'Give, give, we want, we want,' until the man could only give and steal? Dubinsky was a weak man and always I knew it. A weak man you do not tell to hold the world on his shoulders without help and think the world will still be there when next you look. No, Jerome, I would not do it."

At first, he merely said no, he would deal with the troubles in his own way. The pressure mounted. My grandfather resisted. He said, "You think if you find Dubinsky, you will find the money, also? You are crazy. What you will find is nothing, only Dubinsky. All the trips he took. You are going to sell them and get money? How much will you get? You are going to take the clothes off his back and sell them? How much will you get for rags? The furs, the diamonds, the jewels, the clothes he bought for his wife and her daughters. You think you will find them, even? And if you find them, for how much will you sell them? The food he ate. You can sell that, too, and get money? The house and the fine things in it. Ashes they are now. What will you get for the ashes?"

"There must be something," everyone insisted.

"Dubinsky you do not know if you think there is anything," he said. "There is nothing. If there was something, he would not have run."

"He must be punished," they said.

"You think he is not punished?" my grandfather said. "He is with that woman and her daughters. That is punishment worse than prison. You think they will stay with him when there is nothing? You are crazy. Like the snow in the spring they will disappear. And if they stay, he will wish he was in a real prison with bars and doors that lock. Dubinsky will have nothing and he will have no way to earn. The rest of his life he will be in the poorhouse. The rest of his life he will look over his shoulder. The rest of his life he will be afraid someone is coming for him. You think he will be able to look in the mirror? A mirror he won't have, even. You think I am poor now because Dubinsky did this thing? I tell you, it is Dubinsky who is poor. It is Dubinsky who will hide in the dark the rest of his life, not Jacobson. It is Dubinsky who will be afraid of the sun, not Jacobson. Do you think Dubinsky will go to the synagogue again, on Rosh Hashanah or Yom Kippur, even? Dubinsky will be afraid of the synagogue. Dubinsky will die alone and no one will say the kaddish. Dubinsky will lie in a grave, without a mark, outside the cemetery. You would bring back Dubinsky? He would thank you. Maybe already he is hoping you will find him and bring him back. Maybe already he is waiting. He should only wait and hope."

Despite the barrages from every side, despite the threats and the rage, my grandfather would not be moved. He refused to sign a warrant for Dubinsky's arrest. He refused to discuss Dubinsky and the crimes with the police. When they came to him, he insisted there was nothing to discuss; he insisted there had been no trouble; if the company owed money, it would be paid. The police went away. He went to the creditors and told them they had nothing to worry about; they would be paid every cent they were owed. He went to the workers, now out of jobs and ready to kill, and told them they would be paid their wages and would be given a little extra to tide them over until things got better.

He did what he said he would do. He sold off the bits and pieces of the company that, somehow, had escaped Dubinsky's grasp. He went to his competitors and sold them the manufacturing and design innovations he had developed. He emptied out his own savings and sold off all his investments. He sold his house and land, the cow and the chickens, everything he owned. And when he had finished, there was enough to pay dollar-for-dollar all that was owed.

"I took a cloth and I wiped the blackboard clean," he said.

5

NOW HE HAD TO BEGIN again. He could have stayed in Lowell, stayed in the shoe business if he wanted. Three of his competitors, despite their anger at him during his prospering years, offered him jobs. He turned them down. To stay in the shoe business was something that was out of the question. He could not and he would not do it. The Meyersons, despite their fury and their disgust, offered him a job in their store, offered to open up another store that he could manage. He would not do that, either.

"But what are you going to do?" they asked.

"You think I know?" he said. "I will find something."

"What are we going to do, Mr. Jacobson?" demanded Deborah, my grandmother, who was then pregnant with my Uncle Abner, the first of her five children.

"I will find something."

"What? You turn down the Yankees when they forget their anger and offer to help. You turn down my father and his brothers when they try to help. You, with eight children who are about to be nine. You, with two sons in college, already, and you say you will find something. What is the something?"

"The something will be something. But, first, we will move away."

"From my father, from my uncles, from my cousins, from my family? You would take me from them?"

"You want to go back to them, back to Boston?"

"I did not say that. You are my husband. You are the father of the child that stirs in my womb. I will not leave you. But where will we go? How will we live?"

"Where we will go, we will go. How we will live, we will find a way."

All he had left were his horse and carriage, though the carriage he traded for a wagon, and precious few belongings besides the clothes on their backs. He packed what he had into the wagon, loaded the children into the wagon, and set out along the Albany Post Road, heading west and then south when they reached the river. They traveled about a hundred miles, far enough so that there were not many reminders of what had been and what might have been, yet not so far that the ties to family and friends would be irrevocably lost. They reached Hartford. My grandfather looked and, for reasons even he was not certain of, he decided this was the place to settle.

"We moved into a little house," he told me, "and for a day, I sat and said, what should I do in this place? Only a day it took me, Jerome, to find out. A man, a peddler, comes along with a wagon to sell food. What he was selling you wouldn't believe. The lettuce was black, it was rotten. The tomatoes, you touched them and the finger went through, and covered with mold they were. Everything. You wouldn't put what he was selling into the garbage can, even."

He walked around the wagon, examining the produce. He looked at the peddler. He said, "You want money for this?"

The man shrugged. "You want to eat, you buy. You want to starve, you don't buy. It is up to you."

My grandfather said, "Maybe I will buy from somebody else who sells better."

The peddler laughed at him. "If you think anybody has better, you're crazy."

"So, Jerome," my grandfather said, "I knew what I would do. If people would pay money for the things this man was selling, then somebody who came along and sold better would make a fortune. Maybe not a fortune, but a living."

He became a fruit and vegetable peddler. He had his horse and his wagon (and, later, he would have a truck). It was simple enough to find out where the wholesale markets were, to seek out the best local farmers who would be willing to sell to a peddler. Most of the local peddlers did all their buying at the wholesale market. It was simpler; they could arrive, make all their purchases at one time, fill their wagons at one place, and then go on their way. My grandfather decided he would do things differently. He toured the farms, made contacts with the small farmers, struck bargains where he would buy directly from them, get first choice of their produce, and, since the middlemen were skipped, would pay them a little more than they would get from the wholesalers and yet not as much as he would have to pay if he bought from the wholesalers. It worked to both his benefit and the farmers'. And anything he couldn't get from the local farmers, he would buy at the wholesale market.

Every morning, long before dawn, he rose, hitched his horse to the wagon, drove out into the country, touring the farms and stocking his wagon, starting so early that he was still able to reach the wholesale market for whatever else he needed before it opened, before any of the other peddlers arrived. With his wagon filled with the pick of the crop from both farms and market, he returned to the city and began to carve out a clientele in the richest and most exclusive neighborhoods. "From Chaim Jacobson," he said, "they got only the best, so everyone wanted to buy only from Chaim Jacobson."

He was satisfied. It was enough. When he had been in the shoe business, he had been filled with ambition, had aimed always to grab the ring of success and fortune. Now he was content to make enough to live on and have a little left over. He had had riches, had learned the price of riches, and he did not want to pay that price again. It was enough to have his regular customers, to know they prized him, would buy only from him. Six days a week, he rose in the dark, did his buying, made his rounds, sold everything in his wagon before noon, and had the rest of the day to read his newspapers, to read the books that he had thirsted to read and had not had time for until then, to write a little just for his own satisfaction (though he never gave a thought to try-ing to publish anything, never even showed what he wrote to anyone, eventually threw everything away), to think, to make and see friends, to do things that had nothing to do with business or earning money, even to have a little time for his family. It was as though he had decided that at least in a small way he would give the scholar in him a chance to emerge, if only for himself; for all the years, the scholar had been buried beneath the busi-nessman; now the businessman would move aside.

Deborah, my grandmother, did not like it at all. She had mar-ried an ambitious, driven man, a man who would give her a life of ease and plenty. Her children—my Uncle Abner and, within the next decade and a little more, my Uncle Eli, my Aunt Esther, my Uncle Michael, and, finally, my mother, Ruth—were just as de-serving of luxury and opportunity as (perhaps even more so than) the children of Ruchele and Sarah, whom she was raising, watching grow until they went off to make their own lives, and she fully expected that my grandfather would provide. What had happened to that man she had married? Where had he gone, to be replaced by a husband who seemed to have lost ambition, who was satisfied with small things, who was satisfied to sit with his books and his papers in his den through the afternoon?

As I have said, I never knew my Grandmother Deborah; she died soon after my mother and father were married and, so, a couple of years before I was born. My mother talked about her often to me, always described her as a warm, generous, self-sac-rificing woman dedicated to the welfare of her children, and to the children of her predecessors in my grandfather's life. There was, she said, nothing my grandmother would not do for them, no sacrifice too great to make if it would help them have an eas-ier time. "It's too bad you never knew your grandmother," my mother used to say to me, said to me often all the time I was growing up. "She was the most wonderful woman I ever knew. It was always a miracle to me that a woman who was so tiny— she was just five feet tall and your grandfather towered over her—could be such a pillar of strength. Everyone leaned on her. When things were really bad, she held the family together. Your grandfather never realized all the sacrifices she made in her own life so things would be easier for him and for us when we were children. She could make food for one meal stretch for three meals and no one would complain because we didn't know she was doing it. She could take clothes that one of the children had worn, run them through her sewing machine, and the rest of us never even realized we were wearing hand-me-downs. I'm sure your grandfather always thought she was going out and spending more money on new clothes for everyone when she was doing just the opposite. And, Jerome, it's hard to believe, but that tiny little woman was the only person in the world who could stand up to your grandfather and give as good, and as loud, as she got."

My grandfather, of course, did not see things quite the same way. "Your grandmother," he told me, "was a good woman, Jerome. But what she didn't understand you could write a book about. She thought if she bought oysters, which, God forbid, she never did, she would find a pearl in every one, maybe ten pearls. She thought the world should be the cards and the Mah-jongg, with a woman to come to cook and clean and dress the children. If I said to her, 'Deborah, there is enough,' she said, 'Mr. Jacobson, there is not enough.' If I said to her, 'Deborah, how much is enough?' she said, 'Mr. Jacobson, when there is enough I will know how much is enough.' If I said to her, 'Deborah, for you, all would not be enough,' she said, 'Mr. Jacobson, give me enough and I will show you I know when enough is enough.' "

What probably galled my grandmother more than anything was my grandfather's willingness to settle now for a life with a horse and wagon and a life with books and paper when she knew, when she had seen, that he was capable of so much more. And when he turned down opportunities, and there were plenty of those, her fury at him was limitless and the walls of their house reverberated, nearly crumbled and fell, from the artillery fired by this tiny woman at her tall husband and the cannon fire he returned. Peace and quiet were things their house did not know.

My grandfather was the kind of man for whom opportunity was always in the offing, for whom success could have been easy if he had only reached. But he had been there and he was not going to reach again. He had become a master of his new trade as he had been a master of the old one, could walk onto a farm and know in an instant the quality of the produce being offered him, could stride into the wholesale market and before he was even through the doors know which wholesalers had the pick of the crop and which were trying to pawn off second-rate wares. His reputation spread, among those he bought from and those he sold to. He could not take care of all the potential customers who clamored to buy from him, not with just one horse and wagon, and later with just a single truck.

There was, for instance, Roger Jessup. When my grandfather mentioned his name, I stared at him with disbelief and awe. "Did you really know Mr. Jessup?"

"You think I would tell you what was not the truth?"

Roger Jessup. I don't think there was an eight-year-old growing up in Connecticut who hadn't heard about Roger Jessup, who didn't know the history of the family. They were direct descendants of the *Mayflower* and Plymouth Rock, of the founders of both Connecticut and Hartford, of signers of the Declaration of Independence and framers of the Constitution, of heroes of every war. The family tree was heavy with branches containing the names of senators and governors and business tycoons. All over the state, there were buildings and streets and statues bearing the name, and towns they had founded. And Roger Jessup himself. He was dead by then, but his name was written in large letters in our history books. He had been an attorney, the best attorney in the state, the books said, had later become governor and later still senator, and later still a member of the president's cabinet. But no matter what office he held, his door had always been open to anyone from Connecticut; he had answered every letter personally and seriously, had considered every request as though it were the most important one ever made of him. He was, our history books said, a statesman and a man of the people.

"You really knew him, grandpa?"

My grandfather smiled. "I knew him, Jerome."

He had been almost the first customer my grandfather had when he became a peddler. He had also been, though my grandfather didn't know it that first day when he drove up to the house, as he didn't know whose house it was, the lawyer for some of Jadin Shoes' creditors and so had met my grandfather twice before, once to discuss the debts and once to accept the payments that would clear away those debts.

One of the first decisions my grandfather made when he went into the fruit and vegetable business was to solicit customers along Prospect Avenue and Blue Hills Avenue and the streets in that area. Jessup lived in one of the mansions there. That first day, he was just leaving the house as my grandfather was pulling his horse and cart to a stop on the street in front, was just getting down, was just preparing to go to the servants' entrance to discuss his business with the cook or the butler or whoever did the ordering.

Jessup saw him, noticed something familiar, ordered his driver to stop, called out, "You there."

My grandfather stopped and looked. "Yes. You are wanting something?"

"Come here." My grandfather approached. Jessup looked at him. "Don't I know you?"

My grandfather studied him, said slowly, "We may have met, maybe."

Jessup examined him carefully. "I do know you," he said. "Tell me your name."

"The name is Jacobson. Chaim Jacobson."

"Of course," Jessup said. "You're the man who ran Jadin Shoes."

"I am the man," my grandfather said.

"What on earth are you doing here? I thought you lived in Lowell."

"Now I live in Hartford. And now I sell fruit and vegetables."

"Now why would a man with your ability be doing a thing like that?"

"A man must do what he must do. He must feed his family."

"Are you telling me that nobody up in Lowell, up in Boston, offered you a decent job? A man with your ability?"

"People offered. I said no."

Jessup looked at him for a long time. "So, now you're peddling fruit and vegetables. Is that it?"

"That is what I do."

"And you're looking for customers, is that it?"

"I am looking, yes. The finding, it is not so easy."

Jessup nodded. "Well, Mr. Jacobson, you just go up to the door in my house and you tell my cook she's to buy all our fruits and vegetables from you from now on."

"It is not charity I want, Mr. Jessup," my grandfather said. "You should only try for a week and you will see that you will get only the best."

"I'm not offering charity, Mr. Jacobson. I know I'll get only the best from you. If you remember, I dealt with you before so I know what to expect." He told his driver to go on.

Jessup obviously talked about my grandfather to his friends and it was not long before he was supplying every kitchen in the area. It was enough for my grandfather, but it was not enough for Jessup. He managed to meet my grandfather often as the deliveries were being made, spent long minutes in conversation with him, trying to figure him out, to make a decision about him. It took several months before he was sure and then, apparently, he waited for the right moment. It came on a summer day just as my grandfather had finished making a delivery and was turning to leave the Jessup kitchen. Jessup stopped him just inside the door. "Wait a minute, Mr. Jacobson."

My grandfather looked up, surprised to see Jessup in his own kitchen. "Mr. Jessup," he said.

"I've been looking for the opportunity to talk with you."

"So, talk and I will listen."

"Walk with me to my carriage." They walked together out the back door, stood together in the drive. "You know, Mr. Jacobson, you're crazy doing what you're doing."

"And why am I crazy?"

"Because there's not a reason in the world why you should spend your life as a peddler."

"What else should I be?"

"Whatever you want. You're a businessman, Mr. Jacobson, and believe me, you're an extraordinary businessman."

"So, now I am a businessman in the fruit and vegetable business."

"That's no kind of work for a man like you. Look at the success you made with Jadin Shoes before your partner ran out and left the company bankrupt. You started with nothing and built that company into one of the most important in the industry. And how many men would have done what you did when it went under? How many men would have sold everything they had and paid everybody dollar for dollar? Believe me, Mr. Jacobson, not half a dozen. So, I'll tell you what you should be doing. You should be running a real business, a big business."

"Jadin is a dead business," my grandfather said, "and now I am running a little business with no partners."

"A man like you? No, Mr. Jacobson. That's not for you."

"You have a better idea?"

"A dozen better ideas. I have friends all over this state, all over New England. You just give me the word and I'll have a job for you in a dozen firms, an important job. I've already talked to some of my friends about you and they're just waiting."

"Mr. Jessup, I thank you. Believe me, I thank you. But for someone else I do not think I can work. Too many years now I have worked for myself. I could not work for another."

"Well, I can understand that. But, I have another idea. Now, just hear me out. You know that everybody in this neighborhood buys from you now."

"Not everybody, Mr. Jessup. There are some who do not."

"All right, Mr. Jacobson, not everybody. Almost everybody. We all know what you sell, the quality, and believe me, since we've been buying from you, we've all been eating better than we ever did. I don't know what your secret is, but whatever it is, it's something special. Nobody else who ever sold around here has ever been able to come near to matching you. Tell me, could you buy more produce of the same quality if you had to?"

"If I had to, yes."

"Could you buy twice as much, three times as much, ten times as much?"

My grandfather stared at him. "Ten times as much? About that, I do not know. Maybe."

"That's what I thought."

"But ten times as much, I don't have to buy. Not even twice as much. I buy what I need for my customers."

"And right now you're turning away customers, isn't that so?"

My grandfather shrugged.

"Now, you listen to me, Mr. Jacobson. I'm going to make a suggestion. You ought to open a store, a market."

"I should open a market?"

"Of course. Isn't that what I just said? My Lord, if you opened a market, you could serve ten times as many people and you'd be making ten times the money. People would be lined up outside your market trying to buy from you. I know what I'm talking about, believe me. I've talked about this with some of my friends and we all agree. We even have the ideal spot where you could open, not too far from here, which would make it convenient for everyone."

My grandfather listened. He said, "Mr. Jessup, you think I want to make ten times as much money?"

"I think so, yes. Who doesn't?"

"So, you think I am not satisfied now?"

"How could you possibly be satisfied? My Lord, man, you were a rich man in Lowell. You can be rich again. I'd say you could be as rich as you were then, given your brains and your ability."

"You think if I was rich I would be happy?"

"Yes, I think so," Jessup said.

"You are so sure?"

Jessup looked at him. "Well," he said, "maybe I don't know whether being rich would make you happy. But, I'll tell you this, Mr. Jacobson, I've lived long enough to know that being poor doesn't make you happy. I've never seen a happy poor man and I know plenty of rich men who aren't exactly unhappy."

"And me, Mr. Jessup, I have seen rich men who are unhappy and poor men who are happy. It is not the money that makes for happiness."

"Maybe so," Jessup said, "but lack of money certainly doesn't make for happiness. Listen to me, Mr. Jacobson, think about it. Think about giving it a try. What have you got to lose?"

"I could not tell you so you would understand."

"Are you worried about the money to start? Is that it? Well, that's one thing you don't have to worry about. You can set your mind at ease about that. There are plenty of us around here who'd be willing to advance you the capital to get established.

If you ran the market like you ran Jadin, or like you run that wagon of yours, we'd all make a fortune."

My grandfather shook his head slowly. "Can I say how I thank you, Mr. Jessup?"

"Don't thank me. Just do it. That's all the thanks I want."

"I could not do it. A businessman with a store? For me, I don't think so."

"Now, Mr. Jacobson, don't go off half-cocked. Nobody's offering you charity. It's strictly a business proposition. Think about it. Really give it some thought. Talk to your wife about it. You'll see I'm right."

"So, I will think about it."

Through the next weeks, half a dozen other customers on the route pressed my grandfather with the same proposition. All offered to invest in the market. He said only that he would think about it, though he knew what his answer would be. When finally the pressure intensified and he could no longer put off an answer, he said no, he said he could not open a store, he could not explain why so they would understand, only that for him a store could not be. He was satisfied with things as they were, he had no desire to be more than a peddler with his few select customers. No one understood his refusal, most did not believe it until they had no choice. And then there was talk, and he heard it from the servants in the kitchens, that he was a man without ambition, a man who did not want to take chances for real success, a man who was afraid, a man who did not want to work hard, and so he was a man it was silly to waste time worrying about. There was little understanding of how hard he already worked, of the hours he was already putting in, of the fact that it might actually have been easier for him to do as they wanted. They believed what they wanted to believe and from that day on, most of them simply ignored him, left the dealing with him to the cooks and the butlers.

Only Jessup still cared and still tried. "Mr. Jacobson," he said, "I wish I understood."

"It is enough to know I am grateful," my grandfather said, "but I could not do it."

"I don't want your gratitude."

"Still, I give it."

"What I want is to understand."

"I could not explain it so you would understand. It lies here, inside. It is what I must be."

"Well, I suppose it satisfies you even if it doesn't satisfy me. But I believe you could have done it, Mr. Jacobson, if you tried."

"Yes, Mr. Jessup, I could have done it. But I would not try. For me, now, there are other things."

"I can see that. But, Mr. Jacobson, if you ever change your mind . . ."

"My mind I will not change."

"I suppose you won't. But I'm still your friend, Mr. Jacobson. Don't ever forget that. If you ever need any help, if you ever need any legal advice, anything, you just come to me. Do you understand? I'm not joking. I mean it."

"I understand, Mr. Jessup. And I thank you."

He did not, of course, tell my grandmother about the offers and the possibilities. But she found out, as she was bound to. She couldn't believe it at first, then was forced to, and her rage, her disgust, were monumental.

She faced him, straightening, rigid as a steel beam. "Mr. Jacobson, what have you done?"

"Done? I have done nothing."

"Nothing you call it? The rich goyim want to make you rich and you say no and you call that nothing?"

"Rich I have been."

"Rich you're not."

"When I was rich, I had Dubinsky. You want another Dubinsky?"

"You think Mr. Jessup is a Dubinsky? You think Mr. Marlow is a Dubinsky? Mr. Reeves? Mr. Branner? Mr. Whitman? You think the rich goyim are all Dubinskys?"

"One Dubinsky is plenty of Dubinskys. The world does not need another. I do not need another."

"And who would be another? For your children you would not do it. For me you would not do it. For yourself you would not do it. Mr. Jacobson, explain it to me. I do not understand."

"Enough I have."

"For you, it is enough, maybe. For the children, for me, it is not enough."

"Then go back to Boston. Go to your father. Go to your uncles."

"You want I should go to them?"

"Go. Tell them Jacobson is a bum. Tell them Jacobson does not put food in your mouth. Tell them Jacobson puts rags on your back. Tell them Jacobson sends his children into the world naked. Tell them Jacobson takes the roof from your head. Tell them. Tell them. You think they will welcome you, go to Boston."

"And should I tell them you threaten me?"

"When do I threaten you?"

"You raise your hand to me."

"When do I raise my hand to you?"

"It is at your side now?"

"On your head it should be." He slapped the wall beside him with his palm, feeling pain. "But I would not do such a thing. You think I am a man who would hit a woman?"

"With your hand? Never. But you hit me, here, in my heart, every day of my life."

Because he was not rich as he had been in Lowell, and because it was obvious that he would never be that rich again and had no desire for such riches, neither my grandmother nor my grandfather realized then, and my grandmother apparently never realized, that they were not exactly poor, that they were, in fact, fairly comfortable. He made enough peddling to be able to buy his house, not a large one, not like the one in Lowell, but big enough so that he and Deborah and the children were not cramped for space. He made enough so while there were no maids or servants, there was always enough food and nobody went around in rags. He made enough to send all his sons to college, though all had to work to help support themselves, and to help pay George, Reuben, and Michael's way through medical school, Joseph and Joshua's way through law school, Abner's through dental school, Samuel's through engineering (what Eli would have been, no one ever knew; he was introspective, scholarly, brilliant; when World War I started, he enlisted immediately, went to

France, and is buried there). He made enough so that all the girls could go to secretarial school and both my Aunt Esther and my mother to college. He made enough to put savings in the bank, a bank that, fortunately, was to weather the crash and the depression, though the money he invested in stocks, at the urging of my grandmother, he might just as well, he said later with a kind of angry resignation, have stuffed in Dubinsky's pocket.

And as a peddler, he had time for other things, for those battles large and small that added so much zest to his life. If he became convinced that he was right, that there was an injustice being done, a wrong to be faced, he was not afraid to take on anyone or anything. Certain his children were all brilliant and the schools were holding them back with emphasis on mediocrity, he charged on the board of education, presenting a list of books in literature, the sciences, more, presenting a curriculum he had compiled after careful study of books on education, demanding to know why his children, why all the children of the city, were denied access to the best. Week after week, he charged into the board's office after finishing work, harassing, arguing, shouting. He carried his campaign to the office of his alderman, to the mayor, to the political leader of his district. He would not listen to the excuses, to the attempts at explanation about money, about teacher training. He demanded and he demanded and, finally, he was rewarded with the promise, that took years before it was kept, of change in the direction he was pointing.

There were books he wanted to read that the library did not have. He was told the demand for those particular books was not great, and since the library had only limited funds, it could not purchase them at the expense of more popular ones. He was outraged. Why should the library discriminate against him? His taxes went to support the library, to help buy the books that people read. So, why shouldn't his taxes be used to buy the books he wanted to read? He went to the alderman. The alderman kew him by then and knew what he would be subjected to if he tried to ignore my grandfather. His help was promised. The books appeared on the library shelves.

Like many of his contemporaries and friends, he had joined a Workman's Circle, an Oxie as he called it, soon after he settled in Hartford. It was a place where he and his friends could come together and argue about politics and the world. It was also an organization that helped its sick and needy members and their families at a time when there was neither private insurance nor public assistance. It was also a burial society. The Oxie bought land for a cemetery in a then sparsely settled section of the city and went to the zoning board for a permit. The board turned them down; according to long-range planning, this would eventually be a residential area, and if a cemetery occupied a section of it, people would not build houses there and so property values would decline. My grandfather was furious. He stormed into a meeting of the zoning board. If the permit was not granted, he thundered, he would personally bury a body in that ground in the middle of the night, would put up a tombstone and then stand guard. What would the board do then? Would it send in the soldiers to move him? Would it dig up the body and throw it in the river? People died. Everyone died. They had to be buried. The Oxie had bought the land, owned it, had a right to use it for the reasons it had been bought. A reporter for the *Hartford Times* was covering the meeting; his story made the front page the next afternoon. The following day, there was an editorial lamenting the arbitrary actions of appointed boards which denied citizens their most sacred right, to bury their dead in sanctified ground, perhaps because members of those boards had some vested interest in the area. The political leaders of both parties read the story, studied the editorial, conferred, issued orders to their hirelings on the zoning board. At its next meeting, the board, explaining that it had not previously thoroughly studied the issues, reversed itself and granted the Workman's Circle a permit to establish its cemetery. (At its own next meeting, the Oxie passed a resolution praising my grandfather and proceeded to elect him its president, an office he did not want, reluctantly accepted, and then held for another decade.)

Gas and electricity, sewer lines, and telephones were beginning to reach the homes of the rich. Construction in the poorer neighborhoods was somewhere way down on the list of priorities. My grandfather's neighbors complained, grumbled, seethed in frustrated and ineffectual silence; they were newcomers, most of them, afraid from bitter experience in the old countries to raise their voices against the decisions of the powerful. My grandfather was never one for silence. He marched into a meeting of the board of aldermen, rose, and shouted that he and his neighbors paid their taxes just like the rich, so why should they be denied while the rich got everything first?

Don't worry, he was soothed, the utilities would soon reach him and his neighbors.

"When is soon?" he demanded.

"Soon."

"Soon is not soon enough."

"It takes time, Mr. Jacobson," he was told by the mayor. "You just have to be patient. You'll have your gas and electricity, your telephones and sewers. Don't worry. We haven't forgotten you. It's just that it takes time."

"So," my grandfather said, "you should be patient about our taxes, maybe. It takes time to pay them. Maybe when the utilities come, then the taxes we will pay. You should only be patient, Mr. Mayor, and don't worry."

There were reporters at the meeting and the next day both the *Times* and the *Courant* ran not only stories but pictures of my grandfather on the front page, and editorials inside condemning the mayor and the aldermen for their cavalier treatment of those who were not rich and powerful. The papers kept up the attack, and before a month had passed, construction crews were beginning to move into my grandfather's neighborhood.

If my grandfather was winning a certain fame—some would have called it notoriety, and even a little power—my grandmother was looking for a payoff that never seemed to come. "For the world," she complained to him, "you will do everything. For your family, you do nothing."

"For my family, there is nothing I will not do," he said.

"You say. Did you open the store when people were begging? No. The world people hold out to you and you look the other way."

"You are not starving," he said. "You have a house, food, clothes. I do what I must do."

One afternoon, my grandfather arrived home from work to a

scene he would never forget. Perched on the sofa in the living room in a frock coat, balancing a cup of tea on his knee while my grandmother fluttered nervously about the room, was Moses Whitcomb, the power behind the mayor, the silent counselor to the governor, the undisputed political leader of the city and much of the state (while the Irish had seized the power in Boston and in New York by then, Hartford was still a bastion of the old Yankee families). He rose, deftly setting his cup and saucer on a table, when he saw my grandfather. He held out his hand. "Mr. Jacobson," he said, "you have no idea how good it is to see you again. Do you remember when we met in my office over that cemetery business? I'm Moses Whitcomb."

"You I remember," my grandfather said. "Did I forget to thank you for the help?"

"Of course not. I was glad to do what I could."

"So, what can I do?"

"Well, I thought I'd drop by and see how you were getting along."

"I am getting along."

"No little problems I can help you with these days?"

"No problems I cannot take care of myself."

"Glad to hear it." For the next ten minutes or so, Whitcomb chatted idly about the neighborhood, about the city, carrying on a monologue since my grandfather merely sat and watched and waited. Finally, Whitcomb said directly to him, "Now, Mr. Jacobson, the real reason I dropped by this afternoon is to talk to you about the election this fall."

My grandfather nodded and waited.

"You know that George Edwards represents this ward on the board of aldermen."

"I know. But represent I wouldn't call it."

Whitcomb laughed a little. "I know exactly what you mean. George is a nice man and he wants to do the right things. But when he was first elected twenty years ago—it doesn't seem that long—this ward was a lot different than it is now. You know what I mean."

"How should I not know?"

"The ward's changed. The people who elected George, they've

moved out, to other places in the city, and a lot of your people have moved in. We're not sure that George is exactly the right man to represent you people. And, then, he's thinking of running for Congress, anyway. So, the mayor and I and a few others have been talking about who ought to run in George's place. That's why I've come to see you."

"You want my advice?"

"Well, you could call it that. You see, we think you've emerged as one of the spokesmen for your people, and so who else would we come to?"

"A spokesman for myself is all I am."

"Don't be so modest, Mr. Jacobson. I can't think of anyone who's done as much for your people here as you have over the last several years."

"Ten, a dozen I could name. More."

"I'm not going to ask you for their names right now. To tell you the truth, I'm not interested in them. It's you I'm interested in."

"From me you want what?"

"I'll put it bluntly. We want you to run for George Edwards's seat on the board."

My grandfather laughed. "Mr. Whitcomb, a politician I'm not. What I am is a peddler."

"You may say you're not a politician, but listen to me, Mr. Jacobson. I've been in politics all my life and I'm telling you that I've never seen a better politician than you. Do you know what a real politician is? He's somebody who gets things done. And who around here has gotten more things done than you?"

"I could name you a dozen."

"Frankly, you couldn't name me one. I'm beginning to think you don't realize your own power among your people, Mr. Jacobson. You should walk around this ward and listen to what they say. If they want something done, they say, 'Mr. Jacobson will get it done.' That's the kind of man we want on the board. If you agree to run, I can guarantee you'll win in a walk. Why, you could sit on your front porch like President McKinley did in the old days and not make one single speech or promise and you'd still get eighty or ninety percent of the vote. So, what do you say? Will you do it? Not for me but for your people. They need someone like you to represent them. They need someone like you to give them a voice in government."

My grandfather said later that he could not believe his ears when Whitcomb was flattering him like that. "Why should the Yankees want a Jew like Jacobson?" he said. "I tell you, Jerome, since the beginning of the country, the Yankees had been running the city, the state, everything. Even when the Jews, the Irish, the Italianers, the rest moved in, the Yankees was still the big bosses. So, why should they need a Jacobson all of a sudden? Because a Yankee could not win in this ward with so many Jews? Never. In those days, the Yankees put up a candidate, his name could be anything, he won. So, why Jacobson? I said to myself, idiot, think, better to have a Jacobson with you than have a Jacobson against you."

So my grandfather listened to Whitcomb's flattery and Whitcomb's persuasion, and he said, "Mr. Whitcomb, I should thank you. You make me proud. You should come to Jacobson and say he should run for office in this country, which would never happen in the old country."

"You'll say yes?"

My grandfather shook his head. "I will say no. I must say no."

"I'm afraid I don't understand."

"There is nothing to understand. A politician I am not. To run for election is not my way. My way is to go my way. But, I tell you what you should do, if you want to listen. You should go to Seymour Melman or Wolf Cantorwitz. They are good men. Everybody knows them. They are ambitious. They are what you want, not Jacobson."

Whitcomb tried to argue with him. My grandfather would not change his mind. Whitcomb sighed, got up to leave, said, "Look, Mr. Jacobson, don't give me an absolute no this minute. Why don't you think about it for a few days? You do that and you'll see I'm right. Just think about it and in a week we'll talk some more."

But my grandfather, though he agreed to think, to consider, had no intention of changing his mind. He would not be co-opted. He would go his own way as he had always done. And so, a week later, he told Whitcomb he would not run. Reluctantly, Whitcomb abandoned the pressure. He picked Wolf Cantorwitz as his candidate and, of course, Cantorwitz won. But over the next decade, until he died and until a new generation of political bosses moved into power, Whitcomb seemed to consider my grandfather if not exactly a friend, at least someone he could call on once a month or so to test the political climate of the ward, someone who would speak the truth to him. A few more times he broached the subject of running for office, but always with a kind of defeated resignation, knowing my grandfather by then would only laugh and suggest someone else.

Near the end of his life, during one of their afternoons together, Whitcomb said, "Mr. Jacobson, you're a real hell raiser, did you know that? I just wish I'd had you with me all these years instead of against me."

My grandfather said, "Mr. Whitcomb, I was never against you and I was never with you. I was only with Jacobson and what Jacobson believed."

"Don't I know that," Whitcomb said.

My grandmother, of course, was anything but pleased when, listening behind the door, she heard my grandfather turn down Whitcomb's proposal. "He wants to give you the world and you turn him down," she shouted at him.

"He wants to shut me up is what he wants."

"He wants to make you important, so everybody should know the name of Chaim Jacobson, and you want to be a nobody."

"I know the name of Chaim Jacobson, so what should I care if anybody else knows?"

"You are a fool, Chaim Jacobson."

"So, I am a fool."

"What am I going to do with you?"

"Do? You should do nothing. You should close your mouth. You should not listen behind doors."

"If I don't listen, I don't learn."

"So, you shouldn't learn."

All my grandfather's battles through the years were not, of course, played out in a public arena on a grand scale over large issues. Small, private wrongs stirred him just as much. He went to war with his next-door neighbor whose howling dog shattered the night, growled threateningly at every passing child, got loose one day and bit my Uncle Eli when he was a small boy. My grandfather finally called the pound, which came and took the dog away. The neighbor bought another dog, the battle went on for years, shouts hurled over dog barks across the fence that separated their properties. Another neighbor turned him to raging fury when he refused to rake his leaves in the fall and they blew into my grandfather's yard, forcing him to rake day after day. He ranted and howled continually at a close friend who, he said, cheated whenever they played pinochle, and yet they played a couple of times a week.

He didn't win all his fights, of course, but I don't think he ever expected he would. It was the fight itself that engaged his passions. As my father said, everywhere he looked there were windmills that looked like dragons and there were real dragons, and he would battle both, always had his lance and his steed ready, prepared to charge with a fury, a righteousness, a will, and a conviction that he was defending the right against the forces of darkness.

Until he was in his late seventies, he drove his truck, went out to the farms and the wholesale market before dawn, made his purchases, catered to his customers six days a week in every weather. By then, his children had begun to urge him to slow down, even to retire. After all the years of hard, unceasing work, it was, they said, time for him to relax and enjoy himself, to go off with Deborah and just have a good time. He did not even hear their words. He had worked all his life and would not know what to do if he stopped. It was not until my mother and father married and he and Deborah were alone at last in the house that the stray thought entered his mind that maybe he was getting old.

And then that thought became real, had to be taken seriously. He could not remember a time in all his life when he had been too sick to work; the only time he had ever abandoned thought of work was during those months after Sarah died, and even then he had gone to the office a few hours a day. That February, there was a spell of freezing rain and bitter cold. It did not stop him. Deborah kept insisting it was no weather for an old man to be riding around in. He would not listen. He went to work as usual every day, and every day came home drenched and frozen, even a hot bath not thawing or warming him. The rain, the sleet, the cold continued. He woke in the morning after a week or so of it with a bad cold, gasping for breath. Deborah insisted he stay home that day. He refused; what would his customers do for their food if he didn't appear? They would find a way, she said. They depended on him, he said, and so he left the house, made his rounds, and returned home burning with fever, hardly able to walk. He collapsed in the living room on his way to his bed.

He had pneumonia. The doctor came, examined him, summoned an ambulance to rush him to the hospital. He lay in a semi-icoma for a week. The doctor did not think he would live. His children rushed to Hartford from all over the country to take up the deathwatch. My grandmother wailed hysterically. She hovered over his bed, pleading with him to live, to get better, begging his forgiveness for all the harsh words of thirty years and more, crying that she could not live without him, that life would mean nothing to her if he should die. He did not. The will to live was strong; after a week, he came out of the coma and began to get better.

"For a young man," my grandfather said to me that summer so long afterward, "a cold is nothing. For an old man, a cold becomes pneumonia before you can say Jack Robinson, and pneumonia is nothing to sneeze at. For three weeks I was in that bed in the hospital. When you lie in a bed in a hospital, Jerome, you see only the cracks in the ceiling, and you see your thoughts. I asked myself, Chaim Jacobson, what is it for? You work and then you die and what have you done? Money I did not need. Money I made and a little money I had. And making shoes and peddling the fruits and vegetables is not writing midrash. I said to myself, Chaim Jacobson, it is time you used your brain. Maybe the children are right. Maybe they know something you don't know. Maybe you are an old man and it is time to turn the world over to the young men so you can rest a little."

He went home to recuperate and, during those weeks, he

came to his decision. "This man I knew, a young man, Isidore Kaplowitz was his name. For years, he had been *hokking* me to sell him the truck and the route. Always I said to him, 'Kaplowitz, you are crazy. Why should I sell? You think I want to sit and do nothing?' So, now I called Kaplowitz. I said, 'Kaplowitz, this is Jacobson. You are still interested in the truck and the route?'"

After all the years of asking and being refused, Kaplowitz was stunned. "Mr. Jacobson," he said, "you are selling?"

"I am thinking," my grandfather said. "So, make me an offer."

Kaplowitz made an offer.

"You are crazy," my grandfather said. "I will go back on the route. Maybe I will drive the truck into the river and tell the customers to buy from the stores."

Kaplowitz made a better offer.

"You are still crazy."

Kaplowitz made still a better offer.

My grandfather refused.

Kaplowitz sighed and raised the price. "I can do no better," he said. "Take it or leave it, Mr. Jacobson."

"Okay," my grandfather said, "I take it." The final offer was better than he had expected. "The truck is yours. The route is yours. For a day, a week maybe, I will go with you. I will introduce you to the farmers. I will introduce you to the best in the market. I will introduce you to the customers. Then it is yours."

"You won't be sorry," Kaplowitz said.

"What's to be sorry?" my grandfather said. "Only, don't cheat the customers. You should give them only the best."

"I'll give them only the best, Mr. Jacobson," Kaplowitz said. "You'll see, another Chaim Jacobson they will call me."

"And did they, grandpa?" I asked that summer years later. "Did they call him another Chaim Jacobson?"

"Isidore Kaplowitz was what they called him," my grandfather said. "Chaim Jacobson he could not be. There is only one Chaim Jacobson." He grinned at me. "Like there is only one Jerome Greif. Like there is only one of everyone."

"I mean, grandpa, was he like you, with the truck and the customers and everything?"

"He could not be," my grandfather said. "He was like himself.

He was a young man, not fifty yet, and I was old already. The young are not like in the old days. And it was not like in the old days, even, when I started on the horse and wagon. Then the customers bought only from the peddlers. When Kaplowitz took the route, there were stores already everywhere. Not like the big stores your mama goes to now, but plenty of stores. So, it was harder with the truck. And Kaplowitz was a stranger. The customers did not know him. A month, two months maybe, and the customers were calling. 'Mr. Jacobson,' they said, 'how are you?' 'I am fine,' I said. 'When are you coming back?' they said. 'I am not coming back,' I said. 'If you come back,' they said, 'we will buy from you. But not from Kaplowitz. He is not like you.' I said, 'Give Kaplowitz a little chance. He knows the business. He is learning every day a little more. You will not be sorry. But I cannot come back.' "

He and my grandmother began to plan for his retirement. They thought they might go to Florida for a little while, perhaps even to California. My Aunt Frances was married to a man in the hotel business in Miami and she had been urging them to come for a visit, perhaps even to settle in Miami permanently. My Uncle George was practicing medicine in Beverly Hills and he had been trying to get them to go west to him.

But, in the middle of their preparations, my grandmother began to complain of excruciating pains in her stomach. She would stop in the middle of a conversation and double over in agony. My grandfather took her to the doctor. He examined her, rushed her to the hospital. She was operated on that afternoon for cancer of the stomach. She died on the operating table.

So, my grandfather was alone. His children began a new campaign. George wanted him to move to California immediately, Frances insisted he move to Florida, Joseph wanted him in Boston, Reuben in Washington, Miriam in Chicago, my mother into the home she had just set up with my father. Everybody had a different place they were sure he should go to live out his years.

"I did not go to Florida or California or anywhere. I went to the home instead," he said.

6

DURING THE SUMMER A YEAR or so ago, my wife and I and our children drove up to visit my parents. I had been back often enough, of course, in the years since I had left to go to college and then to make my own way, but those visits had rarely been for more than a weekend spent with my parents around their home. The few times I had ventured into the center of Hartford, I had been stunned by the changes in a city that had, while I was growing up, seemed eternally the same and unchanging. More than once, I had gotten lost and been certain I would not be able to find my way back from what had, in my absence, become a strange and different and alien place.

Over the years since that spring he had left the insurance company to set up his own accounting firm, my father had prospered. His company had gotten its first clients the week it opened its doors, had grown steadily, now occupied an entire floor of one of the new office towers downtown, and its clients, corporate as well as individual, came from all over southern New England. Our old house had been sold long ago, while I was in college, and my father had built the home of his dreams on a couple of wooded acres on the slopes of Avon Mountain in West Hartford. He and my mother had become world travelers; at least once a year they went abroad, had learned after half a dozen visits the secret byways of most of the major cities, and a lot of the smaller ones, in Europe and Latin America, and in the last few years had begun exploring Asia, with a side trip the year before to Australia. There was little they hadn't done that they had once dreamed of doing with little expectation that those dreams would ever come true.

It was hard for me to believe that my father was growing old, that he was in his mid-sixties, but that weekend he talked a lot about retiring and just enjoying himself while there was still time. He had, that week, bought himself a new Buick and on Saturday morning, he asked me if I'd like to go for a ride in it with him. In air-conditioned comfort, we drove down the mountain and around West Hartford, my father slowing to point out the new buildings, the changes that had taken place since I had left.

We passed my old elementary school. It still stood, a plain, functional brick monstrosity, was still in use, but my vision was distorted by the changes. Some architect had put up a glass-and-steel addition on one side, bigger and, in its way, uglier than the original building to which it was attached. The playground was still there in the back, but the swings on which I had once stood and tried to pump hard enough and high enough to spin over the top bar, and failed (one of my friends had succeeded, and had fallen off in the process and broken his arm), were gone, and so were the slides and the seesaws. In their place were contraptions of old tires swirling around poles, grotesque shapes and structures that I could recognize as playground equipment only because my own children's school contained the same. The baseball field was still there, though, and through my mind went the memory of the day I had hit the ball over the fence for a home run; the fence had seemed so distant then, but now I realized how close it had actually been.

We drove on, up Fern Street. "Remember that?" My father pointed. Where he pointed were a score or more of Cape Cod houses, identical except for color and landscaping that had been added and altered over the years. It took me a minute to know where we were. Once there had been a hill there; it was where I had learned to ski on old barrel staves and had broken my nose when I crashed into a tree. The hill had been leveled. The pond was gone, too, covered over for the rows of houses and the new streets, the pond where I had learned to ice-skate and play hockey in the freezing cold of New England winters, unaware of the cold or even of the danger of thin ice until a friend fell through one March day when we were twelve or thirteen and nearly froze to death before we could pull him out.

My father turned down a street. It was our old street. "I'll bet you can't pick out our old house," he said.

"You're on," I said. And a minute later, I said, "Stop. Right here."

"I didn't think you'd remember," he said, pulling the car to a stop at the curb.

"How could I ever forget? I grew up here, remember. It's the only house in this town I ever lived in."

We sat in the car and looked out at the house. It hadn't changed much over the years, perhaps gotten a little smaller, or maybe I'd gotten a little bigger. Whoever owned it—how many owners since we left?—had given it the same kind of love and care we had. The paint was fresh, the brick front clean and solid, the grass and the trees tended and lush. A sprinkler was going, throwing a wide spray across the front lawn, turning dark the curving walk to the front door.

"It was a good house," my father said.

"It sure was."

"They don't build houses like that anymore."

"I don't suppose anyone can afford to."

"You know, Jerry, I paid more for this car we're sitting in than I paid for that house back in '39. When we sold it, we got three and a half times what we paid for it. Your mother was in a panic. She was sure we were cheating the people who bought it. They had two little kids and she wanted to cut the price. I'll bet you couldn't buy it for a hundred thousand today."

"It was a good house to grow up in," I said. "Full of good things, good memories, good times."

"It was that," he said.

"We were the last house on the block then. The woods started right there, just beyond our driveway. God, how many times in the spring and summer did I go into those woods to pick wild strawberries and blueberries and just to explore. I remember one time I found an Indian arrowhead when I was digging under a bush. What a find that was."

"What I remember," my father laughed, "was the time you got poison ivy wandering around in those woods. You had it so bad you were out of school for a week."

"How old was I then? Thirteen?"

"About." He sighed. "Just look at it now." Now there were houses as far as the eye could see, and the street, paved and neat, ran off into the distance. "But," he said, "I guess that's what it's all about, change. Everything changes. Nothing stays the same."

"Much as you may want it to," I said.

He nodded. "Much as you want it to." He sighed. "That old house brought us a lot of luck. I left it to go to war and came back to it without a scratch. It was in that house that I made the decision to go into business for myself. That was the smartest move I ever made."

"I remember that," I said.

"You do? You couldn't have been more than eight then."

"That's right. I was standing outside the window when you and mom were talking about it. It was right after grandpa came to live with us."

"My God," he said, "what a memory. I'd forgotten your grandfather was there then. That was some old bird, your grandfather. To take himself up and walk out of the home the way he did, at his age."

"I wonder what the home's like now," I said.

"Oh, I don't even know if it's still there," he said. "You know they built a new place, way out toward Windsor. I don't even know what happened to the old one. I haven't been in that part of town for years."

"You want to go and see?" I asked on impulse.

He looked at me, grinned. "Sure, why not?"

We never got out of the car at the house, just drove off down the street, the street that had not been there, that had just been my woods when I was growing up, a place where I could lose myself for hours, pretending to be an Indian, pretending to be anything I wanted to be.

The streets, once familiar, were unfamiliar, the neighborhoods so changed, as we passed through them. My father made a turn into the North End, onto Vine Street, another turn onto a street that ran into that avenue on which I had vague memories of once riding a trolley car. The houses, most of them, were wrecks now, shambles that barely seemed able to stand. My father slowed briefly and pointed to an old house on a corner lot. I guess it must have been built in the 1890s, with gables, a wide front porch, a large, sweeping lawn. It looked now as though a strong wind would turn it to dust, the wood seemed so dry and cracked, the paint so long peeled off and never replaced, the places where shingles had once been now barren and brown and rotting.

"That was your grandfather's house," he said, "when your mother and I got married. When you look at it now, it's hard to believe the way that man kept it."

A couple of black kids, maybe fifteen or sixteen, were standing on the walk leading to the house. They looked up as we slowed, their faces expressionless but their eyes hot as they stared at us, waiting, not moving. My father stepped on the accelerator and we moved on, made a dozen more turns, went on another couple of miles. He slowed, his eyes beginning to search. "It was somewhere around here," he said. But what we were looking at was an expanse of low-income apartments, three stories, stretching on for five or six blocks. We drove by, passed a few old houses and then another low-income development.

My father sighed. "It was right around here," he said.

"I guess it's gone," I said.

"Well," he said, "that's one place nobody's going to miss. They should have torn it down years ago." He laughed. "And I guess they did."

It was old and deteriorating even then, when my grandfather moved into it. If anyone had asked, he would probably have said that he chose this one because it was the closest to his old home, that it was part of his old neighborhood even though on its fringes. I think, though, that he chose it because he sensed it would be a battleground and he was not yet willing, if he ever would be, to give up his wars.

He need not have feared. The war began before that first day was over, began, actually, with the moment he walked through the front door. It was, I suppose, somehow fitting that one of the crucial issues in the initial struggle would be an issue in his final battle—his chair. He arrived in the morning, unannounced, his cab driver, under his supervision, depositing his luggage and his chair in the middle of the lobby. He paid the cab driver and then walked across the lobby to the stunned volunteer at the reception desk who had been watching the scene with open mouth.

"I am here," he announced.

She stared at him. Like others who worked in the home, both professionals and volunteers, she recognized him, knew him by name. He had been, of course, a familiar figure in the Jewish community for years. But, more important now, he had been in and out and around the home a dozen times during the last month (as he had been through the other homes in the city), inspecting the facilities, asking questions, preparing his way. But now, seeing him with his luggage, with his chair, she did not know what to say. She could only gape at him.

"Shut the mouth already," he said after a moment, "or the flies will get in and they do not taste good. I am here." He was growing impatient.

"Yes, Mr. Jacobson," she gasped finally.

"So, where is my room?"

She stared at him, stared at the papers on her desk, stared back at him, spluttered, "But, Mr. Jacobson, there's nothing here about a room for you."

"So, tell them there should be a room. I will wait." He walked back across the lobby, settled comfortably in his chair, his baggage close beside him.

For moments, the woman could only stare, frozen, paralyzed. Then she picked up the house phone and made a hurried, frantic call. A few minutes later, Bernard Rubin, the director, came striding down the hall from his office, halted abruptly when he saw my grandfather, studied him with disbelief, then moved hesitantly toward him.

"Mr. Jacobson," he said, "what are you doing here?"

"What does it look like I am doing? You think I came like this to say hello?"

"But, Mr. Jacobson, when you were here the other day, you didn't say anything about deciding to join us."

"The other day, I didn't know. Today, I know. So, I am here."

Rubin was spluttering. "But, Mr. Jacobson, you can't just walk in out of the blue like this without any warning. We have to know in advance. There are forms to fill out, to prepare. We have to set up a room. We have to have time. It can't be done in five minutes, on the spur of the moment."

"So, I will wait. I am going no place."

"But, Mr. Jacobson, it just can't be done."

"Mr. Rubin, anything can be done if you should want it to be done. I will sit and wait. You will go to your office and make the forms. I will sign them. You will have the room for me and I will move into it."

"Mr. Jacobson, you don't understand. It can't be done like that. It takes days, sometimes weeks. I'm not even sure we have a room."

"You are telling me I should go away?"

"You have to give us time to get ready for you, Mr. Jacobson. We're very pleased you've decided that you want to come and join us, of course. But you have to give us time."

"And where should I go while you look for time?"

"Why don't you go home, Mr. Jacobson? I'll get right to work on everything and I'll call you this afternoon and let you know when you can move in. How would that be?"

"It would not be," my grandfather said. "My house I have sold, all the things in it, even, except what is in the storage place."

"Oh, my God," Rubin said.

"You could give me a tent, maybe," my grandfather said, "and I could set it in the park and live in the tent while you look for the time."

"Oh, my God," Rubin said again. "No. no. You just sit there, Mr. Jacobson. Don't move. Don't do anything. Give me a few minutes to see what I can do." He hurried away. My grandfather settled back in his chair, took a book from his pocket, and began to read, oblivious to the curious stares from people who passed. Within an hour, an aide appeared, took the luggage, glaring at my grandfather though offering no objection when he was ordered not to forget the chair, and led him down another corridor to a room.

My grandfather unpacked, put his clothes in drawers and in the closet, moved his chair under the window, then relaxed in it, picking up his book again.

In the middle of the afternoon, his door was thrown open—"without a knock, without an invitation, even," he said—and Rubin entered. "We did it, Mr. Jacobson," he said.

"What else?" my grandfather said.

"I hope everything is satisfactory."

"Everything is hunky-dory. What else should I tell you?"

"I'm certainly glad of that," Rubin said. "And now that you're here, I want you to know we'll do everything we can to make sure that you're happy and contented."

"Who said a word about happy?" my grandfather said. "It is a place to live and here I will live. That is enough. Happy is for the young who look ahead. When you are old, ahead is behind and it is enough to live for the day you are living."

"Now that's a pessimistic outlook if I ever heard one," Rubin scolded. "Everyone here looks ahead. We try to make everyone happy. They know there's plenty up ahead for them. That's the kind of home this is."

"Up ahead is the grave. That's where they look," my grandfather said.

"Mr. Jacobson!" Rubin was aghast.

"You think to die is a bad thing, Mr. Rubin?" My grandfather shook his head. "For the young, it is a bad thing. For the old, it is a thing that will be and it is not so bad. I will die, everyone here will die, someday even you will die, Mr. Rubin."

"Mr. Jacobson, you shouldn't talk that way. You shouldn't even think that way."

"I shouldn't think what is true? I shouldn't talk what is true? Mr. Rubin, I am ashamed of you." My grandfather shook his head, then he grinned and laughed. "But, I tell you this, Mr. Rubin. You, you will not die. You will not even grow old."

Rubin stared at him, then stuttered a little laugh himself. "Mr.

Jacobson," he said, "I'm beginning to wonder what I'm going to do with you."

"Don't wonder. We will both find out."

Rubin turned. "Anyway, I'm glad you're here and any time you have a problem, I want you to know you can come right to me." He started toward the door, then stopped. His face reflected a thought that something wasn't quite right with the room, something was out of place or foreign, he wasn't quite sure. His eyes searched the room, came to rest on my grandfather, fastened on the chair in which my grandfather was rocking. "Mr. Jacobson," he said, "what is that thing?"

My grandfather's hand caressed the arm of the chair. "This thing is my chair."

"What's it doing here?"

"It is doing here because I brought it."

"Well, you'll just have to get rid of it."

"Something is wrong with the chair?"

"We have rules, Mr. Jacobson, regulations. I explained all that to you during one of your visits a few weeks ago."

"I remember."

"Do you remember that I told you the home supplies all the furniture, all the furnishings for the people who live here?"

"I remember."

"Well, maybe you just didn't understand. When I said we supply all the furniture, I meant just that. We buy all our furniture from one supplier. We furnish all our rooms just alike so nobody will feel discriminated against, if you know what I mean. If everybody has the same, then nobody thinks somebody else has better. Do you understand?"

My grandfather nodded. He waited.

"That means there can be no deviations. All the rooms have to be furnished with what we supply. Nothing more and nothing less."

"You are telling me I cannot have my chair?"

"That's exactly what I'm telling you. The chair will have to go. There are other chairs in this room. You can use them."

"My chair, it is hurting somebody?"

"You're not listening to me, Mr. Jacobson. That's not the point. If we let you keep that chair in here, then everybody's going to want to have something of their own, something different, and pretty soon this place would look like a secondhand furniture store, like a junk shop. Believe me, if we let you keep the chair, it would be violating all the rules of the home and then what would happen to the rules, to order? The chair will have to go."

"Mr. Rubin, you tell me. Somebody else has brought a chair?"

"No, because we don't permit it."

"Somebody else has brought maybe a dresser, a wardrobe, a rug, a bed, even?"

"Of course not. Because we won't permit it."

"Somebody else has asked?"

"No, of course not. Everybody who comes here knows the rules."

"If nobody else has done it, Mr. Rubin, how can you know what they will want to do?"

"I know, Mr. Jacobson."

"You don't know, Mr. Rubin."

"I don't want to argue with you, Mr. Jacobson."

"Who wants to argue?"

"I don't think I care to answer that, but I'm beginning to think I know. I didn't believe all the stories I used to hear about you from my father, but I'm beginning to believe them now."

"Your father was a good man, Mr. Rubin. But about my chair your father had nothing to do. I will make a bargain with you, Mr. Rubin."

Rubin sighed. "What kind of a bargain, Mr. Jacobson?"

"I tell you, Mr. Rubin, somebody else wants a piece of furniture in their room, you come to me then and we will talk some more. Until then, my chair stays."

"You haven't heard a word I've been saying."

"Mr. Rubin, this chair is hurting who? This chair I have had for fifty years, maybe more. This chair I have taken everywhere. The world is not the same, the chair is the same. Everything goes, the chair stays. And now you would take this chair from an old man who has nothing else. I am ashamed of you, Mr. Rubin, ashamed.

Your father, he would turn in his grave he could hear you."

Rubin sagged with resignation and defeat. He left the room. My grandfather's chair remained.

"How about all the other people, grandpa?" I asked. "Did they get all upset the way Mr. Rubin said they would?"

"Of course not," my grandfather said.

"Well, did they do what Mr. Rubin said they would? Did they all want their own chairs and dressers and rugs and things?"

My grandfather smiled and nodded. "Not all, Jerome, but some."

"What did Mr. Rubin do?"

"He did nothing. Mr. Levine got a dresser, Mrs. Markson a chair, Mr. Hyman a rug, this person this, that person that. Mr. Rubin you should have seen, Jerome. Like a cloud with a storm in it he was every time a mover came with something. Mr. Jacobson, he said, it is all your fault. The home, it is looking like a junk shop because of you. So I said to Rubin, 'Mr. Rubin, you think this should be a prison so the people should not have a little something of their own to make it like a home? You want convicts? You should only hear your words, Mr. Rubin, and you would sink into the earth you would be so ashamed. There is something wrong with a little couch, a soft chair, a rug, so the people should be comfortable, so they should have something nice? You let them, Mr. Rubin, they will make this place a home, not a prison.' "

That was the opening skirmish in the ten-year war between my grandfather and Bernard Rubin, a war that did not end, in which there was no real truce until my grandfather finally walked out of the home. They battled about everything, as though the mere sight of one walking peacefully along a corridor or sitting serenely in the lounge were a spark that forced the other to open fire.

They fought about the furniture in the rooms, of course, and then about the forbidding sterility of the lounges. Rubin maintained, and rightly, I suppose, that the home was run on a tight budget, that there were no funds to fix up the lounges and make them more inviting. My grandfather would hear none of that. If the home would just let anyone who wanted to furnish his own room do so, there would be plenty of money for the common rooms, perhaps even a new radio the people had been begging for and Rubin had been saying was out of the question, just could not be fitted into the budget. Eventually, a compromise was reached. Rubin no longer objected to personal furniture in the rooms, but he would not spend on the lounges. If my grandfather and the others wanted, however, he would have no objections to their soliciting contributions of furniture from stores and private families for the common rooms, just so long as what they got was in good condition. That was all my grandfather had to hear. "Mr. Weinstein was in the furniture business before he retired and he knew everybody. So he got on the telephone. Some of my old customers I went to see. Everybody, they did something." Pretty soon, the two lounges had been decorated and, instead of repelling the residents, now lured them into a community. And each had a radio: one appliance store donated a new Stromberg-Carlson, and another an Atwater-Kent.

The lounges furnished, my grandfather turned to the idea of a library. When he arrived at the home, there were few books or magazines available to anyone, and those that were, were tattered and long out-of-date. For Rubin, the only solution would have been to allocate money, and money was the one thing he never had enough of. My grandfather, of course, thought in other terms. He went to the local libraries to ask for donations of discarded books, to bookstores, to people he knew. The books and only slightly out-of-date magazines began to pour in, cartons lining the corridors.

Rubin accosted my grandfather. "All right, Mr. Jacobson," he said, "you've got your books. Now just what do you propose to do with them?"

"Build a library, what else?"

"And just how do you propose going about that?"

"You think I have not thought? You are wrong. The room with all the junk, with the broken furniture, where everything is dumped? You know to what I am referring?"

"I know."

"We clean it out. You call the junk man and he takes the junk away and we have a room. Mr. Segal, he was a carpenter. I have talked to him already. The shelves he will build. He knows a place that will give the lumber cheap, maybe for nothing, even, if he talks to them nice. So, the books will go on the shelves in that room. And Mrs. Moscowitz, she was a librarian. Now she will work again. A regular library we will have. And, tell me, Mr. Rubin, it cost what?"

Then they argued about the condition of the home. My grandfather was appalled at the filth. Mr. Rubin insisted the cleaning people did the best they could.

"You should give the people a broom, a mop, a dust cloth," my grandfather said. "Their own rooms they will clean. The halls, too. Everything. The people we got, they think a broom is to sleep on, not to clean with. So, you can fire them and you will have more money for the home."

"I can't fire them, Mr. Jacobson," Rubin said. "They need the work, they need their pay. What would they do if we let them go? Would you really like to see them out on the streets, starving?"

"You think I am a monster? So, you keep them. Only, you should let the people do what they can and things will be better, cleaner. You think the cleaning people will care if somebody does their work and they get paid?"

"Are you really serious, Mr. Jacobson? Do you think I could ask people in their seventies, their eighties, to do that kind of work?"

"I am in my eighties. I would do it."

"Maybe you would. But what would their families say? They pay money to live here and you want me to turn them into housemaids?"

"You should only ask them."

"I can't ask them."

"Ask. It won't hurt. A snake will not jump up and bite you. But, you leave things like now, a cockroach you will find in your shoes you should take them off."

They discussed it, they argued about it for weeks until, finally, Rubin said, "I'll tell you what we'll do, Mr. Jacobson. We'll let anyone who wants clean his own room. But that's as far as I'm willing to go. Now, let's not talk about it anymore."

When the war started, my grandfather was determined to do

whatever he could to defeat Hitler. He couldn't join the army, of course, as my father did, but he was sure there were things an old man was capable of. He set about organizing the residents of the home into brigades to go out into the neighborhood as part of the never-ending drives to collect scrap paper, tin cans, rubber, all kinds of discarded waste that might be used for the war effort. Rubin knew nothing about it until one day he spotted a group of the elderly, led by my grandfather, marching in ranks toward the front door.

He called after them before they could leave. "Now, just where are you people going?" he demanded.

"To help with the war," my grandfather said.

"Now what's that supposed to mean?"

My grandfather explained. They were going to go from house to house to collect old newspapers. Rubin ordered them to turn around and march back to their rooms. There were plenty of other people doing that kind of thing. The war didn't need a bunch of eighty-year-olds who could hardly carry themselves around, let alone bundles of newspaper.

"You do not want to win the war?" my grandfather said.

"Winning the war has nothing to do with it. I'm responsible for the safety and well-being of all you people and I can't permit you to endanger yourselves."

"So, we should sit on our behinds and let Hitler win?"

"You should do what you're capable of doing, and that doesn't include acting like a pack of twelve-year-old boy scouts."

Rubin did not permit them to leave that day. But on other days, when Rubin was not quite so alert, my grandfather led his troops on their forays, though whenever Rubin learned of what they were doing, my grandfather had to suffer a bitter and furious tongue-lashing from Rubin, and had to suffer in silence, for this was something where Rubin would not listen to him, would not even let him speak.

Still, my grandfather persisted and their battles over what the old could and could not do for the war raged all during those years. Perhaps the most convulsive struggle, though, came when my grandfather volunteered his own services as an air raid warden. Rubin heard about it when the civil defense officials called the home to check. He called my grandfather to his office.

"Mr. Jacobson," he said, "I've just had a call from civil defense."

"So, Mr. Rubin."

"They tell me you want to be an air raid warden."

"I have offered myself."

"Well, the offer has just been unoffered."

"You will not permit it?"

"I will not permit it."

"And if I should do it?"

"You are not going to do it, Mr. Jacobson."

"You think I am ten years old you should give me orders like a child?"

"I think you're past eighty years old even though you're acting like you're ten."

"What should it hurt if I look at the sky for Nazi airplanes?"

"If you want to look out the window of your room for bombers, go right ahead. I won't stop you."

"And if I should go to the tower?"

"You'll go over my dead body, Mr. Jacobson."

"What could happen?"

"If you don't know, there's no way I can explain it to you. But I'm telling you right now, if you try, you'll regret it to the day you die."

Rubin was not joking. That was so clear that my grandfather for once admitted defeat and did not go ahead with his plane-spotting plans. His other war efforts, though, he did not give up.

These skirmishes were, of course, all part of the continuing war between Rubin and my grandfather through the years. My grandfather was convinced all he was trying to do was make the home a better place to live in, to give its residents, himself included, a purpose, purposes, perhaps even to remain part of the world outside. Rubin, I think, was just as certain that my grandfather was a troublemaker who was making a nearly impossible situation, the care of the old on a very limited budget, the care of people many of whom had lost the ability or the desire to care for themselves, impossible. Both were convinced they were right, and so they fought without end.

There was the situation with the food.

It was an early struggle, one that began soon after my grandfather moved into the home. "Such food you would never eat, Jerome," he said. "If you were starving even, you would throw it into the garbage can."

For a few months, he kept his silence. He went to meals, picked at the food with growing distaste, pushed it away after a few mouthfuls, walked out of the dining room and went to a nearby diner. When he had had enough, he went to the director.

"Mr. Rubin," he said, "you eat the same food as the people here?"

"Sometimes, Mr. Jacobson," Rubin said cautiously. "I eat my lunches here. Why?"

"You like the food?"

"Food is food."

"You think that? You should only know."

"All right, Mr. Jacobson, so it's not the kind of food you'd get in a fancy restaurant downtown."

"Not even in a not so fancy restaurant."

"I'll even grant you that. But it's not easy to cook for this many people. We do the best we can. We have a trained dietician who plans the meals to make sure they're nutritious. We have a trained man who buys the food, the best he can on the budget he has to work with. We have trained cooks who prepare the food. We do the best we can and I don't think anyone can do better."

"Mr. Rubin, this food you should serve to Hitler."

"All right, Mr. Jacobson, what's that supposed to mean?"

"What it means is, you could do better and it wouldn't cost so much."

"You think so? Let me tell you, with the kind of money we have, it would be impossible to do better."

"Impossible it would not be. It would not even be hard."

"Why don't you just leave things to people who know something about them, Mr. Jacobson? We'd all be better off if you'd just do that."

"You think I don't know. About food, I know."

"Whatever you may know, it doesn't have anything to do with what goes on here. Now, I'm very busy. So, if you don't mind, I'd like to get back to work."

If Rubin would not listen, then my grandfather would have to deal with these problems on his own. He planned a campaign step by step, went over it again and again to make sure he had forgotten nothing. First, he enlisted the aid of the other residents. He went from room to room and asked everyone to think of exactly what they would like to eat at every meal for a week and then to sit down and write out their menus.

"You wouldn't believe, Jerome, what some of those people wrote on the papers," he said. "You think maybe they wanted bagels, lox, sturgeon, steak, even? You should think again. I could not believe my eyes. One man, he wanted pheasant; another man, venison; a lady, she wanted caviar, and somebody else, artichokes. I couldn't list all the things. Believe me, they wrote down food they never tasted in their lives, food maybe they heard about in a story somewhere."

He went back to them. "You should be serious," he said. "I am not joking."

They said, "We are serious."

He said, "Serious you're not. Foolish, yes, serious, no. Dreaming, yes, awake, no. You think I am doing this for my health?"

They said, "If not for your health, Mr. Jacobson, for what?"

He said, "So you should maybe eat good sometime, not like a pauper that has to pick at the garbage cans in somebody's backyard."

They said, "You are going to do that?"

He said, "I am going to try to do that. Only, from you, I need a little help, I need a little sense."

Rubin heard what he was doing, of course, and summoned him to his office. "Just what do you think you're doing, Mr. Jacobson?"

My grandfather said, "What do you think I am doing?"

Rubin said, "Who's running this home, Mr. Jacobson, you or me?"

My grandfather said, "Who else should be running it, Mr. Rubin, but you?"

"Then maybe you'll let me run it the way I think it ought to be run."

"God forbid I should stop you."

"I'm trained for my job, Mr. Jacobson. I went to school to learn how to do this. I think I know what I'm doing. I think I know what's best for the people who live here."

"Mr. Rubin, who is arguing?"

"Mr. Jacobson, since when do you do anything else?"

"Mr. Rubin, on little things maybe I can help a little. Some things I know about and so maybe a little help I can give you. That's all I'm doing."

"Mr. Jacobson, I don't need your help."

"Mr. Rubin, my help you could use sometimes. God you're not. Not even Moses. A little help everybody can use. Maybe even God."

My grandfather went on with his plan. It did not go quickly or easily, but eventually he had his menus from nearly everyone capable of planning them. He went over them slowly and carefully, drawing up a master menu spanning a full week.

It was, at least, a beginning. But there was still much to do and much, he realized, he did not know. Maybe what he had in his hands was a menu that would satisfy the people, but what would Rubin, what would a nutritionist say about it? Would they say he had developed a diet that would kill the whole home, that would at the very least make everybody sick? He knew a lot about food, but next to nothing about scientific nutrition. And he also didn't know much about quantities. How much did one buy to feed fifty, seventy-five, a hundred old people? He was sure it was not just the simple matter of multiplying the amount needed to feed one by fifty or seventy-five or a hundred; there had to be other factors involved, but he didn't know what they were. He needed help.

"I went to the university," he told me. "I went to the extension where they train the dieticians, and I asked this lady if maybe they could give me a little help. She asked what kind of help did I need and I told her help in how to feed a place full of people older than me. She said did I run a home for old people and I said no, but I lived in one and so maybe it would help should I know. I tell you, Jerome, you never saw such people. The lady, she tells me I should wait and then she tells me to go to this office and there I meet another lady who tells me she's the one who teaches everyone to be a dietician. So, I give her the menu and I say, 'Please, would you tell me if eating like this would be terrible for people who are old like me.' For an hour, she sat there and she read the menu and she studied it and she wrote little things on a piece of paper and then she said to me, 'Mr. Jacobson, I have a few little suggestions that I will give you, but I can tell you if you served menus like this, the people would all live to be a hundred and never get sick.' "

That was fine; that was exactly what he wanted to hear. Now he was ready with his next question: how would he know how much to buy to feed seventy-five or a hundred people? There were formulas, the professor told him, though ultimately it depended on the ages and the activities of the people who would be doing the eating. The people, he told her, were between seventy and death, and what they did most of the time was sit on their behinds and argue about what program they should listen to on the radio. She gave him a formula so he could calculate how much he would need to buy to feed seventy-five to a hundred sedentary old people.

On his meticulously organized plan, the next item was: how much is there to spend? He could not, certainly, move one inch further until he knew how many dollars were available. He knew he could not walk into Rubin's office and ask how much the home was spending for the food it bought. But he knew that the home had to file a report with the state and with its trustees every year itemizing all its income and outgo. He got a copy of that report, and with it was easily able to calculate the food budget.

"You know what I did then, Jerome? I went back to the market where I had not been for a year, maybe, more even. The dealers, they saw me come in the big doors, their mouths flew open like they wanted the birds to go in and build nests, so wide they were. 'Mr. Jacobson,' they shouted to me, 'we have missed you. Without you, it has not been the same. You are coming back to work?' I told them to work on a truck was not for me anymore; I was too old and old men belong in old people's homes, not on trucks. They laughed and they told me they never saw an old man so young. I told them maybe they should go to the doctor and buy new glasses."

If he was not planning to go back into the business, then why had he come back to the market? he was asked.

"What's the matter," he said, "an old man cannot come in to say hello to his friends he hasn't seen in a year? A man cannot take a little time to shmooz with the friends he knows for thirty years, maybe more?"

"What's to shmooz about?" one of the old traders asked. "You think anything's changed around here because you've been away a year? Nothing changes around here except the faces."

He asked about this person and that person, was told most of them were well, a few had retired, a few others had gone out of business with the spreading of the big food market chains like the A & P around the city, others had gone to work in some of the plants that were once more, the depression easing, beginning to hire.

"And how," he asked, "is that Kaplowitz that bought my truck and my route?"

"You haven't heard?"

"I have heard nothing. The last I heard, a year ago, maybe a little more, he said everything would be fine."

"Everything was not so fine. Kaplowitz didn't last even a year. Near where you used to sell, the A & P opened a store, and the other way, another market, and in between, still another. The people out there, most of them buy from the stores now. Let me tell you, Mr. Jacobson, it was a good thing you weren't around the last time Kaplowitz came in, when he said he'd gone broke. The things he called you, you wouldn't say such things about your worst enemy."

"His enemy I wasn't. I was his friend."

"A friend like you he didn't need," one of the traders said. "It would have been better you should have been his enemy. Then he never would have bought."

My grandfather nodded, then he laughed a little. "If Kaplowitz hadn't bought, what would I be doing for a little money in my old age?"

There were grins. One dealer said, "I should have so much money."

"If you had so much money, you would be in the poorhouse."

"I'll bet," said another. "I hear you're living in Florida these days, with all the rich."

"You heard I was in Florida? Who would say such a thing?"

"I don't remember. Somebody said that right after you sold out to Kaplowitz you and your wife sold the house and went down to Florida for good. I can't say I blame you. From what I hear, that's the place to be, not like here with cold and snow like it was the North Pole in the winter and the fires of hell in the summer. They tell me the weather in Florida is always perfect. So, we all thought you'd done the right thing moving down there."

My grandfather shook his head. "No, I was thinking. But Mrs. Jacobson died all of a sudden so we did not go."

"Then where are you living now?"

"I am in the Zion Home."

"In an old people's home? Why would you want to live there?"

"Where else should an old man live?"

"I don't know," one of the men who had gathered around him said. "You've got plenty of kids. With one of them. Where else?"

"You would live with your children when you are old? Any of you?"

"Not me. I'd live in the cemetery first."

"I am not ready for the cemetery," my grandfather said, "so I live in the home."

"What's it like, to live in a place like that?"

"It is not so bad. Except for the food. That I could do without. The rest?" He shrugged.

There were a few knowing looks, a few wise grins. "Aha," somebody said, "it's out in the open at last. Now we know why you came to see us, Mr. Jacobson."

"Now you know?"

"You think you're dealing with a bunch of dummies? A few of us have the brains we were born with."

"What is it you think you know?"

"That place, they all of a sudden realized what they had living there, so they decided to put you in charge of buying the food. Figured they'd save a few bucks and eat a lot better."

"It should only be," my grandfather sighed.

"It's not?"

"It is not. But," and my grandfather held a pause for a long time, looking from one wholesaler to another, "maybe it could be."

"What do you mean, maybe?"

"With a little help."

"What kind of help?"

My grandfather reached into his pocket and pulled out the list he had prepared. "If I should want to buy . . ." and he read off the list and the quantities . . . "you would charge me how much?"

My grandfather had put them in a position of bidding against one another not for a reality but for a possibility. But they knew my grandfather, figured the chance was worth taking, that they had nothing to lose anyway, and so for an hour they calculated, added and subtracted, haggled and bargained and bid, until at last my grandfather was satisfied. "If it happens," he said at last, "I will come back to you and these prices I will expect."

"Unless the market changes, Mr. Jacobson. You know that. These prices are today."

"That I know. But it cannot change much."

He walked out of the market with a sense of triumph. He had gotten his bids on everything the home would need—fruit, vegetables, staples, meat, milk, butter, and all the rest. And the cost was two-thirds of what the home was then spending for less and for poorer.

It had taken more than six months for him to reach this point. He had, after all, done it all by himself, without a staff, without experts on a payroll, and he had done it in semisecret.

"You think," he told me that summer so long afterward, "I went to Rubin then with all my papers and said, 'Ha, Mr. Rubin, so you did not need Jacobson's help? Look with your eyes and then tell me that.' You think I did that, Jerome? You are wrong. The best food, if you don't know how to cook it, like garbage you can make it taste. But I knew a man from the market who had a restaurant on Front Street. I went to him. I walked into his restaurant. He was standing in the front, saying hello to the people who came to eat. I said, 'Mr. Shapiro.' "

Shapiro looked up. He smiled broadly. "Mr. Jacobson. Where have you been? Have you been hiding from your old friends?"

"Mr. Shapiro, I am living in the Zion Home, if that is hiding."

"You, in a home? Mr. Jacobson, that's no place for a man like you."

My grandfather sighed. "Where else should I be? A man gets old, he has to live someplace."

"Someplace, yes, but there, no."

"Maybe you're right, Mr. Shapiro, but what's done is done."

"What's done can be undone."

"Maybe you are right. But for me, the home is not so bad. Not good, but not so bad."

"And the food?"

"Should I tell you?"

"You don't have to tell me. I know."

"Unless you ate it, you wouldn't know."

"You want me to eat it?"

"You think I want you to die?"

Shapiro laughed. "So, you came to me so you could eat a good meal for once in your life."

My grandfather said, "A good meal I will welcome, yes. And while I eat, I will ask you a question."

"Ask. But, first, you should eat." He led my grandfather to a table in the rear, would not let my grandfather order, ordered for him, and sat with him while he ate, refusing to listen to my grandfather's question until the meal was finished. When my grandfather at last pushed away his plate and leaned back, Shapiro said, "Okay, so now ask."

"Mr. Shapiro, you are an expert in cooking."

"An expert, Mr. Jacobson? No. But a few things I know."

"So, Mr. Shapiro, maybe a few little things you can tell me."

"What should I tell you?"

"You want to cook for seventy-five, maybe a hundred people so they can eat good, how would you do it?"

Shapiro studied him. "You are going to open a restaurant, Mr. Jacobson?"

My grandfather laughed. "The home is not a restaurant."

"You are going to be the cook in the home?"

"No, of course not. But, if I was, what would I do?"

"The first thing you would do," Shapiro said, "is buy the best food you can. Sometimes you can disguise the taste of bad food when you cook for one person, two or three maybe, but not when you cook for seventy-five or a hundred."

"I know that already," my grandfather said. "Suppose I get the best food. What do I do next?"

"It depends on the food. You do one thing with beef, something else with lamb, something else with chicken, and a dozen different things with all of them. You cook vegetables different, soup different, everything. Every meal is a different thing, every dish you cook a different way. So, what should I say? You should hire a cook is what you should do, maybe three, four cooks."

"Suppose I got the cooks and they do not know how to cook?"

"Then you fire the cooks and hire cooks who know how."

"Suppose I cannot fire the cooks?"

"Then you are stuck like a stick in the mud."

"But there must be something."

"You teach the cooks to cook, that is all you can do. You give them instruction, you give them directions they have to follow. If you are lucky, they will learn and not ruin the food."

"You could teach the cooks?" my grandfather asked.

"Who knows?"

"Suppose I gave you some menus. You could tell me how to cook everything so people who can't walk even would run to the dining room?"

"You want I should give you all my secrets? You tell me you are not going to open a restaurant and now you ask for all my secrets."

"Your secrets you can keep. The restaurant, too. What do I know from restaurants? What I want is so the old people in the home should be able to eat the food, so they shouldn't put it under the table for the mice, so they shouldn't get sick from eating and die."

"Mr. Jacobson, tell me, you are running the home now? That boy, Meyer Rubin's son, I thought he was in charge."

"He is. You think I would take his job? I am just giving a little help."

"This Rubin, he wants your help? He asks for it?"

"Who knows what he wants always? What he needs is different. You bring a man a little gold, you think he will throw it in your face and tell you to give it somebody else?"

"So, you come to Shapiro."

"To who else? To who better?"

"You know what you ask? You ask a stranger, five hundred dollars, a thousand maybe, more he would charge you. You want a cookbook like from Fannie Farmer or the Settlement."

"You want me to pay? I will go to the bank and get the money."

"Stop." Shapiro held up his hand. "Who said you should pay? Is Shapiro asking for your money?"

"You said it would cost."

"I said from a stranger it would cost. Since when is Shapiro a stranger? Besides, Mr. Jacobson, I owe you."

My grandfather looked at him blankly. "For what do you owe me?"

"For what I owe you, I could never pay. When my mama and papa died, you know where they were buried, God rest them? In the Oxie cemetery, where else? And why is there an Oxie cemetery? Because of you, Mr. Jacobson, who else? So, if not for you, where would my mama and papa rest? So, for what I owe you, I could not pay."

"You think I would be paid for that?" My grandfather gave him a black look.

Shapiro waved a hand. "Who said anything about pay, you to me, me to you? What I say is, I would not charge you. Give me the menus. I will talk with the cook, we will look at them, we will see what we will see."

"So, Mr. Shapiro, I thank you. Now I owe you."

"Nothing you owe me. For the old people, I do it. For my mama and papa, I do it."

"And I can have them when?"

"You want miracles? Miracles I don't make. In a week, two weeks, better three, you should come back, have another meal like you couldn't get better anyplace, and then maybe I'll have a little something."

Three weeks later, to the day, my grandfather dined once more with Shapiro in his restaurant. When they were finished eating, Shapiro handed him a thick notebook. It was filled with recipes, the instructions for every dish explicit and simple and detailed—"An idiot could not make a mistake with that book," my grandfather said.

The moment had come to confront Rubin. His troops in order, their weapons loaded and ready, he charged into battle, stalking the director, cornered him in a corridor, demanded that the engagement begin. Rubin sighed, took my grandfather into his office.

"What is it this time, Mr. Jacobson?"

In my grandfather's arms was the ammunition he was sure would win the day, a heavy, bulging loose-leaf book filled with results of his labors, from the menus prepared by the residents to the nutritional findings of the university expert to the names of the wholesalers and their prices to all the instructions from Shapiro. He dropped the book with a thud on the desk in front of Rubin.

Rubin stared at the book, looked up at my grandfather. "What's this, Mr. Jacobson?"

"You should look with your eyes and you will see."

Rubin reached for the book, pulled it across the desk with some effort, opened it, flushed at what he saw, anger and a dozen other emotions reddening his face, stiffening his body. He closed the book. He looked up at my grandfather with flaming eyes. "Mr. Jacobson," he said tightly, struggling to control his voice, "I thought I told you months ago, not once but a dozen times, that food is none of your business."

"If I have to eat the food, it is my business."

"It's not your business. I told you we had experts who know

a lot more than you do who take care of the food."

"So, sometimes even the experts are wrong. I went to experts. They said different from your experts. If you read, you will see."

Rubin glared at him, tried to relax, leaned back in his chair and folded his arms, deliberately avoiding touching the book, as though it were contaminated. "You think I'm going to take the time to read all this?"

"You have the time, you should take it. You would not regret it, believe me."

"I'm a very busy man, Mr. Jacobson."

"So, don't be so busy for once. You will not be sorry."

"Well, I can tell you this. I certainly don't intend to do anything with this—with whatever it is you've thrown at me—while you're standing over me, watching."

"So, I will go and we will talk later."

My grandfather waited. He began to fret. Whenever he saw Rubin, the director ducked out of his way, avoiding him. A week passed. Two weeks. Then, a summons came. Rubin wanted to see him. My grandfather hurried to Rubin's office. The secretary told him to go right in, Rubin was waiting.

As my grandfather went through the door, Rubin looked up from behind the desk. He rose from his chair and stepped to one side. "Mr. Jacobson," he said, "sit down, here, in this chair, behind the desk."

My grandfather looked at him, uncertain. "You want me to sit in your chair, behind your desk?"

"That's exactly where I want you to sit. If you want to run this home, then you have to sit in the director's chair. So, sit down."

"Why should I want to run the home?"

"God knows why anyone would want to run this place," Rubin said. "But, God knows, you're doing your best to try."

"Mr. Rubin, you are wrong. The chair is yours, the desk is yours, the job is yours. I would not have them."

"You don't want them, Mr. Jacobson? Then, would you please tell me exactly what it is you're trying to do?"

"What I am trying to do is help a little, that's all."

"Your kind of help I don't need," Rubin said.

"I did something wrong?"

"Something? My God, do you want a list?" Rubin picked up the heavy book from his desk. He waved it, almost a threat, at my grandfather "This . . . this thing. What do you propose I do with it?"

"That is for you to decide, Mr. Rubin, not for me."

"Really? Then why did you go to all this trouble? Why did you storm in here and drop this package on my desk if you didn't expect me to do something about it?"

"I am only trying to give a little help so the people should enjoy their food and not get sick because of the meals."

"Nobody gets sick because of the food here. Nobody's ever gotten sick from the food we serve."

"You should only know."

"Don't tell me. I know."

"What you know, you don't know."

"Do you have the slightest idea what would happen if I tried to do anything to implement this?" He waved the book.

"The people would eat better and the home would save money."

"You just don't understand, do you, Mr. Jacobson?"

"I understand all right, Mr. Rubin. All my life I was in business. So, how could I not understand?"

"If you understand, then you understand that this is impossible."

"Nothing is impossible, except maybe to live forever."

"This is impossible. Believe me, Mr. Jacobson, I know what I'm talking about."

"Then you will do nothing?"

"Even if I wanted to, there's nothing I could do."

"You do not want to?"

"Things are fine just the way they are. I like things just this way."

"You should only live here a week, a day, even, and you would see how fine things are. You would see how much you like them."

"I'm here every day seven days a week, from early in the morning until God knows when."

"You go home every night."

"It's useless to talk to you, Mr. Jacobson. It's impossible to get through that thick skull of yours. Do you have any idea what you've done? You wasted the time of all these people who helped you with this. You wasted my time. You wasted your own time. And you got the people in this home all excited over nothing. I told you when you first came to see me about the food that you should leave it to the experts who get paid for doing that kind of thing, who are trained to do it. But you wouldn't listen. Oh, no, not you. You have to go your mule-headed way. And this is the result. My God, Mr. Jacobson, what am I going to do with you?"

"So, you are going to throw it in the wastebasket?"

"That's exactly what I'm going to do with it."

"Mr. Rubin, everything I ask since I came to this place, you tell me it cannot be, the home has no money for these things. So, now I show you how the home can have some money and the people can eat some food that doesn't belong in the garbage and you say you are going to throw it in the wastebasket."

"Mr. Jacobson, you don't know what you're talking about."

"I know, Mr. Rubin, I know."

"You don't know, and you'd better believe me for once. Now, will you just go away and forget the whole thing and leave me in peace, for just a few minutes, at least? If you want to try to run this home, then come here and sit in my chair and try, and let me tell you, you're welcome to it. Otherwise, just go back to your room and read a book, go to the lounge and listen to the radio, do anything you want, only leave the running of this place to people who know what it's all about."

And that was Rubin's last word. He would say nothing more to my grandfather.

"So, Jerome," my grandfather said, "I went back to my room and sat in my chair and looked out the window. I said to myself, Chaim Jacobson, maybe you should leave this place like your friends say. The world, it changes, everything changes, everybody changes, only the home does not change. It does not want to change. You try to help and you get a kick in the pants. So, maybe it is time you went."

But he did not go because there was, really, no place for him to go, no place he really wanted to be. And then, over the next months, as his passions cooled a little, he began to notice a change, gradual, subtle, but continual. For the people in the home, mealtime no longer seemed to be a time to dread, a time to pick with wry faces. The vegetables and the fruit seemed fresher, the food more recognizable and tastier. And he began to notice that the meals varied from day to day, and that the menus began to include those things the people had told him they wanted. And he sensed that to the people in the home, he had somehow become a hero, had become a man to hold in awe, to approach with respect. "Some of the people came to me," he said, "and they said, 'Mr. Jacobson, you are a worker of miracles. You said you would do it and it is done.' I said, 'I did no miracles. I did nothing. If somebody did something, if somebody you want to thank, then go to Rubin. He must be the one. To me, he would not listen.' "

Rubin never said a word to my grandfather and my grandfather never said a word to him about what had happened. But my grandfather knew. There was no way, after a time, that he could not know. Some of his friends in the wholesale market sent him notes to thank him for throwing the home's food-buying business their way and they wanted him to know that they would maintain the quality and price just as though he were doing the buying personally.

"And you never said anything to Mr. Rubin, grandpa?" I asked.

"Why should I say anything, Jerome? What was there I should say? You think I wanted he should thank me? What I wanted was better food for the people and better food we got. That was enough for Jacobson."

But there was a small footnote that, I think, gave my grandfather no little satisfaction and some amusement. Among his books, he had kept a copy of the home's annual report for the next year. He got it from his room and showed me the director's message to the trustees. Rubin had written:

"Your director is pleased to report that substantial progress has been made in a number of areas of the Zion Home's operation during the past year. These changes have led to greater efficiency, considerable savings, and have made the home a better and more appealing place for the residents, which is, of course, our major concern. Perhaps the most substantial improvement has been in the field of food service. Your director was fortunate enough to engage the volunteer services of an expert of many years' standing in the fields of catering and nutrition. At no cost to the home whatsoever, he and your director worked side by side for many months analyzing and reexamining the entire food operation, from menu planning to food purchasing to the actual preparation of meals. As a result of our studies, we have been able to institute numerous beneficial changes that have led to better and more nutritional meals for our residents while at the same time permitting us to actually cut the cost of our food operation by nearly one-third. You will be pleased to learn that our food operation has recently been cited by the Connecticut Nutritional Association and by the New England Association of Homes for the Aged for outstanding achievement, a model that other institutions should seek to emulate."

Late in 1945, my grandfather began to have some trouble with his eyes. He had worn glasses since early middle age and with them had perfect vision. But now he began to have some difficulty focusing on the print in a newspaper or in a book. The type seemed to blur and waver, and for him not to be able to read was intolerable.

"I went to Rubin and he said not to worry, I probably just needed a new pair of glasses. So, he sent me to this fancy doctor on Asylum Street for an examination. Dr. Reinhold was his name. To him you should never go, Jerome. He put me in a fancy chair and he looked into my eyes with this little light for two minutes, maybe, not even that long. Then he said I should read this chart with lots of letters and numbers that each line got smaller. Another two minutes he took. Then he said, 'Mr. Jacobson, you need a new pair of glasses.' I said, 'You are telling me something I don't know? When the print in the newspapers and the books is so I can't read, then even I know I need new glasses.' He said I shouldn't worry, he would make the glasses for me and I should come back in three days and they would be ready."

My grandfather got his new glasses and everything was fine. He thought nothing more of Dr. Reinhold and the examination. "One day I am sitting in my chair reading the newspaper when the knock comes at the door. I say, 'Who is there? Come in.' The door opens and who comes in but Sol Greenbaum."

Greenbaum stood timidly in the doorway, holding out an envelope. "Mr. Jacobson," he said, "there is a letter for you. I have brought it. From the government it is."

"So, Mr. Greenbaum, bring it already."

Greenbaum tiptoed across the room and handed my grandfather the stiff, long envelope. He stood over my grandfather, waiting. My grandfather looked up at him. "You are waiting for something, Mr. Greenbaum? A tip, maybe?"

Greenbaum said, awe near fright in his voice, "The letter, it is from the government."

"So, it is from the government."

"You are not going to open it?"

"When I am ready, I will open it." My grandfather put the envelope on the window ledge near him and went back to his newspaper. Greenbaum sighed, turned, and tiptoed back out of the room. When the door closed behind him, my grandfather took the envelope and tore it open. Inside was a check for twenty-five dollars. He studied it. His monthly old-age-assistance check was not due for another ten days. He could think of no reason the government would be sending him another check now. He rose from his chair, left his room, and went to Rubin's office.

Rubin saw him enter, sighed, leaned back. "Yes, Mr. Jacobson, what is it now?"

My grandfather put the check on the desk in front of the director. "The meaning?"

Rubin picked up the check, examined it, then nodded. "It's a check to pay for the eye examination you had, and for your new glasses. All you have to do is endorse it and we'll send it along to the doctor."

My grandfather stared in disbelief. "Twenty-five dollars?"

"That was his bill."

"Twenty-five dollars? For a little look and a little glass? I tell you, Mr. Rubin, it is too much."

"Come on, Mr. Jacobson," Rubin said, "what do you care? It doesn't come out of your pocket. The state's paying for it. All you have to do is endorse the check on the back and that will be that."

My grandfather reached across the desk and retrieved the check. "The doctor . . . his name I don't remember."

"Dr. Reinhold."

"Yes, Dr. Reinhold. Now I remember. He is rich?"

"How should I know? I imagine he's pretty well fixed. Most doctors are. But what's that got to do with anything?"

"Well, I tell you, Mr. Rubin, he must be rich if he wants twenty-five dollars for a little look, not five minutes, even, and a little glass. So rich you should be. Let me tell you, Mr. Rubin, in 1911, when first I was having a little trouble with my eyes, I went to Dr. Magnus. You know Dr. Magnus? Your father went to him. Everybody went to him. In Hartford, there was no better doctor for the eyes than Dr. Magnus. He looked into my eyes with this machine, with three machines. For an hour, he looked. He put drops in my eyes so I could hardly see. He said, 'Mr. Jacobson, you come back tomorrow so I can look again when the drops wear off.' The next day, another hour he was with me. He said, 'Mr. Jacobson, you need glasses. It will cost you six dollars. Three dollars for the examination, three dollars for the glasses. You could go somewhere else and maybe get the glasses a little cheaper if you want.' I said, 'Why should I go somewhere else when you are the best?' So, I paid the six dollars and I got the glasses and my eyes were like new."

"That was more than thirty years ago, Mr. Jacobson," Rubin said. "Everything's changed. Everything costs more these days."

My grandfather shook his head. "You say more? Mr. Rubin, I went to Dr. Magnus until 1935, when he died. Always it was the same, times were good, times were bad, always the same. Three dollars for the examination, three dollars for the new glasses. And the examination like you've never seen. Now, this rich Dr. Reinhold, for two minutes he looks at my eyes with a light, for two minutes he wants me to read letters and numbers, he says I need new glasses so new glasses he makes. For this he wants twenty-five dollars?"

Rubin sighed. "Mr. Jacobson, it's not your business to say no to his charge. Dr. Reinhold examined your eyes; he fitted you to a new pair of glasses; he sent the bill to the home; we sent it to the state; the state okayed it; it sent you the check to endorse over to the doctor. There's nothing to argue about. Just sign it on the back and forget it."

"You think I will forget it? You don't know Jacobson." He turned and marched out of the director's office, went back to his room for his overcoat, went out into the cold of winter, into the snow, waited at the corner for the bus, took it downtown, and walked the few blocks to the state office building and up the stairs to the old-age-assistance office on the second floor. He waited at the counter until a young woman approached.

"Can I help you?" she asked.

He held the check out to her.

She took it, studied it. "Is something wrong?"

"Something is wrong."

She looked back at the check, back at him. "Are you this Chaim Jacobson?"

He nodded. "I am Jacobson."

"Then, what's the trouble?"

"The check. It is for too much."

"I don't understand. What do you mean, too much?"

"It should be for six dollars. Maybe ten, but no more."

She stared at him. "You'd better talk to Mr. Barnes," she said. "Don't go away. I'll be right back." She hurried across the room ιο a young man behind a desk, bent over, put the check in front of him, and talked rapidly, gesturing toward my grandfather. The man stared at him while the girl talked. He got up and walked across the room to the counter.

"Hello," he said. "I'm Albert Barnes. Can I do something for you, Mr. . . . ah . . ." he glanced down at the check in his hand, ". . . ah, Mr. Jacobson?"

My grandfather nodded. "The check, you can take it back."

"Take it back?"

"And write another one, for ten dollars, maybe."

"I'm afraid I don't understand."

"Then I will tell you." My grandfather went through his story of Dr. Reinhold and Dr. Magnus and the differences.

Barnes heard him to the end. "I still don't understand," he said. "Just wait here and let me get the records." He went across the room to a wall of filing cabinets, opened drawers, searched, returned with a file. He laid it on the counter and opened it. "Here we are," he said. "Yes, it's all right here. Dr. Reinhold examined your eyes, made you a new pair of glasses, and sent a bill for twenty-five dollars. I think that's pretty reasonable, considering what's being charged these days. Anyway, it's right in line with our standards."

"Reasonable it is not."

"Mr. Jacobson, did or did not Dr. Reinhold examine your eyes and make you a new pair of glasses?"

"A new pair of glasses he made, yes. Examine my eyes, no. He looked at my eyes with a little light, yes, but examined them, no. So, for the little look, maybe he should get fifty cents, a dollar even. For the glasses, three dollars is all right. So, you should make the check for four dollars. You want to be generous, you can make it for ten. But twenty-five dollars? I say, never."

Barnes stared at him. "I just don't know what to say to you, Mr. Jacobson. I've never encountered a situation like this in my ten years in this office."

"So, now you are encountering it. Something new you should be glad about. Who wants life always to be the same?"

"What I'm trying to tell you, Mr. Jacobson, is that everything here is absolutely correct and legitimate and there's nothing for you to question. You were examined; you got your glasses; the doctor sent his bill; we authorized payment. We sent you the check because we have a policy that our clients should be able to pay their own bills themselves rather than having the state do everything for them. All you have to do is sign the check over to this doctor. It's really very simple."

"Simple it may seem. But simple it isn't."

"Mr. Jacobson, you owe the doctor his fee."

"I owe him his fee, yes. But I do not owe him to make him Rockefeller."

"Mr. Jacobson, the state says he's entitled to the amount he charged."

"I am the state also, yes?"

"Of course, of course. We're all the state. But that's not the point."

"To me, that is the point, exactly."

Barnes sighed, frustration mounting. "Just what is it you want, Mr. Jacobson?"

"I want you should tear up the check. I want you should make a new check. You want to make it for six dollars, you make it for six dollars. You want to make it for ten dollars, I will not argue too much. But more than ten dollars, never."

Barnes started looking around for help. An idea came to him. "Mr. Jacobson, do you have any idea how much it would cost to destroy this check and make out a new one?"

My grandfather waited.

"It would cost at least five hundred dollars."

"That I cannot believe."

"It happens to be the truth, Mr. Jacobson. Let me see if I can explain it so you'll understand. If we destroy this check, we'll have to change all our records, in a dozen different places. We'll have to write a letter to the doctor explaining what we've done and why. We'd have to draw another check. If the doctor objected, he might decide to sue, not just you and the home where you're living but the state as well, and that would mean we'd have to get a lawyer to prepare a brief and go into court to defend the action, and then we'd probably lose and have to pay the twenty-five dollars anyway plus the court costs. Now, you wouldn't want to see that happen, would you?"

"It would not be my fault."

"Whose fault would it be?"

"The doctor who tried to cheat and the state which was willing to be cheated. Since I am the state, I am not willing to be cheated."

"So, you won't endorse the check?"

"To Dr. Reinhold? You are joking."

Barnes sighed again, sagging. Suddenly he brightened. "I've got an idea that will take care of this whole thing."

My grandfather nodded, waited.

"Mr. Jacobson, this check is made out to you."

My grandfather nodded.

"Legally, you could do anything you wanted with it. Did you know that?"

"You think I am a thief?"

"Of course not. If you were, you wouldn't be here. What I'm trying to tell you is that you can take this check to the bank and cash it, then you can send this doctor whatever you feel he deserves together with a note explaining why you're disputing his bill. Everybody will be at least partially satisfied that way; the doctor at least can't say you've ignored his bill."

"And the rest of the money? What would I do with that?"

"Whatever you want, Mr. Jacobson. Put it in your pocket, buy a new necktie, a book, a good meal. Flush it down the toilet. Give it to charity. What you do with it is your own business." Barnes turned away from the counter.

"Young man . . ."

"Look, Mr. Jacobson, I've said all I'm going to say. You just do what you want to do."

My grandfather stared at his retreating back. He shrugged and walked out of the old-age-assistance office. He walked into the center of the city, went into a bank, cashed the check, and collected two ten-dollar bills and a five. He walked up Asylum Street to the office building, rode the elevator to the tenth floor, walked into Dr. Reinhold's office, waited in front of the receptionist's desk.

She looked up. "Yes?"

"I have come to pay."

"Oh? And your name?"

"Jacobson. Chaim Jacobson. You are so busy you cannot remember a patient?"

She spun in her chair, pulled open the drawer of a low filing cabinet, searched and found and took out a folder. "Oh, yes, here we are. Mr. Jacobson. You were in last month to see the doctor." She smiled. "You know, it wasn't really necessary for you to go to all the trouble of coming in personally to pay the bill. You could have mailed it in."

"I could have, yes. It was better I came in person." He reached into his pocket, took out a ten-dollar bill, and placed it in front of her on the desk. He spun and started toward the door.

"Mr. Jacobson," she called after him.

He halted with his hand on the door. "You are wanting something?"

"I'm afraid you've made a little mistake. The doctor's bill was for twenty-five dollars. You only gave me ten."

"For a little look and a little glass, ten is plenty. It is too much, even. Tell Dr. Reinhold, my name is Jacobson, not Astor, and his name is Reinhold, not Rockefeller."

He strode out of the office then and retraced his route back to the old-age-assistance office. He waited patiently at the counter until the girl approached him again.

"Oh," she said, "it's you."

"Mr. Barnes I would like to see."

"Just a minute." She walked across the office to Barnes. He looked up, saw my grandfather, shook his head, held back, then rose reluctantly and came forward.

"What is it now, Mr. Jacobson?"

My grandfather reached into his pocket and took out the ten-dollar bill and the five. He laid them carefully on the counter in front of Barnes. "You should buy yourself a new necktie," he said. He turned and walked out of the office and rode the bus back to the home.

"And what happened to the fifteen dollars, grandpa?" I asked when he had finished. "Did that Mr. Barnes buy a new necktie?"

My grandfather looked at me and shook his head. "What happened? How should I know?"

"Did Mr. Rubin ever say anything to you about it?"

"Mr. Rubin? No, never. Why should he say anything? It was over."

7

SPRAWLED ON THE GRASS IN the backyard that summer, listening to my grandfather as he relived for me the wars of his life, those of the long past, those with Rubin, there were moments when, young as I was, I could not miss a wistfulness in his voice, a faint undertone even of regret that those wars were over and now he had only his memories. Once, I asked him if he didn't miss his old friends at the home, if, perhaps, he didn't miss those running battles (though I'm not sure I used that phrase; I don't really remember what I called them) with Mr. Rubin. I said that most of my friends were away for the summer, at camp or the beach or somewhere, and I knew I missed them. In a way, I even missed this one particular kid I never really liked, who was my special enemy. We used to fight all the time and while I was sure I didn't like those fights at the time and hated the thought of them, now that he was gone for the summer, I suddenly realized that I actually missed them. So, I guessed he must miss his friends, he must even miss Mr. Rubin.

He laughed. "Ah, Jerome," he said, "it is different when you are a young boy. A boy's world is his friends, his enemies, even. For an old man, his friends, his enemies, even, they are here," and he tapped his chest above his heart. "What would I need with Rubin? I am with my grandson now, with my family. I have a little quiet, a little peace, a little rest, a little time to sit and enjoy the sun. What I don't need is to fight with Rubin."

Yet, there was something in his voice when he talked about Mr. Rubin that did not escape even a small boy. And half a dozen times that summer, Mr. Rubin called to ask about my grandfather. My mother faithfully reported her conversations with him. "I think he'd like to come and see you, pa," she said.

My grandfather snorted. "Once more Rubin will see me if he wants," he said. "But Jacobson see Rubin? Never in this life."

"Oh, pa," my mother said, "don't talk like that."

"What did grandpa mean, mom?" I asked.

My grandfather smiled. My mother dismissed the question. "Nothing, nothing at all, Jerry. Grandpa was only joking."

If there were many things about my grandfather I sensed and absorbed quickly, still there was a lot I missed for a long time, probably because we were together so much that I stopped thinking of him as old, as a man of any determinable age, only as my grandfather who would be there always as he was. I know I looked forward to those hours with him each day, looked forward to his stories, the remembered wars now that he seemed to have no more to fight, and I saw nothing strange in a boy of nearly nine and a man of nearly ninety becoming close companions, becoming more than friends.

But it was apparent that our relationship worried my mother and father. My mother would watch us together with a concerned expression, a frown creasing her brow, an anxious note in her voice when she suggested that it might be a good idea if I let my grandfather rest and went off to the playground at the school or explored the woods or did something a boy should do. And I sometimes heard my mother and father talking after I went to bed.

"Jerry's spending too much time with pa," my mother said. "A child his age ought to be out playing baseball, doing something with children his own age. He shouldn't be sitting around all day listening to an old man talk about a lot of nonsense."

"You're home all day with him," my father said. "If you're so worried, why don't you do something about it? You could always drive him to the lake for a day."

"How can I leave pa alone?"

"Ruth, he's a grown man. He can still look after himself if he has to."

"Have you taken a close look at him lately, David? I'm starting to get worried."

"He's all right."

"We should have sent Jerry to camp."

"Maybe. But where was the money going to come from? It's taking everything we can scrape up to get the office started. I hope things will ease up in the next couple of months. But until then, we'll just have to go slow."

"We could always have asked pa. He said he's got some money put away. I don't know how much, but he would have been glad to help."

"Do you really think I'd ask your father for a handout?"

"Oh, David, he wouldn't have looked at it as a handout."

"He wouldn't have, but I would."

"If only there was some way."

"But there isn't. We're just going to have to make the best of it this summer. Besides, I'll make you a bet Jerry's getting an education listening to your father. He'll end up knowing more about your family than you and all your brothers and sisters put together."

"At least you might talk to him."

"What do you want me to say? That he's spending too much time with his grandfather? That would be a hell of a thing to throw at him."

"We ought to do something."

"Maybe. But I'm a total blank. All I can think about is getting the business going. So, I'm completely open to any suggestions."

"That's the trouble. I haven't got any. I thought maybe you would."

"I wish I had. But right now I don't see any way out. I expect the best thing is just to do nothing. The summer will be over in a couple of weeks, then Jerry's friends will be home, school will be starting again, and I figure we can all get back to normal."

"I hope you're right, David. I hope we haven't done Jerry any harm by keeping him home this way all summer. You never know what can affect a child, how it will come out later."

"You've been reading too much Freud, Ruth. Forget it. The kid'll be all right. What the hell, how many other kids get to hear the kind of stories he's been hearing? Most kids just read about history. He's been hearing it from somebody who was there."

"I suppose so." Her voice sounded dubious.

"Besides, look at it another way. You say you think your father's going downhill. I don't see it, but maybe you're right. It doesn't really matter. We both know he can't have all that much more time, not at his age. So, this summer's been kind of a gift to him, having Jerry around, having someone to talk to who'd listen. That's not such a bad thing for an old man coming to the end."

Was my grandfather really getting that old, going downhill, nearing the end? I looked for the signs after I overheard that conversation, but I couldn't see any. He seemed the same to me most of the time as he had been since that day in May when he had come to live with us. Maybe he was sleeping a little more in the middle of the day, after lunch, but nobody could blame him in the stifling heat of August; even I had begun to take a short nap after lunch, something I hadn't done at least since I was five, but then the bedrooms with the shades drawn were the coolest places in the house. And maybe there were times now and then when he would start to tell me a story and then digress partway through and never quite get back to the point, or times when he seemed to lose track and just stare off into space. But it was possible to blame that on the heat, too, and besides, we all do that sometimes, not just old people. They say the heat isn't supposed to affect kids the way it does grown-ups, but I know that by the middle of August, when, except for a couple of late thunderstorms, it hadn't rained in nearly a month and the temperature had been in the nineties nearly every day, I was a lot more edgy and fretful and even forgetful than my grandfather.

So, I wasn't aware of any great change in him. He still took his walk every morning after breakfast, alone, to get his paper and his ten cigarettes from the store and maybe it took him five or ten minutes longer, but so what? He still listened while I talked to him about the Red Sox and the pennant race and other things, and seemed to share my excitement even if he didn't understand all that much about baseball. And I think he was as anxious as my mother that I not become too dependent on him, that I not center every moment of every day on being with him. He could, at times, be just as direct and adamant and insistent as she that I go off to the playground at the school, which I did for an hour or so every day, though there were rarely more than two or three other kids there, and they were older than I, so I had free use of the swings and the slides and the sprinkler that ran all the time, though there was no one to sit on the other end of the see-saw. And there were days when he ordered me to just go off in the woods and explore. It would be good for me to be alone for a while, he said. I did what he ordered and invariably came home with a bucket of wild berries that we then sat in the backyard and shared.

But something was missing. I knew it, could not put a finger on it at first. And then finally I realized what it was. In May, I had seen him march off to war, had seen him in action. Since then, I had only heard about his battles, his victories and his defeats. What I wanted, desperately, was to be a witness once more, just once, maybe even to be a participant, to be a Sancho Panza to his Don Quixote. But he seemed beyond the wars then, or above them.

And then, near the end of August, the years fell off him like strips of dead bark from a tree in spring, and he was putting on that armor, picking up his lance, and preparing to ride to a final struggle.

I was in the backyard late in the morning, playing what had become a daily game of pretend baseball, the Red Sox against the Yankees, with a tennis ball against the cellar hatch cover, when he appeared up the driveway from the store, carrying his newspaper. He was moving in a funny kind of run, the kind of way an old man who hasn't run for a long time would move when he had to try. He saw me and shouted, "Jerome!"

I let the ball fly off the sloping hatch over my head, didn't bother to chase it. I stared at him. "What is it, grandpa?"

He sped across the yard and sank into his canvas chair, beckoning me. He thrust out the newspaper to me. "Look! Tell me what you see."

What I saw was the front page of the *Daily Forward*. What I saw was a page full of type in Yiddish, broken by several blurry, indistinguishable photographs. "What, grandpa?"

His finger jabbed sharply against one of the photographs near the bottom of the page. "You see this? You see this picture?"

I looked at it. It was a photograph of three men sitting around a table at an outdoor restaurant somewhere, cars moving in the street behind them. I didn't recognize any of the men.

"This man," and his finger touched the figure in the center, "you know who this man is?"

I shook my head.

"This man is your cousin."

"My cousin?" I had dozens of cousins. Some of them I had met and those I had never met I had seen pictures of. But I had never seen a picture of the man at whom he was pointing.

He nodded, a tremor of unquenchable excitement passing through him. "Your cousin. My nephew, Mendel."

"Mendel?" As far as I knew, I had no cousin named Mendel.

"Your cousin, Mendel." He pointed to the printing in Yiddish beneath the photograph. "You see what that says?"

I looked at the print. "I can't read Yiddish, grandpa."

"You cannot read Yiddish?" He shook his head ruefully. "You must forgive an old man. I forget sometimes. English they teach the young in this country, but not Yiddish. So, maybe if I have time, I will teach you, so Yiddish shouldn't die when all the old ones die. But, now, you listen and I will tell you what it says so you should know. Here, under the picture," and his finger ran across the caption, "it says that this man, the one in the middle, is Mendel Yakovson who escaped from the Russian army and came to Paris for safety. He is in this café with some people from the newspaper. Look good, Jerome, so you should know your cousin."

I peered as hard as I could at the photograph, at the figure in the center. Like most newspaper photographs, it was smudged and fuzzy, the features difficult to distinguish. About all I could make out was that the man seemed youngish, in his twenties, was clean shaven, and had what appeared to be dark hair, but with a newspaper photograph, that was impossible to say for sure. I looked back up at my grandfather. "How do you know he's my cousin, grandpa?"

He waved his hand. "Wait, Jerome. You should wait. I will tell you what the newspaper says and then you will know." He gestured at the story that ran alongside the picture, read it over for what must have been the third or fourth time, turned to an inside page, and read down another column of type, nodding over and over. When he finished, he turned back to check himself and told me what the newspaper said about my cousin, his nephew, Mendel Yakovson.

According to the story in the *Forward,* over the past months, as tensions between the East and the West had been growing, an increasing number of Russian soldiers, especially those who were Jews, had been fleeing the Soviet army and seeking asylum in the West. Mendel Yakovson was one, the latest the newspaper's correspondent had found. He had been interviewed a few afternoons before in an outdoor café on the Left Bank where many Russian emigrés seemed to hang out. And there he had told his story.

Until a month earlier, Mendel Yakovson had been a corporal in the Soviet army, in which he had served since 1941. He had been conscripted a few days after the Nazis had attacked the Soviet Union, had served in a regiment that had been in action almost continuously until the war's end. He had been wounded five times, never too seriously. He had been decorated six times, and his medals included both the Order of Stalin and the Order of Lenin. Near the end of the war, most of his comrades by then killed, he had been promoted to corporal even though he himself was not a Communist. He had, however, considered himself a patriotic Russian and, as his wounds and medals demonstrated clearly, a brave and loyal soldier whose sole desire was the total annihilation of Hitler, Nazism, and Germany so that he could return home to peace.

Through those four long years, from June of 1941 until the war ended in 1945, he had not been home and he had heard not a word from or about his family. That was not unusual; the same thing was happening to many of the men in the Soviet army, for their homes, like his, had been in the path of the invading Germans, had been captured and liberated by Russian counterattacks not once but several times. Still, he was filled with fear. He had heard many rumors of what the Germans had done to the Jews, and to the Russians, in the towns they overran; he had seen the results in the areas he had helped to recapture, had seen things in the parts of Russia that had been occupied and in Poland that were too horrible to imagine, that could not be described, that none who had not seen them for themselves could possibly believe.

And so, when the war ended, he was desperate to get back to his home in the town of Nezhin near Kiev in the Ukraine. His pleading was at first ignored, but then his commanding officer gave consideration to his long service, his wounds, and his medals and he was told that he could have a week's leave. He made his way as fast as he could from his unit's base near Leningrad across Russia to Nezhin, praying and hoping. When he arrived in Nezhin, he knew he had arrived in the center of hell. There was nothing, hardly even ruins left. The Nazis had swept through and destroyed everything, and what they had not destroyed, the Russian army had finished in its counterattacks. The day he reached the ruins, a few peasants were picking their way through the rubble, a few young men he did not recognize were organizing crews to begin rebuilding. He asked after his family. No one knew anything. Then a peasant recognized him, not him by name or from friendship or even acquaintance, but merely as one of the young Jews who had lived in the town before the war. The peasant told him that the Nazis had marched all the Jews away, to a valley a few miles distant. There, they had killed all the Jews.

He went out to that valley, to that mass grave, raged and mourned, knew he would never find the graves of his parents, of his relatives, for they were all buried together. He went back to his regiment.

A few months later, the regiment was sent to East Germany for duty in the occupation. Yakovson had already begun considering his future. With his family dead, with his home destroyed, he was certain there was nothing left for him in Russia. Indeed, he wondered if he might actually be in some danger should he return home, or anywhere in Russia. He was tainted. He was Jewish, to start with, and all his life he had tasted the bitter potion of Soviet repression of the Jews, a repression his father and other relatives had told him was different only in minor degree from the lash of the czar. And he was suspect because his Uncle Avram, his father's brother, who had been an early Communist, had been a supporter of Trotsky; he had been a commissar of a factory in Kiev after the Revolution until he had been accused of Trotskyite treason in the purge trials of the 1930s and executed. That, Mendel Yakovson knew, would forever cast a dark shadow across his future, at least as long as Stalin lived, and there were those who said Stalin would live forever.

And there was more yet, besides his Jewishness and the Trotskyite treason of his Uncle Avram. His father, Yitzhak, and his grandfather, Moishe, had not been workers or peasants; they had been innkeepers in Nezhin and until he had been conscripted, he had worked in the inn, had thought that when his time came, he would own it.

So, he planned and he waited and finally, late one night, he crept out of his regiment's base, traveled only in the dark across the Soviet zone, traveled in the dark across all of Germany, hiding in fields and barns and ruins, until he reached France, where he could walk in the sunlight, until he reached Paris and the hope of freedom.

Now that he was in the West, the interviewer asked, what were his plans?

It was too soon to say, Yakovson replied. He might stay in France, if that was possible, and try to find work in a hotel, for that was his trade. Or, perhaps, he might go to America. He had an uncle in the United States named Chaim, though he had never seen him for the uncle had left Russia long before Mendel was born, when Mendel's father, Yitzhak, was still a child. There had been some letters, but nobody had heard anything from Uncle Chaim since the middle of the 1930s. Uncle Chaim was probably dead anyway, for he would be close to ninety. But there had been three children who had followed him to America. Yakovson thought their names were Gershon, Fagel, and Yussel or Iosif, he wasn't exactly sure. Some of them must still be alive, though he didnt know that as he didn't know them or know whether they were even aware of his existence, but he would like to try to find a way to get in touch with them even if they couldn't help him go to America. They were, as far as he knew, his only living relatives.

My grandfather finished. He smiled at me in a kind of triumph. "You see that this Mendel is your cousin, my nephew."

I had listened closely, had tried to make sense of what my grandfather had been telling me. Some of it seemed familiar, but not all. I said, "But, grandpa, his name is Yakovson and your name is Jacobson."

"Yakovson, Jacobson, they are the same," he said, waving a hand to end my objection. "In Russia, the name was Yakovson. In America, Jacobson. But listen, Jerome, let me explain so you will understand without a doubt. He is Yakovson, I am Yakovson, and my family were the only Yakovsons in Nezhin. He had an uncle named Avram who was murdered by the Communists. I had a brother named Avram who even when he was a boy talked nothing but revolution. He had a grandfather named Moishe who owned an inn in Nezhin. My father was Moishe and he owned an inn. He had a father named Yitzhak who was a boy when another uncle, Chaim, went to America. I am Chaim and I had a brother named Yitzhak who was a boy when I left. Chaim's children were Gershon, Fagel, and Yussel, who are your Uncle George, your Uncle Joseph, your Aunt Frances. He says his Uncle Chaim, if he is alive, would be ninety. I am alive and I am ninety. So, Jerome, this is my nephew and we must do something and must do something now."

He seemed to spring from the lawn chair toward the house, gesturing me to follow. He picked up the telephone and thrust it toward me. "I do not see so good today. You should make the call for me."

"Who should I call, grandpa?"

"You should call the operator and tell her you want to talk to the *Daily Forward* in New York, and then you should give me the phone." I did what he said.

My mother was in the kitchen, as usual. She heard us in the hall at the phone. She called, "Pa, who are you calling?"

He had the receiver pressed tightly against his ear. He did not answer, just waved a hand in her direction to silence her.

I said, "Grandpa's calling the *Daily Forward* in New York."

"He's calling who?" She came to the doorway and stared at him. She opened her mouth.

"Be quiet," he snapped.

"Jerome," she said, "what are you two up to?"

"Grandpa's calling about my cousin, my Cousin Mendel."

"Your cousin who?"

My grandfather turned angrily toward her. "Ruth, be quiet. You think I can hear the long distance when such noise you are making?" He listened into the phone. He began speaking Yiddish. He talked and he listened and he talked more, and the conversation went on and on, his voice rising in excitement, anger, frustration, falling into a tone of agreement, of understanding. He nodded and finally hung up.

My mother was tapping her foot, her own anger growing. "Now what was that all about?" she demanded.

"Your Cousin Mendel," my grandfather said.

"My Cousin Mendel? I don't have a Cousin Mendel."

"You should only know. A Cousin Mendel you have only you didn't know it until now."

"You'd better start explaining, pa."

"In the *Daily Forward* this morning," he began. He was too impatient, too excited to get out much more. He thrust the paper at her. "Here, you should read for yourself."

I hadn't known she could read Yiddish, or it had never occurred to me. Sometimes, when they didn't want me to understand what they were talking about, she and my father would talk Yiddish, but I had never seen her reading it. She read slowly, with obvious effort, while my grandfather loomed over her, practically dancing with agitation, so eager for her to finish. I could see the disbelief in her face slowly altering, changing to wonder, to incredulity, finally to acceptance.

She finished, closed the paper, looked at my grandfather. "What," she asked, "can we do?"

"I am doing already," he said. "You think I would call long distance to the *Forward* in New York if I wasn't doing?"

I'm glad I never saw our telephone bill for the next two weeks, glad I didn't have to pay it. My grandfather was too impassioned to do the dialing himself, to wait for the long-distance operator to come up with numbers and ring them, so he kept me by his side, made me do all the details, and then took the phone himself. He called the editor of the *Forward* in New York every day, no conversation lasting less than fifteen minutes. He talked with half a dozen people at the State Department in Washington, none of whom seemed to quite understand what he was talking about, all of whom insisted that he put his requests in writing and mail them to them before they could act. So, he sat down and wrote a dozen letters, making me sit with him so now and again he could check an English word, as if I then had the vocabulary that could help him. The letters were mailed at the post office, special delivery, not at the letter box on the corner. He waited two days for an answer and when none came, he began making those calls to Washington again, was shuttled from one bureaucrat to another, was told to be calm and patient, that his requests were moving through channels and it would take time.

"Time?" my grandfather shouted into the phone. "You think I have time? Soon I will be ninety, so how much time do I have? My nephew waits in Paris, alone; he knows nobody. You think he has time?"

But, from the State Department he could not get speed. He called the French embassy in Washington and the consulate in New York, was told once more to put his requests in writing and they would then investigate. He wrote more letters, waiting a few days, called again, was told to be patient, it would take time.

He called both our senators in Washington and our congressman, never got beyond staff assistants who told him he should explain the situation in a letter and they would investigate and see what could be done. So, he wrote, waited, called, was told to be calm, be patient, they were doing their best.

He called the governor, the mayor of Hartford, the town manager of West Hartford, the state senator, the assemblyman, councilmen, everyone he could think of. The replies were always the same—put the story in writing and then they would do what they could. His days were filled with the calls and the letter writing and seething impatience, growing anger. "If Moses Whitcomb was still alive," he said, "he would not ask for a letter. If Roger Jessup was still alive, he would not want a letter. They would do and it would be done." He said that not only to me and my mother and my father, but to everyone he called. There was only blank ignorance from his listeners. Roger Jessup they may have known about; everybody did. But Moses Whitcomb had been dead a long time and most of those he talked to had never even heard the name. When my grandfather said it to my mother, she had one of those blank expressions. "Who was Moses Whitcomb?" she asked.

He glared at her as though the question was not worthy of an answer. I answered for him. "He was a big political leader a long time ago. He was grandpa's friend. One time he asked grandpa to run for alderman."

"Really? I never heard that story."

But my mother and father, both convinced that Mendel Yakovson was, indeed, what my grandfather claimed, tried to help. They made a few calls on their own, wrote a few letters, too, and got about the same results as my grandfather.

My grandfather tried to enlist the entire family. He called Uncle George in Beverly Hills, Aunt Frances in Miami, Uncle Sam in Boston, Uncle Reuben in Chicago, Uncle Joseph in New York, Uncle Joshua in Washington, Uncle Abner and Uncle Michael in Philadelphia, Aunt Rachel in San Francisco, Aunt Miriam in Dallas, Aunt Esther in Cleveland. Except for George, Frances, and Joseph, who had been born there, none of them was exactly certain where or what Nezhin was, had hardly realized that they had had relatives who still lived in Russia, or who had lived there until the Nazis came. They heard him out, promised to do what they could (though I later came to think that most of them would have said anything to humor their father then and actually did nothing).

He raged around the house, unable to sit down and relax for more than a few minutes, rushing to the phone every time it rang, pacing behind the front door when he thought the mailman was due with the morning and the afternoon deliveries, shouting angrily about the collapse of the world if the mailman was a little late. Letters arrived. He tore them open with anticipation and excitement, only to discover that they were acknowledgments that his letters had been received, notices that this bureau or that politician was investigating and he would be kept informed of any progress.

What news there was, was not designed to foster optimism. A letter arrived from the State Department. The department regretted to inform him that its diplomats in Paris had been unable to discover the whereabouts of a former Russian soldier named Mendel Yakovson. If my grandfather had an address, he should send it to the department and further inquiries would be made. If he heard from Yakovson, he should tell the man to present himself at the embassy in Paris or at the nearest American consulate and request a visa for entrance into the United States and that request would be acted on promptly.

There were more calls to and from the *Daily Forward,* but without promising results. The paper sent a glossy photograph of Mendel, taken that day at the café, to my grandfather so that we would have a better likeness. But that was about all it could supply. Its Paris correspondent, who had been the one to interview Yakovson that day, had cabled back that the man had moved from his rooming house leaving no forwarding address and, despite a number of inquiries, no one seemed to know where he had gone. The *Forward*'s man would keep looking, but he was not hopeful that he would turn up anything. Soldiers who had deserted the Russian army and fled to the West had a way of disappearing without a trace and no one was ever sure whether they had done so on their own, deliberately, or it had been done for them or to them.

By then, it was the beginning of October. My friends were back, of course, school had started again, and so had my piano lessons, so I was out of the house much of the day, home only for lunch and then late in the afternoon. But my grandfather continued to consider me his one true confederate in this battle who would not lose hope and abandon the fight. When I was in the house, he would enlist my help in making a telephone call, would report in detail anything that might have happened, would let loose his fury at all that had not happened, at all that was not being done.

"If I was a young man still," he said, "I would find Mendel. I would go to Paris, today, even, and I would bring him home with me. If I was eighty again, even."

For a week, that early October, there was nothing, no letters, no phone calls. It looked as though we were at a dead end and the matter of Mendel Yakovson was going to die inconclusively. As I came home for lunch from school, my grandfather, dressed in his best suit, was standing by the front door preparing to leave. My mother was trying to detain him.

"Where are you going, grandpa?" I said.

"To the governor."

"Pa," my mother said, "you know that won't do any good."

"If the letters do no good, if the telephone does no good, maybe Jacobson in person cannot hurt. Besides, I remember the governor and maybe he remembers Jacobson. When I was with Moses Whitcomb sometimes, he was a boy, a young man at Whitcomb's elbow. So, maybe he will remember and maybe if he remembers, he will do something."

"Pa, what can he do that hasn't already been done?" my mother said.

"If he can do anything, it is more than anyone has done." He could not be deterred. He strode out of the house, down the street to the bus stop.

It rained that afternoon, one of those sudden, torrential storms of early fall that seem to come from nowhere, drown the world for an hour, and then vanish just as suddenly. I had gone back to school in brilliant sunshine, the sky a blinding blue without a cloud. An hour later, it was as black as a starless night, shredded by lightning, split by terrifying crashes of thunder, rolling one on top of the other. In an hour, it was over, and by the time school ended, the sky was washed clean, all the clouds gone, and even the sidewalks and the streets, littered with fallen leaves and branches, were beginning to dry. I went to my piano lession and then started home.

As I reached the house, a long black official limousine, on the license plate only the number *1,* was pulling to a stop at the curb. A chauffeur in uniform jumped out of the front seat, raced around and opened the rear door, reached in, and then I saw my grandfather emerge slowly in his grasp. My grandfather's hair, always so meticulously combed and brushed, was a wild, damp mop flying around his head. His clothes were sagging on him, soaking rags, clinging in places like paste, impeding his movements. The chauffeur held his arm tightly, led him unresisting up the front walk toward our door.

I raced after them, shouting, "Grandpa! Grandpa!" I had a tremor of fear.

The chauffeur pressed the doorbell. My grandfather heard my voice, looked back toward me, smiled a little weakly. "It is nothing, Jerome," he said when I reached them. "A little rain fell on me and the governor told this man to drive me home in his car. I told him it was not necessary but he said it should be."

My mother opened the door. She fell back at the sight of my grandfather and the chauffeur, her face alarmed. I don't think she even noticed me at that moment. "Pa," she cried, "what happened?"

"The old man got caught in the storm," the chauffeur said. "He showed up in the governor's office looking like a drowned rat. The governor was plenty worried, believe me. It seems he remembers the old man from a long time back. Anyway, we tried to get him dried off as best we could, gave him a little hot soup, and then the governor told me to drive him home."

"It was not necessary," my grandfather said. "The bus I could have taken." His voice was weak and the way he looked, even I knew he would never have made it on the bus.

"Sure," the chauffeur said, "like I could have flown."

"Thank you," my mother said to the chauffeur. "I don't know how we can ever thank you and the governor enough. I was worried sick when the storm started."

"I can believe it," the chauffeur said. "You'd better take him inside now and get him out of these clothes before he gets pneumonia."

"That's exactly what I intend to do." She reached for and took my grandfather's arm, began to pull him into the house.

My grandfather resisted just a little. "The governor," he said to the chauffeur, "you should tell him I will be back. There is an important matter I must talk with him about."

"Sure," the chauffeur said. "I'll tell him. And you can bet he'll be waiting to see you."

"How can we thank you?" my mother said again.

"Don't thank me, lady," he said. "Thank the governor." He patted my grandfather on the back, told him to take care of himself, that when he was ready to see the governor again he should just call and they'd send a car, and then he turned and went back to the limousine.

My mother led my grandfather into the house and up the stairs. She noticed me then. "Jerome," she said, "fill the bathtub while I get grandpa undressed. Fill it as hot as you can, scalding."

"I am not a child," my grandfather protested.

"That's exactly what you're acting like," she said. He did not argue again, let her lead him to his room. I went to the bathroom and filled the tub.

My grandfather began to cough that night, deep, racking coughs that seemed to choke him, to leave him breathless. His face was terribly flushed and even to come near him was to feel a scalding heat. My mother called the doctor. He got to the house within an hour. He was in the room with my grandfather for a long time. My mother and father sat, rose, paced nervously around the living room, waiting. I could feel their concern, their fear; it was infecting. I didn't know for sure what was happening but I was growing terribly afraid.

The doctor came down the stairs. My grandfather was asleep, fortunately. He was a very sick man. The last thing a man his age needed was to get caught in a storm like the one we'd had that day and then to hang around in wet clothes for a couple of hours. He was running a high fever, though at that moment, it didn't seem that there was any fluid in the lungs. We'd all better pray that it didn't turn into pneumonia, which was a distinct possibility. Perhaps it might be best to send him to the hospital right away.

"Is that necessary?" my mother whispered.

"No," the doctor said, "it's not necessary now. It would just be a precaution. He'd be looked after in the hospital in case . . ."

"I can look after him here."

"I'm sure you can. But it won't be easy."

"I know it won't be easy. But he's my father."

"Well, have it your own way. I still think he'd be better off in the hospital, but if you want to keep him home, I won't argue." He wrote out several prescriptions and said he would be back the next morning.

My grandfather was in bed in his darkened room for a week. Those first days, my mother was in the room all the time; she put a cot there and slept beside him on it so that she would be near if he needed her. The doctor came twice a day to examine him and those first days his face reflected his own concern. Several times he mentioned the hospital, but every time my mother vetoed the idea and my father, worried about her and seeing how she was acting, reluctantly backed her.

She called all her brothers and sisters, half brothers, and half sisters to tell them what had happened, her voice dropping to an inaudible whisper when she saw me hanging around, her hand gesturing vigorously to me to make myself scarce. But I stayed near, heard, "Pa's very sick. . . . Yes, the doctor's been here, every day, twice a day . . . I don't know. We're worried. The doctor's not sure. . . . No, not yet. Not until it's absolutely necessary. I'd rather have him here. I think he's better off here with people he knows. . . . No, no. There's no need yet. I'll let you know if there's any change."

"Mom, is grandpa going to be all right?"

She stared at me. "Little pitchers have big ears," she said.

"I heard what you were saying."

"I know you did. Of course, grandpa is going to be all right."

"But you're so worried. And the doctor's here all the time."

"Of course, we're worried. Who wouldn't be? Grandpa's very old, so when he gets sick, it is natural that everybody worries. But he's going to be just fine. In a few days, he'll be up and around just like always. Don't you worry your head about it. You've got better things to do."

But, of course, I worried. And, late in the week, when I had the chance, when my mother was off doing something around the house, I went to my grandfather's door, opened it a little, and peeked in. He was propped up on several pillows in his bed. For the first time, he looked to me like a very old man. His face was waxy, sunken, and his hands on the blankets were gnarled and mottled. He seemed to have shriveled, faded. His eyes opened. They were a very pale blue and clouded. After a moment, they cleared. He noticed me in the doorway.

"Ah, Jerome," he whispered in a very old voice, "so you have come to see your grandpa at last."

"They wouldn't let me in before, grandpa."

"They wouldn't?"

"No, mom said you had to be very quiet and I should stay away. Are you going to be all right, grandpa?"

His mouth moved in an effort to smile. "Of course, I will be all right. You are worried?"

I nodded. "Really all right?"

"You think I would miss your birthday?"

"It's your birthday, too."

"Jerome, what are you doing in here?" My mother was standing behind me, glaring.

"I came to see grandpa, mom."

"It is all right," he said. "I am happy to see the boy again."

The fever broke at last, the cough became only an occasional hollow rumble deep in his chest, his color got better. He had, somehow, escaped the feared pneumonia. On the tenth day, he got out of bed, dressed, and came slowly downstairs, and each day after that he was a little stronger.

But his illness had obviously taken a toll, had aged him as life itself had not. He was a little stooped and moved more slowly than before, tired easily. He had to give up his morning walks to the store, asked me instead to buy his newspaper and cigarettes—though when my mother heard that, she screamed at him in fury, forbidding the cigarettes. So, on my way home at lunch, I stopped at the store and got his newspaper at least.

What bothered me most, I think, was that he seemed to have lost interest in his search for Mendel Yakovson. I asked him, and he just shrugged. A letter came from the *Forward.* The search was proceeding but there was nothing else to report. He read it, sighed, and put it away.

Our joint birthday was a Thursday near the end of October. By then, my grandfather was well enough for a celebration. My mother informed us that the end of the week would be the time for a big celebration. Thursday would be just for us, my grandfather, me, my mother and father. We would have dinner together, maybe she would bake a cake, and there would be presents. Saturday afternoon, I could have a party for my friends; there would be another birthday cake and ice cream and then maybe my father would take us all to the movies. The biggest party would be Saturday night. All my aunts and uncles and a lot of my cousins, too, would be coming from all over the country to be with my grandfather for his ninetieth birthday; we would all go to a restaurant downtown where a special room had been reserved for the occasion.

Thursday arrived. I knew my mother well enough to understand that even though it was my actual birthday, I could expect no special dispensations, that I would have to go through the usual routine of the day, at least until dinner and that small party.

Still, since it was my birthday, I was sure the rules could be bent just a little. I dawdled on the way home from school, stopping at the playground for a while, fooling around with my friends, doing a lot of things that meant nothing except to tell me that this was a different kind of day. When I finally got home, I went around to the backyard, got my ball from the garage, and began to play a game of baseball against the cellar hatch.

My mother had been waiting, watching for me out the kitchen window. "Jerome," she called at the first throw, "come in the house."

"Aw, mom, I just got home."

"Jerome, did you hear me?"

"In a few minutes."

"Now."

"Five minutes."

"Now."

"Do I have to?"

"Jerome, will you just stop arguing and get in here."

"Aw, mom."

"In. Now. The piano's waiting."

"Aw, mom, it's my birthday."

"Birthday or no birthday, the piano's waiting."

"I'll wake grandpa."

"Don't worry your head about that. You just get in here this minute, young man, and march yourself into that living room and sit down at the piano and don't leave for the next hour. Do you hear me?"

There was no use arguing anymore. "Yes, mom, I hear."

"Then get to it, now. And I want to hear every note, fortissimo."

"Even when it says to play pianissimo?"

I heard a small sound, like a muffled laugh. "Now, no wise remarks out of you, young man. Just do what you're supposed to do."

So, I walked away from the ball, leaving it on the grass, and went into the house. My mother was preparing things in the kitchen, the makings of the cake laid out on the counter. I started to go by. "Wash your hands first," she ordered. I started for the sink. "In the bathroom."

I detoured for the bathroom, washed my hands, or, rather, let a little cold water touch them, and went to the piano, ran through some scales to warm up, as Miss Marcus always told me to do, opened the book of pieces, and began to play the Chopin études I had been working on with some limited success and a little confidence since the spring, delaying the inevitable necessity of grappling with the new. Miss Marcus had given me the first three Chopin preludes opus 28 to learn by Monday. I knew that I would be able to read the notes, strike most of them correctly, perhaps even memorize the first prelude. Anything beyond that was far in the future.

And there were distractions. I could hear the noises from the kitchen, the discordant clashing of pots and pans against enamel sink and wooden and tiled counter tops, the scurrying of my mother as she darted from stove to counter to refrigerator, all the sounds of cooking and preparing. There was more. There were noises upstairs. I heard my grandfather's door open, the resisting squeal of the attic door on its hinges as it was pulled open, footsteps climbing those steep stairs, moving heavily, slowly, with obvious effort, from one tread to another. Since I knew the notes of the études by heart, after all this time, I could play them with little concentration, could turn at least part of my mind to the sounds above. I was sure I heard a rustling in the attic, as though someone, my grandfather, was pulling and crumpling brittle old paper. A little later, I heard the heavy footsteps descending the attic stairs, heard them muffled by the upstairs hall carpet, heard the bathroom door open and close, heard the roaring of the shower, strained into the silence, heard the bathroom door open and close again, the muffled footsteps, my grandfather's door closing, in a little while opening, the beat of his feet on the stairs descending to the first floor.

My mother's voice, from the kitchen, startled. "Pa, what are you doing?"

There was mockery in his voice. "What I am doing is celebrating my birthday. It is against the law?"

"Now, just stop that." She sounded like she did when I had done something to annoy her. "What do you think you're wearing?"

He laughed, mocking. "What I am wearing is my birthday suit."

I buried my head against the keyboard, putting my hand over my mouth so nobody would know I had heard, so nobody would hear the sudden laughter that rose from my stomach. I hit some notes, any notes, to cover the sound. To me then, a birthday suit meant only one thing and I rocked at the idea of my grandfather standing in the middle of the kitchen in his birthday suit. I couldn't play a correct note with the music in front of me; my eyes were blurred with the tears of welling laughter. I had to see. I flew off the piano bench and into the kitchen.

My grandfather was standing in the center of the kitchen. He was dressed in an ancient, faded uniform. It must once have been a blue, though the years had faded it so that the color of a summer sky was now the pale of fall. There were brass buttons, still tarnished despite some strenuous rubbing and polishing of the last minutes, in a double row, parading up the front of the tunic. The gold braid on the sleeves was tarnished. A red stripe ran up on the outside of the trouser legs. The trousers were tucked into shiny black leather boots, though the leather was aged and there were cracks and creases. In his hand, he was holding a small black leather case.

My mother was staring at him, taking everything in. "Now, just where did those things come from?"

"From Russia, where else?" He laughed again, amused. "You think maybe I stole them?"

"Pa, stop that this instant. You know that's not what I meant." She spotted me. "Jerome, what are you doing in here? You're supposed to be practicing the piano. Now just get back where you belong."

"But, mom, I heard you and grandpa."

"I don't care if you heard the devil himself. You belong at the keyboard, not in the kitchen." She glared at me until, reluctantly, I turned and obeyed. Even before I was out of the room, she was back at my grandfather. "Now, will you please give me an answer? Where did those things come from?"

"From my trunk. Where else would I get them? You think maybe I waved a wand and did some magic?"

"Pa, I just don't know what to think, and that's the God's honest truth. Do you mean to stand there and tell me that you've had that . . . that thing . . . I suppose you'd call it a uniform, all these years?"

"And why not?"

"You're asking me that question?"

"If a question you ask me, why shouldn't I ask a question of you?"

"You just stop that. Act your age."

"And how should ninety act?"

"Not like nine. Will you please tell me what ever possessed you to go up to the attic and dig around in your trunk and pull that thing out and put it on? Today of all days?"

"When better than today? It is my birthday."

"Don't I know it. You don't have to remind me. I'll just bet you haven't worn that thing, even looked at it in . . . well, I don't know."

"The last time was when I left Russia."

"Oh, pa, what am I going to do with you?"

"You should do something?"

There was resignation in her voice. "Well, I suppose you have to humor an old fool on his birthday." I could hear a loud sigh. "All right, pa, you do what you want to do. Only, will you please get out of this kitchen so I can finish what I'm doing." There was a moment of silence, then her voice again, louder. "Jerome, what are you doing? I don't hear that piano."

I ran a string of notes from the Etude no. 10, called, "You weren't listening, mom."

"Louder," she shouted.

My grandfather came into the living room and sat in a chair near the piano, where he always sat when he watched me practice. He grinned at me. I grinned back, strangled a laugh. I played some more. It was time to move on to the preludes. I took the book, opened it, studied the notes for a moment, struck the first ones. Out of the corner of my eye, I saw my grandfather open the leather case in his lap. He took out a flute, fitted it together, slowly and carefully polished it on his sleeve. He raised it to his lips, blew into it, his fingers barely touching the key mechanism. He made no sound, merely had his lips against the embouchure, moved his fingers at first stiffly, a little awkwardly, and then with increasing agility on the mechanism. He took the flute away from his mouth and smiled at me, nodded. I stared back, stumbled over the notes. He put the flute to his lips again and suddenly from the instrument came the notes I was trying to play. He smiled with satisfaction, gestured toward me to play. I played. He played along with me, duplicating what I was playing, only there was a feeling, some sense of emotion or understanding, in his playing that I could not capture on the piano.

My mother appeared in the entrance to the living room. She stared from him to me. "What is going on here?" She saw the flute, heard the sounds. "My God," she said, "a duet." She stared at my grandfather, stunned. "Now where did that thing come from, pa?"

His expression did not change. He moved the flute just a fraction from his lips. "The same place as the rest. Where else?"

"How should I know? I don't think I'm going to be surprised at anything that happens around here today."

He made a gesture at her with his head. "Go away, Ruthie. You cannot see that we are playing? You are disturbing the music. Go back to the kitchen."

She did not move for a moment, remained in the doorway watching with disbelief. My grandfather put his lips against the embouchure, his fingers on the keys, began playing the first prelude. He nodded to me. I picked up from the book where he was, struck the keyboard. We played together. My mother watched, sighed, turned, and left.

I think he led and I followed and for the next fifteen minutes, we played preludes without pause, and his playing and mine, too, got better and better with each minute. It was an experience I had never had at the piano before, total immersion in the music, total enjoyment in the playing and the sounds I was making. Then, exhausted, we paused. My grandfather settled back in his chair. He held the flute and looked on it with contentment.

I smiled at him and he smiled back. "I didn't know you played the flute, grandpa." I had forgotten that early in the summer he had told me that when he was a boy, his father had made him study the flute. Then I remembered. "Oh, now I remember," I said. "You told me. But I didn't know you could play like that."

"It is a long time," he said. "I play not very good."

"It sure sounds to me like you play pretty good."

"I play the flute like you play the piano." He laughed. I was sure he was joking; I had all I could do to strike a correct note on the piano; he not only played the right notes on the flute but the sounds that emerged were filled with things I had not known were in the music. He shook the flute vigorously. A spray of saliva danced away from it like mist. He wiped it away, wiped the mouth hole on his sleeve. "It is a good flute." He nodded.

"I didn't even know you had it still."

"I have had it for more than eighty years. But I have not looked at it for nearly seventy years."

"For seventy years?"

He nodded. "The last time I played this flute was also for a party. Not a birthday but a wedding. It was when the grand duke was married. I sat in a tree and made the flute sound like a bird singing."

I didn't know what to say. I thought, grinned, said, "Were you wearing your birthday suit then, grandpa, for that party?"

He started, stared at me as though he didn't quite understand. Then he started to laugh. He could not stop. He took out a handkerchief, took off his glasses, and wiped the tears of laughter from his eyes. He put the handkerchief away. He grinned at me. "Yes, Jerome, I was wearing my birthday suit that day. Only, that day it was called a uniform."

"Oh, I know that. I know it's a uniform. Like my daddy wore when he was in the army, only different."

"Only different," he agreed. "Not the same army."

I studied the uniform. "I never saw one like that before," I said. "It's like the one the man wears who stands in front of the Bond Hotel downtown. Only different."

He smiled and nodded. "It is different. Your grandpa has been many things in his life but never a doorman at the hotel in Hartford or any city. This, Jerome, is the uniform I wore in the army, the uniform they said was for special occasions."

"Gee, I didn't even know you were ever in the army, grandpa. You never told me. Did you fight in the war? What army were you in?"

Oh, yes, he said, he had been in the army, though his was an army that didn't exist any longer and nobody made or wore uniforms like his anymore, nobody had made them or worn them in many years. The army he was in was in the old country, in Russia, before he came to America. He made a sour face as though he had just taken a swallow of my mother's lemonade and had forgotten to put the sugar cube between his teeth. "It was," he said, "the army of the czar."

"The czar was like a king, wasn't he? Like King George of England."

He looked at me and shook his head sadly. "Like King George? What do they teach the boys in the schools today? Like Hitler, maybe. Like Stalin, maybe. But like King George, never. The czar had a hand of steel and a knout in his hand for the people. He lived in palaces like a king, in Saint Petersburg, in Moscow, he had palaces and dachas everywhere. He said the people should love him like he was their father, and they should call him their little father, the father of all the Russians. But, I tell you, Jerome, the czar had many children but he was not the father of all the Jews in Russia, or all the Russians in Russia, even, and the people did not love him. If the czar was a relative, he was a wicked uncle."

I thought I knew what he meant. In school, we had been reading about King Arthur, the teacher had even arranged our desks in a circle around the room like the Round Table and given all of us the names of knights and ladies (I was Sir Gawain), so I made an immediate connection. I said, "Like Modred?"

He gave a little laugh. "You think I do not know about King Arthur?"

"Oh, I'll bet you read about him in school, like we do."

"No, in the *cheder* we read about Haman, and in the Russian schools they read about Ivan and the boyars. About King Arthur I read after I came to America and learned to read English."

My mother, a little strident and impatient, came from the kitchen. "What's going on in there? Stop that talking and get back to the piano, Jerome."

I ran a scale. "I was just turning the page, mom." I turned the page, struck the first notes of the third prelude. My grandfather picked up the flute. But this time, when he blew into it, the sound that came out was pitched in an imitation of my mother's voice. I smothered a laugh. My grandfather winked at me, then began to play the notes of the prelude. We played our duet for a while.

"Miss Marcus should hear you play Chopin, grandpa," I said when we reached the end.

"I did not think I remembered," he said.

"I didn't even know you could play it on the flute. I thought it was just for the piano."

"Anything you can play on any instrument." He put the flute to his lips again, played something I didn't know, nodded to himself with satisfaction.

"Did you play the flute when you were in the Russian army, grandpa?"

"I played the flute."

"And did you carry a gun and fight in a war?"

"A gun I did not carry, only the flute. But a war?" He twisted a little in his chair, pulling around the back of his tunic to show me a jagged tear in the fabric. "This is the scar from the war I fought."

I stared at it. "It couldn't have been a very big war if that's all that happened."

"Like the war your papa was in it was not big," he said. "But when you are in a war, any war is a big war."

"Were there lots of battles?"

"Like your papa saw? No. But there were battles."

"Did you kill lots of the enemy?"

He smiled just a little and shook his head. "It is hard to kill the enemy with music. It is hard to kill the enemy when you do not know whether the enemy is with you or facing you."

I didn't understand that and I told him so.

"Then, maybe, I should tell you about the Russian army and you will understand."

There were wars in Russia all the time he was growing up; there were always wars, but nobody understood what they were about except the czar and his nobles and the rich. The wars didn't concern him or any Jew, they didn't even concern most Russians except when the czar sent his agents to collect more taxes or the Cossacks to seize the young men and take them away to be soldiers. For the Jews, there was always fear when the Cossacks appeared. Sometimes it was because the czar had decided he wanted a pogrom and so he sent the Cossacks to burn the Jewish homes and kill the people; sometimes it was because the czar only wanted the young men for the army and so he sent the Cossacks to take them. The czar may have hated the Jews, but he was just as willing to put them in his army as to kill them, just as willing to make them soldiers as he was to make soldiers out of ordinary Russian peasants. So, when the Cossacks came riding across the steppes, the people never knew whether they were going to be killed or whether their young men were going to be taken away. What they usually did when they saw the Cossacks in the distance was to run and hide in the fields, especially the young men.

One day, the Cossacks came. My grandfather was in his room in the inn reading and he did not hear the alarm. His brothers hid themselves safely but when he realized what was happening, there was no time. He was seized by the Cossacks and told that he was now a soldier in the czar's army. He tried to explain that he was married to Ruchele, that he had two children, Gershon and Fagel, and what would they do if he were taken away? The Cossacks said that was their problem; the czar needed young men for the army and he was a healthy young man.

As they were about to take him away, together with a few other young men who had not had time to hide, his father appeared from his hiding place and went to the hetman. He said that he knew that his son would have to go with them and that while he did not want to see it happen, he knew that the czar's will was not to be questioned by any loyal Russian and he was a loyal Russian. But, he said, the hetman should know that this young man was a gifted musician, that he had been playing the flute since he was a boy. So, perhaps, the young man could better serve the czar and all Russia by playing his flute in an army orchestra for the benefit of the officers and the soldiers than by carrying a gun.

The hetman and the other Cossacks who heard this laughed. They said the czar had plenty of men who could play musical instruments. What he needed were men to carry and shoot rifles at the enemy, not serenade them.

My great-grandfather said he was sure that was true, but, still, there must be a place for a truly gifted flutist. He rushed into the inn and came out with my grandfather's flute, handed it to him, ordered him to play it for the hetman and the Cossacks. My grandfather played.

The hetman listened, nodded, said the young man played well but the czar needed men to carry rifles, not flutes.

My great-grandfather said he was sure the czar must also need flutists and he was sure that if the hetman tried very hard, he might find an army orchestra that could use someone who could play the flute as well as my grandfather. He handed the hetman a small leather bag tied at the neck with a leather thong.

The hetman took the bag, hefted it in his hand, shook it. There was a clinking jingle inside. He opened the thong and peered into the bag. He smiled and said he thought he might know of an army band that needed a flutist but he wasn't sure. He would have to think about it. It was still possible that soldiers with guns were needed more.

My great-grandfather went back to the inn, returned with another leather bag tied at the neck with a thong, a bag a little larger and a little heavier than the first one. He handed it to the hetman. The hetman weighed it in his hand, jingled it, opened the neck, and looked inside. He smiled broadly. He put the two leather bags in his saddlebag. He said he had suddenly remembered that there was an orchestra being formed by a regiment; the orchestra would need a flutist. He would take the young man there and make sure he was taken care of. Some young men, he said, could better serve the czar by making music to keep the officers and the soldiers happy and contented than by shooting rifles whose bullets would hit nothing but the trees and the air.

My grandfather went off with the Cossacks. Until he reached the regiment, he was not sure whether he would be a musician or a soldier because all too often when such bargains were struck with the cossacks, the hetmans merely pocketed the money and sent the young men into battle anyway. But, when they reached the regiment, the hetman kept his word and my grandfather became part of the regimental orchestra. He played while other young men marched away to battle; he played several times on the tops of hills while the battles were fought in the valleys below, blowing into his flute while he saw men die in smoke and thunder. He played at dances for the officers and while they dined in their regimental messes.

Twice while he was in the army, he was permitted to go home to Nezhin. The first time, he spent the week with Ruchele and his children, telling them about the army, telling them that if he ever had the chance, he was going to run away. The army was not for him. But, Ruchele said, if he ran away, they would be after him, they would take him back and they would kill him. He said not if he left Russia. Where would he go? Where else but to America.

A year later, he was given another leave to Nezhin. He got home to discover that he had another son, Yussel, just three months old. Now, he said, he knew he would have to run away as soon as he could. There was no one to support his family. His children would grow up without him, seeing him once a year. If he did not run away, he did not know when, if ever, he would get out of the army to return to them; the orchestra was filled with old men who had been in the army for ten, fifteen, twenty years. He had no intention of serving the czar a day longer than he had to.

He went back to his regiment, but the opportunity to escape never seemed to come. Then the regiment was moved to Poland and one day the orchestra was marched from its base deep into a forest. Nobody told the musicians where they were going or why. Once in the forest, they were made to climb the trees around a large clearing, were forced to sit on branches and conceal themselves among the leaves. They were told to play in the trees and, under the direction of their conductor, began to learn to play as though they were some new species of birds, filling the forest with gentle music that, no matter how soft and gentle, frightened the real birds and animals away. For ten days, they practiced in those trees until they were perfect, until it seemed that the trees themselves were making the music.

What they didn't know until the tenth day, when they had taken their positions among the leaves and branches, was that they were to provide the music for the wedding of the czar's brother, the grand duke. The conductor gave the signal, the forest echoed and murmured with their songs, and a procession began to make its way along the trails through the forest to the clearing. There were priests, there were princes, dukes, nobles of all kinds. There were generals and admirals. The czar and the czarina came into view. The grand duke appeared in his white uniform, his medals heavy all over his chest, glittering with blinding flashes in the sunlight. The bride, veiled and gowned, her hand on the arm of her father, a prince, came slowly along the trail to stand beside the grand duke before the patriarch of the church.

They played softly through the ceremony. They played while straining, groaning, sweating servants carried heavy tables into the clearing, covered them with shimmering white cloths, loaded them with foods and drinks of a quantity and a kind my grandfather had never imagined even existed. They played while the wedding guests filled themselves. They played when the grand duke and his new bride were handed into a carriage and driven away. They played while the feasting and celebrating went on. They played until their lips were stiff and sore and blistered from playing and they were too hot and exhausted, too starved and thirsting, to play any longer, and still they played without pause or rest until it was growing dark and the last of the wedding guests slowly drifted back down the trails away from the clearing and the servants began to clean up the debris. That day, my grandfather said, must have been like a fairy tale if you were on the outside looking in at it. But if you were in a tree playing the flute through blistered lips and dying for a drink of water, it was more like a dream of hell, and he swore that when it was over, he would never play the flute again.

At last, it was night. The order was given for the music to cease. The men were told to come down from the trees, to fall into ranks and be marched away from the forest back to their base. My grandfather knew at that moment that he would play for no more weddings or dances or dinners or battles, that he would never raise his flute to his lips again for a czar or a duke or a general or an army. Instead of falling into ranks, he turned the other way and, in the darkness of that forest night, began to run into the trees. A Cossack saw him. He began to shout for him to stop. My grandfather ran faster. The Cossack mounted his horse, grabbed his lance, and gave chase. My grandfather dodged through, around, between the trees. The Cossack rode after him, ducking low branches, veering his horse to avoid crashing into trees or stumbling over fallen limbs, thrusting out with his lance. Several times he seemed within striking distance, leaned forward, and drove his lance at my grandfather with a fury. My grandfather managed to slip behind trees, twist, race into even denser forest, managed to escape the lance. The Cossack kept after him, caught up with him, thrust out once more with the lance. It tore through my grandfather's tunic. My grandfather was driven to the ground. The Cossack turned his horse and rode down on him again, thrusting at him with the lance. The lance drove past him, missing by a fraction, digging into the ground. The Cossack pulled it free. The resistance of the ground and the obscurity of the dark must have convinced him that he had run my grandfather through and killed him. He sat on his horse, towering over the body, peering down at it through the darkness, laughing. My grandfather did not move. The Cossack prodded him with the lance. He went limp, let the Cossack and his lance move him as though he were nothing more than a boneless shape surrounded by dark cloth. The Cossack thrust down at the body with his lance again, missed again in the dark, though the resistance of the ground when he tugged his lance free obviously assured him that he had struck mortally again. He laughed, spun his horse, and rode away, wiping the lance clean against the horse's flanks as he rode.

For a long time, my grandfather lay still, not moving, waiting. When he was certain the Cossack was not going to return, when the sounds of men had completely vanished and the natural sounds of the forest night—the rustling of animals among the leaves and underbrush, the calling of night birds from tree to tree—had returned, he rose, brushed himself, and began to walk through the forest toward the west. It was only then that he realized he was still holding the flute, had never once let it go. He took that as a sign that he should keep it with him.

For how many days he did not know, he walked alone and in the dark, always near some place where he could conceal himself if necessary, hid during the days wherever he could find shelter, moving always west. One day, he hid in a farmer's barn, found some old clothes there, and changed from his uniform into them. For a reason he could not explain even to himself, he wrapped the uniform in some burlap that had been discarded in the barn and carried it with him.

He walked through the nights and slept fitfully through the days until he was convinced that he was out of Russia and was safe. He knew that, he said, when he heard some people talking in a language that was neither Russian nor Polish, a language he did not know but that bore a resemblance to Yiddish. He began then to walk through the day and sleep at night without fear. He worked for a day or a week for farmers for food and lodging, then went his way. Finally, he reached the sea and a port. He had no money, but he found a synagogue, came upon people who spoke Yiddish. He told them he had run away from Russia and that he was trying to get to America. He was given work as a janitor in the synagogue, picked up a few other odd jobs around the community, and finally was able to afford a passage on a ship across the ocean.

The story ended there. His voice just faded away and we were both silent. I had a sudden vague thought touched with melancholy, that he had told me a last story and there would be no more, that he had been saving this story for a particular moment and the moment had finally come, that this was his birthday present, not just to me but to himself, too. And, a long time later, remembering, I thought I saw in that story a kind of summing up, that contained in it were the seeds of all that would follow in his life.

But I said none of this to him then, banished it from my own mind almost as soon as it entered. I said only, "And you never threw away the uniform or the flute. You've still got them."

"I still have them. So you can see."

"But you must have played the flute again even after you promised that you wouldn't."

"Never. Until this very day."

"Why, grandpa? I mean, not why didn't you play the flute, but why did you decide to put on your old uniform and play the flute today?"

He smiled. "Because, Jerome, today is my birthday, as it is your birthday. Today, I am ninety years old, which is very old to be. And when you get to be ninety years old, you should do something special, even if it is only putting on an old uniform and playing an old flute with your grandson who is nine."

"I guess so." I was dubious, not quite sure what he meant. "Are you going to wear the uniform all day and tonight, too?"

"That is why I have it on."

"Are you going to wear it for the party on Saturday?"

"I do not think so. Saturday will be only a party. It will not be my birthday, or your birthday."

"Well, aren't you at least going to play the flute again on Saturday, so everybody will know how you can do it?"

He shook his head. "I do not think so. I think I will not play the flute again after today."

"You said that seventy years ago."

"I did," he laughed. "I meant it when I said it."

"And you mean it now?"

"I mean it now, only more so."

I had not heard my father's car in the driveway, had not even heard the back door open. But then I heard his voice in the kitchen, talking to my mother, asking where the birthday boys were and how they were doing. She told him we were both in the living room and I was supposed to be practicing but what I was doing mostly was talking to the other birthday boy. He laughed and said, "Well, it is their birthday," and then he said he'd be right down, after he washed up. He went up the stairs without even looking into the living room or saying anything to us.

My mother came into the living room. She looked at us. She said, "Well, you managed to get out of most of your practicing, didn't you."

I said, "Mom, I practiced harder and better than ever. You should have been listening."

"Oh, I was listening, all right," she said. She looked at my grandfather. "And you're a big help, pa. Sometimes I think you're no older than Jerome."

He lifted the flute and trilled a high, mocking note at her.

She stared at him. She tried to stop a smile but couldn't do it. "Oh, both of you. Just go and get washed up for dinner."

My grandfather and I were the first ones to the table. We sat across from each other in our usual places. He had put his flute back in its leather case and the case was now on the table near his setting. My mother wheeled a serving cart from the kitchen. She had made a very special dinner for us. There was a roast beef on a platter, a carving knife and fork next to it; there were large bowls of potatoes and vegetables. She put the roast on the table in front of my father's place, the potatoes and vegetables in front of hers. She sat down in her chair at the end of the table.

My father marched into the room carrying a bottle of red wine and a corkscrew. He grinned happily at me, at my grandfather, began singing "Happy Birthday" to both of us. He stopped behind my chair and ran his hand through my hair, hugged me around the shoulders, leaned down and rubbed his cheek against mine; that hurt; he needed a shave, as he always did at the end of the day. He went to his chair at the end of the table opposite my mother, started to sit down, saw my grandfather I think for the first time, stared at him, looked across at my mother. "What's he made up for?"

My mother said, "Ask him."

My father laid the bottle and the corkscrew on the table. He sat down. He examined my grandfather carefully. He said, "Are you going to a costume party, Mr. Jacobson?"

My grandfather smiled. "I am going to a birthday party, David. I am going to a birthday party for my grandson."

"And for yourself."

"And for myself."

"So, you decided to dress for the occasion."

"It is not everybody who lives to be ninety."

"You're absolutely right," my father said. "So, you went out and rented a uniform to celebrate."

"I went to the attic and took my uniform from my trunk."

My father's eyes studied the uniform. "I'll bet you haven't put that thing on since you left Russia."

"That bet you would win."

"I'm surprised you even kept it all these years."

"I am full of surprises."

"You're telling me something I don't know?" He shook his head, a little in admiration, I think. "It's too bad there's not a parade. You could march in it, at the head of the line, wearing that getup."

"If there was a parade," my grandfather said, "I would not march in it. Already I marched in too many parades."

"Haven't we all," my father said. "I'll tell you something, Mr. Jacobson. You sure don't look ninety. In that thing, you look ready to march into another battle, full of . . ." he looked at me, smiled, "well, vinegar anyway."

My grandfather waved a hand. "To an old man you shouldn't talk nonsense. I am an old man now and like an old man I look."

Both my mother and father began to protest.

My grandfather shook his head at them. "Why should you argue? You think I have not had a good time in my life?" He looked at me and smiled. "Jerome," he said, "grown-up people worry too much. They worry all the time about things they can do nothing about. Only the old men and the young boys understand." He looked back at my father. "You should carve the roast, David. In your own house, at your own table, you should not sit with your mouth open and a sad look. You should smile and carve the roast so we can eat."

My father smiled, started to reach for the platter, halted, reached for the wine bottle and the corkscrew instead. "I almost forgot this," he said. He opened the bottle, poured a little into his glass, tasted it, nodded, pleased. He poured three glasses, handed one to my mother, one to my grandfather, and kept the third for himself. He paused, looked at my mother. "Should we give some to Jerry?"

"Oh, David, you know he's too young."

"Well, after all, it's his birthday, the last of the single digits."

"Oh, mom, can't I?" I pleaded.

She looked at my father, made a stern face. "You're spoiling the boy."

"One sip of wine isn't going to hurt," he said. He went to the cabinet and took another wineglass, poured a little for me. "Sip it," he ordered, "don't chug." He raised his glass, said, "Happy birthday" to my grandfather and to me, took a sip of the wine, and nodded. I sipped from my glass. It tasted sour to me and burned my tongue and throat. I made a face and pushed the glass away. Everyone laughed.

And then my father carved and we ate and when we had finished, my mother told us all to go into the living room for the birthday cake and some surprises. I raced up the stairs first to get the present I had bought, with what I had saved from my allowance all summer, for my grandfather.

Before we could get started, the telephone rang. It was Uncle George calling to wish his father a happy birthday, to tell him he would see him on Saturday. For the next hour, the telephone did not stop ringing. There were calls from all my aunts and uncles wishing happy birthdays and saying they would see us on Saturday.

Finally, there were no more calls. We gathered in the living room. My grandfather sat in his chair. In his lap, he held the case with the flute. Suddenly, he looked very tired and very old. Until he smiled at me, and then the fatigue and the years seemed to peel away.

My mother came out of the kitchen carrying a chocolate cake with nine candles around the edges and one to grow on in the middle. She put it on the coffee table. My father took a match and lit the candles. He had to use three matches to get them all lit. One candle kept going out. My mother and father told my grandfather and me to come and blow out the candles. They started to sing "Happy Birthday." My mother said, "Make a wish." I closed my eyes, but, for once, I couldn't think of anything I wanted to wish for. My father ordered, "Blow." I opened my eyes and both my grandfather and I blew as hard as we could. The candles flickered and then went out.

My grandfather went back to his chair. He opened the flute case, wiped the flute carefully, put it to his lips, and began to play "Happy Birthday," very softly and very slowly. My father looked at my mother; his look was a little bewildered. My mother shrugged. I listened to my grandfather's playing. The song sounded very sad and lonely the way he was playing it then and I was surprised because I didn't think it was possible to make that song sound that way.

My grandfather took the flute apart and put it away in the case very carefully. He closed the case. He got that very tired and very old look again. My mother and father looked at him and their faces were very worried. My mother said anxiously, "Are you all right, pa?"

He looked up. He smiled and some of the years went away. "I am fine," he said. "It is nothing. I am just a little tired. An old man has been sick, it takes a little time to recover. You should cut the cake now so we can all eat. Jerome is waiting."

She cut the cake and we all had some; I had two pieces. And then came the presents. I said, "Grandpa first." My mother and father smiled at me.

My mother brought him a handful of envelopes. "These all came for you today, pa."

He looked at them. "You open them, Ruthie."

She opened them. They were all birthday cards, from all our relatives, from people at the wholesale market, from his friends. There was a card signed by all the people from the home. There was even a card from Mr. Rubin. My grandfather listened as she read the messages and the names. He nodded, pleased and, now and then, a little surprised. When she read Mr. Rubin's card, he snorted.

My father handed him a long, slim package. "Open it, Mr. Jacobson. It's just a little something we thought you might like."

He pulled the wrapping away slowly, opened the box. Inside, there was a new tie. He took it out, examined it, nodded. "A new tie," he said.

"We thought you could always use another new tie," my mother said.

"Always," he said. "There are never enough."

"And there will be plenty of other presents on Saturday, pa. Everybody will be bringing something for you then," she said.

"I am sure," he said. "I can wait until Saturday."

I walked up to my grandfather then, took my hand from behind my back, and handed him the gift I had bought and

wrapped myself. My mother and father looked at me with surprise. They hadn't known I had gotten him anything. My grandfather took the package. He held it in his hand, looking at it. He
looked at me. He whispered, so low I could barely hear the
words, "Thank you, Jerome. What a surprise." He took out a
handkerchief and blew his nose very hard. He just held on to the
package, not moving to open it.

"Open it, grandpa," I said.

"I will," he said. "In a minute." He kept holding on to the package and then he started to pull off the paper. He held the book
in his hands, read aloud the title, *Tales of the Jewish Heroes*. He
looked at me.

"It's all about David and Goliath and the Maccabees and all the
rest," I said quickly. "The kids ahead of me in Sunday school
have been reading it. One of the teachers I asked said it would
be perfect."

He took out his handkerchief again and blew his nose hard.
He took off his glasses and wiped his eyes. He said, "Jerome,
never have I gotten a nicer birthday present." His voice was hus-
ky, as though something had gotten stuck in his throat. He
turned away so I couldn't see his face. He held on to the book
very tightly.

It was my turn, then. Packages appeared as though from the
air. There was a new baseball glove and an official American
League baseball. There were, of course, new clothes and some
books. There was the new bicycle I had been praying for. My father wheeled it into the room and I couldn't believe it when I
saw it. I was exhausted from the opening and the surprises.

"Jerome," my grandfather said then.

I looked at him.

"I have a present for you, too."

I wondered what. He hadn't been out of the house anywhere
since he had been sick, so how could he have gotten anything
for me?

I went to him. He reached into his lap, lifted the leather case
with the flute. He put it into my hands. He said, "What has been
mine for more than eighty years should be yours."

I looked at the case, at him. I didn't know what to say. I just knew, even though I didn't play the flute, even though I might never play the flute, that it was very special.

My mother said, "Oh, pa."

My father said, "They're determined to make a musician out of you, Jerry."

I held on to the flute case.

My mother said, "Aren't you going to thank grandpa?"

I nodded. I said, "Thank you, grandpa."

He said, "You should only take care of it."

I said, "Don't worry. I will. I'll even learn to play it."

He said, "That is not necessary. If you do, you do. If you don't, you don't. But it is yours."

My father said then that it was getting very late, too late for a nine-year-old. There was still school tomorrow and it was time for me to go up to bed.

I tried to argue. They wouldn't hear it. But the arguments weren't very forceful anyway, since I was too tired to offer much resistance. My grandfather said he was tired, too, and so he thought he would go up to bed at the same time. We both said good night and climbed the stairs together.

For just a moment, we stood together outside the door to my room. I said, "Happy birthday, grandpa. Good night."

He smiled. He touched my head softly, a caress, his hand resting there lightly for just a moment. He said, "Happy birthday, Jerome. Nine is a good age to be."

I went to sleep as soon as I had pulled the covers over me. Sometime during the night I woke into the darkness. My mother would have said it was because of too much cake and too much excitement. But it was not that. Something was different. I strained to understand, to know what. I know now that the difference was silence. I had grown used to the sounds of my grandfather's snores, deep, loud breaths in the night, they had become part of the pattern of night. But there was only silence then, no sound anywhere. I listened hard, gave up trying to figure out what had awakened me. I went back to sleep.

By Saturday, the house was filled with my aunts and uncles and a lot of my cousins, some of whom I was meeting for the first time. They all kept telling me what a big boy I had become and saying, "My, doesn't time fly." And, "You look just like your father."

My mother was wandering around the room, talking to them, making coffee, doing a thousand things to keep busy, but her eyes were very red and she kept wandering off upstairs into the bedroom to be alone, and then my father would follow and pretty soon he'd bring her down again.

And they all kept repeating the same things. "Why didn't you call us before, Ruth? You knew we would have come. Why didn't you tell us he was failing?"

My mother and father both kept insisting there had been no warning, no reason to get anybody before. Everybody was planning on being there by Saturday anyway, and besides, even that night, at the birthday, he had been fine, a little tired, perhaps, but fine and enjoying himself and acting like a boy. So there hadn't been any reason to call.

They kept repeating, "You have to give it to him. My God, to live to be ninety and still have all your marbles."

They kept saying, "Well, it sure gives all of us hope, doesn't it?"

They kept saying, "When it's my time, I should only be so lucky. To go like that."

I listened to all that talk for a while and then I ran out back and got my ball and began to throw it hard at the cellar hatchway, just kept throwing it until my arm was so tired I thought it was going to fall off. A couple of times, somebody opened the back door and glared at me and said, "Boy, will you please stop making that racket."

But my father was always there. He said, "Leave the boy alone. He's doing it his way. He was closer to Mr. Jacobson than anybody."

I went back into the house after a time. My mother was in the kitchen and my father was holding her and telling her everything would be all right. One of my aunts came in and went to my mother and patted her on the stomach and said, "My God, Ruth, why have you been keeping it a secret? When are you due?"

My mother said, "In January."

I stared at her then, at her stomach for I guess the first time, and I realized then what they had been talking about for so long in such a veiled way. It hadn't meant anything to me until then.

There were copies of the newspapers around the house and everybody spent a long time reading and talking about the stories about my grandfather that were in them, long stories telling about how he had come to America from Russia and all the things he had done and how important he was. My aunts and uncles and cousins read what was written and they all said they hadn't realized he had done all that. I started to read the stories and knew, after a few paragraphs, that they had a lot of things wrong, and just put them down and walked away.

I went upstairs to my grandfather's room just when it was getting dark. I opened the door and stood looking in. There wasn't anything to see. I went in anyway and then I sat in his old chair and rocked for a while. A little later, my father came up and found me. He came over to me and put his arms around me and just hugged me very tightly, so tightly it was hard to breathe, but then I was having trouble breathing anyway. He said softly, into my ear, "He was a good guy, Jerry. A real good man. They don't make them like him anymore."

I wasn't going to cry because, I thought then, when you're a man, you don't cry and I was going to be a man. But my father was crying, or at least his eyes were wet and red, so maybe I was wrong. But I wasn't going to cry.

My mother said I couldn't go to the funeral home or to the funeral. "You're too young," she said. "You don't have to go. There's no reason for you to go."

But I had to go. I told her I had to. "He was my grandpa," I said, "and I have to go." I meant more than that, though I couldn't say what else I meant, and I knew I had to go to discover things, to know things for certain, though I wasn't exactly sure what they were.

My father backed me. So, on Sunday, I went with them to the funeral home. The coffin was at the end of the room, just under the altar, and a lot of people had already begun walking by it and looking in. My mother said I shouldn't go, but I wanted to do that, too, so we went behind the coffin and looked. There was somebody lying in it with his eyes closed, somebody who looked like my grandfather only I knew it wasn't my grandfather. It was as though somebody had taken some wax or clay or something and tried to sculpt him, but something was missing, the something that had been my friend and my grandfather and a lot more.

It was, somebody told me later, one of the biggest funerals in Hartford. There weren't enough seats in the chapel for all the people who turned out; there wasn't even enough room for everybody to stand, so a lot of people had to wait outside in the hallway and even outside in the parking lot and on the sidewalks. All his old friends from the wholesale market were there, and a lot of his customers, those who were still alive, and even some of their children who were grown; there were people from his old neighborhood who remembered him and the things he had done when they were growing up; the whole of the Workman's Circle, his Oxie, turned up, but of course he was going to be buried in the cemetery he had helped found, in a special section reserved for former presidents and even in a special part of that section that had been set aside just for him long ago. There were a lot of people from the old people's home, all huddled together and crying as though they would never stop. Mr. Rubin came over to my mother and father. His eyes were red and swollen. He tried to say something but couldn't get words out, just shook his head and put his hand on my mother's shoulder and squeezed very hard and then turned and went away. There were a lot of gasps and surprise when the governor walked into the chapel and went to my mother and told her how sorry he was and how he remembered my grandfather from a long time ago when he was just getting started. I wasn't surprised to see him there.

There must have been a hundred cars in the procession to the cemetery, stretching on and on behind the hearse and the limousine in which I rode with my mother and father and my Uncle Abner and his wife, my Aunt Helen. The crowd was so thick around the grave site that I couldn't see through it to a clear spot. The people were still coming down between the graves when the rabbi started the service.

They put the coffin into the ground then, and I watched as it sank slowly out of sight. My mother started to weep very hard.

My father put one arm around her and held her very close, and he put his other arm around me and pulled me very tightly against him. And suddenly I knew that at least part of my grandfather was gone and I knew I would never see him again or hear any more of his stories or share anything with him again. I wanted to stop being brave then, and my father hugged me a little closer and I held on to him and on to myself.

We went back to the house after that and there were a lot of people in every room, all talking about what a wonderful life my grandfather had had and how pleased he would have been at all the people, so many of them, who had come to his funeral. I didn't want to listen to all that, so I went up to his room and I sat in his rocking chair and I held his birthday present to me in my lap, closed in its leather case. I sat there for a long time, until it got dark and there wasn't any more noise or talking downstairs.

For a month, my grandfather's room stayed as it had been, and then my mother started to clean it out, to put some of his things away, to get rid of the rest. It took her several days to finish the job. She would go into the room and pick something up and just hold on to it while the time passed. A couple of times, I stood in the doorway and watched, even asked if I could help. But she sent me away, telling me she didn't need any help, she could do it all by herself.

But, when she and my father began moving the furniture out, I went into the room and just sat down in his chair, watching. "Jerry," she said, "you'll have to get up now. We want to move these things out."

I sat there. Then I said, "Mom, do you think I could have this in my room?"

She looked at me strangely. "What do you want with that old thing?"

"I just want it, that's all."

"Where would you put it? With all the stuff in there now, there's hardly room for you, let alone that old chair."

"I'll find a place, mom. Can't I have it?"

My father nodded. "I don't see why not," he said. I got out of the chair and he and I hauled it into my room and we made a place for it near the window that overlooked the backyard.

And the room changed. The walls were covered with new, bright wallpaper, new curtains hung on the windows. A crib appeared and a lot of nursery furniture and all the rest of the stuff needed for a baby. In January, my mother went off to the hospital in the middle of a snowstorm and five days later, reappeared with my sister. After that, the sounds that came to me in the night were her cries and her howling demands, and pretty soon, except for an occasional ghost, the room was all hers.

There were times, a long time later, when she was older and I was home on vacation from college, when I tried to sit her down and talk to her about her grandfather. I guess because she never knew him and could never see him real, her attention wandered quickly, she would fidget and finally just jump up, tell me she remembered something important she had to do, and run off. So, I stopped trying.

8

No MAN LEAVES BEHIND A neat package of his life. At the end, there are, finally, a lot of loose threads that have never been gathered. No matter how much time there is, there is never enough time to finish everything and perhaps there is, in the last moments, some hope that there will be someone to finish off that unfinished business. I know that in inheriting my grandfather's flute and his chair and a few other things, I felt, inside, that I had also inherited those dangling ends that had eluded him. It would be a long time before I could do anything about any of them, but in those years of growing and maturing and beginning to find my own way, there was always the thought that someday, somehow, I would try.

After I finished college, I had the chance to go to Paris for a couple of years to study on a fellowship. Going to Paris to live was one of those dreams that had seeped into my mind and obsessed my brain, as, I think, it had with a lot of guys and girls of my generation with the first exposure to Hemingway and Fitzgerald and Gertrude Stein and the visions of the expatriate ferment of the 1920s. The Paris of the 1960s would not be the same Paris, but still it would be Paris.

Yet I knew when I applied for that fellowship and got it, and all the time I was getting ready to go, that I would do something more than study while I was in France. My grandfather had said in that last month that if he had been eighty instead of ninety, he would have gone to Paris and found his nephew, Mendel Yakovson. Well, I was twenty-four and I was going to Paris and one of the things I would do was find my cousin, Mendel Yakovson; I would give my grandfather's memory that; I would tie off one of those loose ends life had not given him the time to do. That I was going to tackle something that was impossible, that I was going to try to do something fifteen years later that more experienced and more capable people had been unable to do when the scent was still fresh, did not concern me. It was just something I knew I had to try.

Before I left New York, I went down to the offices of the *Forward,* talked to one of the editors there, told him what I planned. He stared at me in disbelief, laughed at me, shook his head. Forget it, he said. I'd just be wasting my time. It was impossible. There were better things for a young man to do in Paris than search for old ghosts who did not want to be found. Not without a deep sigh and an obvious reluctance, he did give me some little help. For a couple of hours, he searched through the dusty old filing cabinets and drawers, so obviously disordered and disorganized. But all he could come up with were a faded copy of the photograph of Mendel Yakovson that had originally appeared in the paper (the sharper one that had been sent to my grandfather had long since disappeared) and the name and address of Harry Rabinowitz's widow, Rabinowitz being the correspondent who had interviewed my cousin that summer afternoon fifteen years before. The address was five years out-of-date and whether the widow still lived there the editor was not sure. But if she did, or if she had moved and I could track her down, it was possible that she had kept her husband's papers and would let me go through them.

So, I went to Paris, took a small room in a pension on the rue Lobineau, started classes and my independent work on my fellowship project, began to make some friends and enjoy Paris in the autumn. I was sure there would be plenty of time to start looking for Yakovson once I was settled and acclimated.

After about a month, I met a girl at the Sorbonne. She was

French, from a village near Grenoble, and living in Paris just a little distance from me. And she spoke a lot better English than I
did French. Jeanette and I started to hang out together and then
to go places together, to discover Paris as I think it really has to
be discovered. I was just twenty-four and she was twenty and for
us it was all new and wonderful, beyond description, as anything
is when you stop being strangers and become not friends and go
beyond lovers to be in love.

And so the fall went by and the winter, too. There was plenty
of time, no need to hurry. It had waited fifteen years, it could
wait a little longer. I was too full of Paris and too full of Jeanette,
and when that little itching nagged at my brain, I scratched it,
anesthetized it a little, and went on enjoying myself, and, when
I wasn't playing, worked as hard as I could to make some head-
way that would justify the fellowship.

There were so many things for the two of us to discover and
talk about that I don't think I ever mentioned my grandfather or
much about him to Jeanette until months later, until one night
early in the spring. Maybe it was the return of new life that stirred
something in me, maybe it was the realization that it was finally
time to move. We were lying in bed in my room, and in the lan-
guor of that moment, I said something. I don't even remember
what. She asked a question. I answered, and pretty soon I was
talking. I talked all that night and Jeanette lay on the pillow next
to me, eyes half closed, listening, asking a question now and then
so I knew she wasn't asleep, reaching out to the bedside table
too often for one of my American cigarettes.

The emotions that I had held down for months were stirred,
and the desires and needs that I had ignored through the winter
burst through the hard soil of my soul or mind or whatever. And
there were new passions that came, I think, from sharing something held so long and so close with someone who seemed to
understand and to care.

A few days later, we rented a car and drove across into the still-
scarred battlefields until we reached Romagné and the cemetery
where those who had died on Meuse-Argonne nearly fifty years
before are buried. We got the location and wandered among the

endless rows of graves until we found the Star of David among the crosses, and read the inscription faded by time:

ELI JACOBSON
U.S. ARMY
1899–1918

I looked at it and tried to imagine the uncle dead nearly twenty years before I was born, but it was only one grave among fourteen thousand, only one Star of David among those thousands of crosses and six-pointed stars, only the grave of a stranger.

We went back to Paris the next day and then began to search for Mendel Yakovson.

Mrs. Rabinowitz was not at the address I had. She had moved three years before. There was a forwarding address. We went there, to a small apartment building near the Bois de Boulogne. Mrs. Rabinowitz was in her middle seventies, a pleasant, sad-faced woman with cropped white hair. She greeted us, listened while I told her why I had come, and led us into a sitting room with a view of the Bois. She made us sit while she brewed some English tea. She was very sorry that she couldn't offer us more, not just in refreshments but in help. She seemed to recall vaguely some cables and letters between her husband and the paper in New York in 1946 about a Russian soldier, but there had been so many Russian soldiers appearing in Paris in those months that she had no clear recollection of any particular one. Her husband's papers and records? She was sorry, but when she moved the last time, and it was the third time since he died, she had finally thrown away all that useless impedimenta. No, she had never met Yakovson, she said when I tried to show her the photograph, so it would do no good for her to look at it. She was sorry, but her husband had really kept such things to himself. She wished us luck but was sure we would have none; if her husband had not been able to find my cousin, and he had been intimate with everybody who was anybody in the Jewish community and among the new arrivals, then she was sure there was no hope that we would be able to. We would be searching the city and the country for a hopelessly lost ghost.

A few days later, we went to the American embassy, finally got to see a clerk who didn't want to be helpful. I pressed and Jeanette, suddenly feminine and helpless and pleading, which were facets she had never shown me before, wooed him and he disappeared somewhere into the embassy, to return with an old file. He opened it on the desk, showed us that it contained nothing but copies of cables and letters between Washington and Paris, a copy of a letter from my grandfather to the State Department, and an address in the fourth arrondissement, Yakovson's original Paris address. "You won't have any luck there," he said as I wrote it down. "We sent somebody there back then and the guy had disappeared, nobody knew where."

But at least we had that, another starting point. The building was an old rooming house in some disrepair off the rue des Ecouffes in the Jewish ghetto. The landlady, old and as decaying as the building, spoke no English and, while my French was good, I didn't trust it, so Jeanette took over. The landlady hadn't the slightest idea what we were asking. Jeanette made her understand. She shrugged expressively. So many young Jewish soldiers fleeing the Russian army had passed through her house over the years, especially in those days so soon after the war, how could we expect her to remember one particular young man?

Jeanette asked, "Don't you remember when the man from the Jewish newspaper in New York came to you about a soldier? Don't you remember when people from the American embassy came?"

She thought, nodded slowly. She seemed to remember something, but she wasn't sure what.

I took out Yakovson's photograph, showed it to her. She studied it, shrugged. "There were so many then," she said. "How can I remember one?"

"Is there anyone still in the house who was here fifteen years ago?" Jeanette asked. "Maybe they might remember."

The landlady emitted a sour, sarcastic laugh, looked at us as though we had loose pebbles rattling around in our heads.

"Perhaps you could give us the name of someone who was here then and we could find him and ask."

She looked at us. "People come, people go," she said. "This

is a rooming house, not an apartment building. Nobody stays here long. It is a place to stay for a week, a month, and then to go on. I would have trouble telling you the name of one who was here six months ago. How would you expect me to remember fifteen years ago?"

"Don't you keep records, a register, something?"

She gave us that stare again and laughed. "Go away, young man, take your young lady with you. Forget this. You will never find this soldier you are looking for. Why should you want to find him anyway after so many years?"

For the next couple of weeks, we wandered through the ghetto, up and down the rue des Ecouffes, along the rue des Rosiers and all the other streets and alleys, stopping in every store and shop, every rooming house, pension, hotel, apartment, showing the photograph, asking our questions. A couple of people seemed to recall that they might once have heard the name Yakovson, but that was so long ago they had no idea of the context. One or two studied the picture, said it seemed familiar, that face, but why or how was beyond them. One man suggested we go to a Jewish refugee organization that had helped a lot of Russian deserters in those days. If it was still in business, and he wasn't sure it was, perhaps they could help.

We checked, found that it was still operating, in an office on the fourth floor of an old building two blocks from Les Halles. The office was one tiny room. There was hardly space to move among the battered, tilting wooden and metal filing cabinets, the precariously canting stacks of old newspapers and magazines. A small old man with a yarmulke glued to the back of his head was sitting behind a desk studying papers through a reading lens when we entered. He looked up, peered at us with surprise; I think we were the first strangers to enter that office in years. He didn't even ask us what we wanted, just cleared some of the papers off a couple of chairs so we would have a place to sit. Then he asked. We explained it to him.

He listened intently, nodded several times, went directly to one of the filing cabinets, opened it, flipped quickly through the folders, shook his head, closed the drawer, opened another, went through another line of folders, stopped, nodded, pulled one out, and returned to the desk, brushing a stack of papers onto the floor so he would have a place for the folder.

He nodded to us and smiled with satisfaction. "I remember," he said. "I knew I remembered. I never forget." He opened the file, read through it quickly, nodding, then looked back at us. Mendel Yakovson had been brought to the office in the summer of 1946, right after he reached Paris, by another Russian deserter named Valary Shumansky. Yakovson had asked for help in settling in France, for assistance in obtaining work in a hotel, which had been his trade before the war. The office had made inquiries at a number of hotels in Paris, had even arranged several interviews for Yakovson. But when they had tried to reach him to give him the information, he was no longer there and no one knew where he had gone. The old man shrugged. That was the end of the file.

"How about this Valary Shumansky? Maybe he would know," I said.

"Well, we will see," the old man said. He went back to the filing cabinets, searched, returned with another file, opened it, read through it. His face fell. "I am sorry," he said. "Shumansky died in the influenza epidemic in the winter of 1946. He had no relatives."

Our faces must have reflected the blow in the stomach. The old man smiled a little. "Do not give up hope, young man, young lady. What you are trying to do may seem impossible now, but the impossible has been done before. That some of us were still here in 1946 is the proof. Tell me, have you looked in the telephone books, the directories, for a Yakovson? Have you searched for others who came from Nezhin?"

We had not. It had not even occurred to us, though these were the most obvious things for us to have done.

"The simplest things are the last things we do," he said. "That is what you must do now. If it does not help, come back and perhaps I will have another idea."

We spent a couple of days with the directories. I had no idea there were so many Yakovsons, and Jacobsons (we decided to check them out, too, since my grandfather had taken that spelling), in Paris. We could strike out all the ones who were obviously

Scandinavian—the Nilses and Jenses and the rest—and there were still dozens left, including one whose name was Mendel.

We called Mendel Yakovson first. His wife answered, said he was at work in a jewelry shop on the rue Saint-Honoré du Faubourg. We rushed to the shop. Mendel Yakovson was pointed out to us by one of the clerks. He was a well-dressed, prosperous-looking man in his mid-sixties; there was not the slightest resemblance to the man in the picture. Still, we asked. He looked at us carefully, shook his head. He had come to France in 1927. He had been born and brought up in Odessa. He had never known there was another Mendel Yakovson in France, though he was sure there were plenty in Russia. He looked at the photograph. No, he had never seen the man.

We went home, went through the list of the other Yakovsons and Jacobsons, decided we would call on them personally rather than use the phone. It took weeks, and we traveled by the métro from one end of Paris to the other, discouragement growing, and with it a determination not to give up, to go on until there was nowhere else to go, and then find another place.

There were two Yakovsons in the ghetto. They turned out to be brothers from Lodz in Poland who had survived Auschwitz. They had no knowledge of any other Yakovsons in France, or anywhere else, for that matter; they were sure all the other Yakovsons in the world were ashes.

There was an Henri Yakovson who lived in a penthouse apartment overlooking the Parc Monceau. He was a furrier, his family had been furriers since arriving in France in the nineteenth century. As far as he knew, the only other Yakovsons he had ever met or dealt with were his brother, Pierre, who was his partner and lived in the eighth arrondissement, his nephews, and his sister, who was married and so, of course, was not a Yakovson anymore.

There was a Yakovson who was a tailor and a Jacobson who was a doctor—four Jacobsons, in fact, who were doctors—and a Yakovson who was a policeman, of all things, and there were others, but none of them had any knowledge of Mendel Yakovson who had been a Russian soldier and none of them had ever seen the man in the photograph.

We took the long ride on the métro out to Clichy, to the charcuterie run by a Gérard Yakovson. For a half hour, we stood and waited while he cut meat and finished with several customers, taking his time, chatting with them idly while he worked, though his glance kept darting toward Jeanette and me. When there was a break, he approached, leaned across the counter toward us, and waited silently. He looked very French, with a round face, split by a thick mustache, deep, dark eyes, and a sour expression. I asked if, by any chance, he had ever run across or known a man named Mendel Yakovson.

"Mendel Yakovson?" He appeared to think.

"He was a Russian soldier who fled to France in 1946."

He shook his head.

I took out the photograph and showed it to him. He studied it. He studied me, he studied Jeanette. He said, "Why do you want to know?"

I said, feeling just the beginning of hope, "Mendel Yakovson is my cousin."

He said, "You are not a Russian." He looked at Jeanette. "And she is French."

I said, "I'm an American."

He said, "I could tell that by your accent. What are you doing in France?"

"I'm studying at the Sorbonne."

"She is your *fille?*"

"She's a friend."

"Of course. What else?" He grinned sourly. "What do you want with this Mendel Yakovson?"

"I just want to find him, to meet him. He's my cousin."

"You know him?"

I shook my head. "I've never met him."

"Then why do you want to find him?"

Jeanette explained in rapid French that I could barely follow about my grandfather. Gérard Yakovson listened impassively. He studied me some more. "What would you do if you found him?"

That was a question I had never even considered. I shook my head, trying to form an answer. "For God's sake, I don't know. Say hello. Tell him who I am. I don't know. I haven't thought that far. I just have to find him."

"For your grandfather?"

"Maybe. For my grandfather. For me. I don't know."

"Are you a Communist, working for the Russians?"

"Oh, Jesus, of course not."

"One never knows. One must ask. One must be sure. You do not look like a Communist, but what does a Communist look like?"

"Even if I were, what difference would it make?"

"One never knows."

"You think the Russians are still after him?"

"He was a deserter, you said. Do you think any country isn't after those who desert its army? If you deserted your army, wouldn't the American government be after you?"

"After fifteen years?"

"After a hundred years. You think the Russians ever stop?"

"It didn't even occur to me."

"A deserter has to be somebody else or he dies."

"And did Mendel Yakovson die? Or is he somebody else?"

He was silent for a while, his eyes veiled, watching me, watching Jeanette. He sighed. He shrugged. He said, "Go to Dijon."

"What?" Both Jeanette and I stared at him.

"Go to Dijon. You do not understand French, either of you?"

"To Dijon?"

"To the Hotel Central. Ask for Marcel Leventov."

"He's . . ."

"Who do you think he is? Do you want me to hold your hand and go with you and introduce you?"

"You know him."

"Know him? I met a man, many years ago, who came to Paris from Russia. I had a small shop then, near Les Halles. He saw the sign over the door, came in, said we had the same name. We were not related. We talked. He came in two, three times more. He said he was going to Dijon. He said he was afraid the Russians were after him to take him back. He would have a new name. That's all I know."

"Have you heard from him since?"

He shook his head. "Not one word. So, if you want to find this cousin of yours, go to Dijon."

The excitement so intense we could hardly breathe, we took the train to Dijon the next day, rushed from the station to the Hotel Central, demanded to see the manager, were ushered into his office. I could hardly get words out. Jeanette's French was better, calmer. She explained. The manager listened, nodded. Oh, yes, he remembered Marcel Leventov. The man was working in the hotel when he, the manager, was returned finally from the prison camp in Germany where he had spent the years after the terrible defeat. Leventov had been the night clerk. For a Jew, he was not a bad guy, a little pushy, a little too ambitious, but, and he shrugged, you know how Jews are.

Was Leventov still working in the hotel?

He shook his head. Leventov had left about ten years before.

Did he know where Leventov had gone?

He wasn't sure. But then, he hadn't been that friendly with Leventov, so there was no reason the man would tell him. Why did we want to know?

Jeanette said because Leventov was my cousin.

Oh. The manager peered closely at my face, trying, I suppose, to see the Jew in it. He shrugged. There might be somebody who remembered, he said. He seemed to recall that Leventov had been friendly with one of the other clerks who was still at the hotel. If we would relax and wait, he would ask. He left the office, returned in about ten minutes. Yes, he said, the clerk remembered. Leventov had not been well, something to do with his chest or the climate or something. The doctor had advised him to go to a warmer place. He had told his friend he was going to Cannes. His friend recommended that he seek employment at a hotel there. He thought it was the Majestic, but he wasn't sure.

Another train ride south, a bus, a cab. Another manager. He listened. Yes, he indeed remembered Marcel Leventov. An ambitious man with a future in the hotel business.

I was barely able to get out the question. Was he still at the Majestic?

The manager shook his head sadly. Alas, no.

Where was he? Did he know?

Leventov had suffered a heart attack during the past winter. He had been in the hospital for two weeks. Unfortunately, he had not recovered. He had never married and so there were no survivors.

So we had reached the end and we were a few months too late. Jeanette and I took a cab out to the cemetery above the city. The grave was still a little raw, the grass just beginning to grow on the mound. There was a small stone. It said only:

MARCEL LEVENTOV
MORT 1962

We took the train back to Paris that afternoon.

Last year, a few months after our ride around our city, my father did what he had said he would do. He sold his accounting business and he retired. He and my mother spent the winter in Florida, came north in the spring, and, after a few weeks, decided that Florida was where they wanted to settle from then on. The dream house was put on the market and sold quickly.

The worst of the selling and the moving was going through all the things they had kept all the years, that had survived one move already, been stored in the basement and the attic, but would not survive this last move, to a Florida condominium. Jeanette and I and our children made the trip up for a kind of last look at the house, perhaps even the city, for there was nothing any longer to pull me back but memories of what had been and was no more, and to help sort through and discard what had been amassed.

It was a journey through my childhood, going through those old suitcases and trunks and cardboard boxes, dumping things on the floor and examining them. We'd come on something, hold it up, laugh and remember, and have to explain to the kids, sometimes to Jeanette.

In the middle of everything was an old trunk of my father's. He opened it, looked in, and started to laugh. "Jesus Christ," he said, "will you look at this. I thought I got rid of it years ago." He pulled out his old army uniform and the hat I had put on so long ago on a Memorial Day. "Well, I sure as hell don't need this," he said, and he threw it off to one side, onto a pile of other litter.

And then we found another trunk. It was my grandfather's. I opened it. There was a lot of junk in it that meant nothing to me, that he must have been saving for some reason of his own. But on the top was that uniform he had worn on that last night, folded neatly, the creases irremovable, I think, from all the years. And on top of the uniform was the book I had given him that last night, *Tales of the Jewish Heroes.* I stood for a moment looking down at it. I reached in and picked it up. Except for the layer of dust that had seeped in and blanketed it, it was still fresh and new and untouched. I opened it, flipped a few pages, saw that there were even pages still uncut. But that was natural; he had never really had a chance to look inside. I suppose when my mother or father had been putting his things away after he died, one or the other of them had just naturally put the uniform and the book in the trunk and forgotten them.

I didn't mention it to anyone, went on going through all the clutter, the pile of things to be discarded growing mountainous; there was so little to be saved, so little there would be room for. But later that night, after everyone had gone to bed, I went back down to the cellar, hunted through the piles. I took my grandfather's uniform. I took my father's uniform and the hat. And I took the book. And I carried them out to the car and put them in the trunk.

When we got home a couple of days later, Jeanette saw me take them out of the trunk, watched as I carried them up to the apartment. The uniforms, both of them, I hung in my closet, way at the back, next to the uniform from my own war just a few years past. Why I had kept it I don't know, any more than either my grandfather or my father really knew why they had kept theirs. Certainly, if there is a difference in wars, mine had been closer in its senselessness to my grandfather's than to my father's, and if a certain nobility of purpose clung to my father's, then both my grandfather's and mine were symbols of man's folly that should never be forgotten.

The book, that last living gift, I put on the shelf in my study, next to the leather case with the flute, right above the spot where I keep that old rocking chair I sit in so often to rock and read or just think.

A friend, a musician, was at the apartment a few weeks ago. We were sitting in the study when he noticed the flute case, opened it, and took out the old flute. He examined it closely, said it must be a hundred years old at least. I said at least a hundred years. He fitted it together and played it a little, took it away from his mouth and stared at it with wonder. It's got magic in it, he said. You want to sell it? I could get you a fantastic price.

I shook my head, took the flute from him, and put it back. It was, I said, an inheritance, a special gift. It was a gift you do not sell. You keep it close forever.